Beyond the Lens

By Hannah Ellis

To Fiona

with lots of love

Acknowledgements

I'm so grateful to everyone who has helped with this book.

To my parents for your amazing help and support. I love being able to bounce ideas off you and I value your input so much. It makes it all so much easier and more fun. Anthea Kirk, thanks so much for indulging me in all the book chat and for loving my characters as much as I do. Your help has been invaluable. To Fay Sallaba and Sarah Fraser. Thanks for always making time to help with the book and for being such enthusiastic supporters. Thanks to Dua Roberts and Ashley Bignall for listening to all my rants and keeping me sane.

For this book, I was lucky enough to find an amazing editor. Thank you so much, Jane Hammett, it was such a positive experience working with you and I look forward to working with you on future projects.

Kathy Robinson, thanks so much for proof-reading for me.

A big thank you to Aimee Coveney for a fantastic cover.

To my wonderful husband, Mario. I really couldn't do this without you. Thank you so much for believing in me and for supporting me in every way. You make it possible for me to follow my dreams. You're the best and I love you so much.

To the fantastic people of CLCHQ, it's so great to have you on hand to offer help and encouragement. What a wonderful group to be part of. Thank you.

Finally, a great big thank you to my readers and especially to those who not only read all of my books, but also shout about them to friends, write reviews, post on social media etc. I'm so incredibly grateful to you.

Part 1

Chapter 1

I'd never stolen anything before in my life. I couldn't even bring myself to take a mint from the bowl beside the till at the hairdresser, so I was quite proud of the stapler in my handbag. At first, I'd considered returning it. I'd actually retraced my steps, sure I couldn't live with the knowledge that I was basically a common thief. I turned on my heel as I realised I also couldn't cope with the humiliation of taking it back. I'd have to convert to Catholicism, though; it was clearly calling to me by way of the guilt eating away at my gut.

"I stole a stapler and lost my job," I confessed to my mum over the phone while I sat in the cosy coffee shop, watching the world go by through the window. "Not in that order."

"That's brilliant news!"

An inevitable reaction.

"Mum, are you dancing?"

"Just a little celebratory jig around the kitchen."

I could imagine her, too.

7

"I got made redundant, so I should get some money from them."

"Even better!"

"Most mothers would be concerned, you know?"

"What's to be concerned about? You have to leave your horrible, boring job that you hate. And they pay you to leave, and will presumably give you a reference. It's brilliant news!"

"Well, I got a stapler out of it, if nothing else." I'd been stomping around the office, ignoring the sidelong glances from my co-workers, when I realised I didn't have many personal items around my desk. The dramatic packing-up of my things was going to be wholly unsatisfying. I'd lifted the phone as it rang and slammed it down again, making everyone around me flinch. In a fit of rage, I'd grabbed the stapler and shoved it into my handbag, as though that would teach them to be careful who they let go in future. I came to my senses immediately and rummaged around in my handbag for it, but soon realised it had got lost in the abyss. It gave me time to realise I was being watched. In case no one had seen me steal it, I didn't want to incriminate myself by unloading the item in front of them.

"I'm really happy for you," Mum said. "I only wish this had happened sooner."

"There is just the slight matter of paying my rent, putting food on the table, clothing myself. Those trivial things in life." Mum would genuinely see those things as minor inconveniences. She was all about fun.

"Don't worry about those things. You'll figure something out. In the meantime, have some fun – go a bit crazy for once! Throw caution to the wind." She laughed, and her laugh was infectious. "Why don't we go out tonight and celebrate?"

"Because it's not something to celebrate," I told her. I often wished I had one of those mums who were happy to be your mum and didn't need to be your best friend too. I hated it when she insisted on taking me out to some dodgy club and I had to watch her flirt with random men all night.

"Oh, come on. Be a little spontaneous for once."

"I'll start being spontaneous when you start being sensible," I offered.

"But I'd be boring like you then." She laughed wickedly, making me smile. "Just promise me one thing." She was suddenly serious. "Don't start job hunting this evening; put it off for a week or so. Relax a bit and think about what you really want from life. I've always hated thinking of you sitting in that boring office. I want more for you."

"I'll wait a week, I promise." She had a point. I could afford to be a bit choosy – and adding 'not mind-numbingly boring' to my job criteria probably wouldn't hurt.

"Oh, and be a yes person for a while," she said.

"What on earth does that mean?"

"Say yes to things. You always say no to everything. I bet you don't even realise you're doing it."

"Do me a favour, Mum! Cut down on the daytime TV, will you?"

"There's your sense of humour! Making a little appearance today, is it?"

"I'm not joking," I told her.

"Just say yes!" She laughed again. "Call me tomorrow."

I smiled to myself. I guess it was nice she was positive about me losing my job.

The middle-aged waitress walked past just as I placed my phone on the table in front of me.

"Can I get you anything else?" she offered, picking up my empty coffee cup. I politely declined and asked for the bill.

I navigated the city centre, intent on getting the bus home. It was Friday afternoon and the streets were busy. I zigzagged down the pedestrian zone, unable to avoid a woman with a clipboard who wanted me to do a survey.

"I'm in a hurry," I told her, feeling guilty for some reason. "Sorry."

"Got any spare change?" a homeless man asked me.

"No, sorry." I winced. I really must have been Catholic in a previous life.

Then I almost walked into a young woman, who thrust a piece of paper at me. "Get a free drink tonight with this flyer."

I pushed her hand away, suddenly irritated. "No, thanks."

I stumbled away, feeling like screaming as I thought about my life. My mum was rarely right, but I'd have to give her this one: I did say no to everything. I didn't even think about it; I'd trained myself to automatically say no. Mum would've done the survey and had a good old chinwag with the lady while she was at it. The homeless man would've wished he hadn't chosen her when she told him her life story as she handed him 20p. And she'd have bitten the girl's hand off for a free drink.

I wondered if I was missing anything; if my life would be enhanced by a few random social interactions. Perhaps it wouldn't hurt to be a yes person for a while. I slowed my pace but made it almost to the bus stop without any opportunity to chat to strangers. Typical!

"Excuse me!" The voice behind me was shrill, and I turned with a smile. The sight of a vaguely familiar blonde woman holding a microphone, backed up by three cameramen, caught me out. This clearly wasn't a 'yes' moment!

"Are you looking for some excitement in your life?" she asked theatrically.

No, I wasn't looking for excitement. To be honest, I'd never been a huge fan of excitement. So I was surprised to hear the word 'yes' come out of my mouth. I looked around, but it had definitely come from me.

"How does an all-expenses-paid, week-long holiday sound to you?" Her voice was high-pitched, and it made me wince.

"It sounds great!" I matched her tone, surprising myself again. Had I been possessed by my mother? Something was not right here. I should go back to being a 'no' person before I got myself in trouble.

"Would you like to join us to take part in a reality TV show in sunny Spain?" Her eyes were wide. "The plane is waiting to whisk you away!"

I grinned at her. Surely no one in their right mind would agree to this. Admittedly, a week in Spain might be quite nice, but a reality TV show? I'd never understood why anyone would put themselves through that.

"Okay," I found myself saying. The desire to punch myself in the face was sudden and overwhelming. What was happening? Who was I? How could I make this stop?

The woman jumped up and down, squealing with excitement. It was a bit embarrassing, really. Perhaps my boring office job wasn't so bad after all; at least there I didn't have to make a complete idiot of myself on a daily basis.

She moved to stand beside me and looked into the camera as she grabbed my hand to raise it above my head. "We've found our fourth contestant! Tell everyone your name …?" She looked enquiringly at me.

"Lucy Mitchell," I said.

"Well, Lucy Mitchell, get ready! You're going on a trip to remember!" She screeched into the camera and bounced around like a demented donkey.

"Cut!" a voice called from behind the cameras.

"Oh my God! Couldn't you be a little bit excited?" Microphone lady's energiser bunny performance was replaced by a cold hard stare. "It's like you were trying to make my job difficult. Are we really taking this one?" she called in the direction of the nearest cameraman.

A woman in a cream suit stepped out from behind him and raised her cigarette to her lips as she held out a hand to me. "I'm Jessica," she told me. "Yes, we're taking her." She inhaled deeply then threw the cigarette on the ground to squash it underfoot. I hated people who did that. Why was it okay to litter with cigarettes? I was tempted to tell her she should dispose of it properly, but thought it wouldn't go down well. It rarely did, come to think of it. "We can't afford to be picky at this point in the day," she told microphone woman.

"This is Chelsea," Jessica informed me. "You've probably seen her if you watch any TV shows crappy enough to indulge D-list celebs."

"Oh! You're Chelsea Cartwright!" I had, in fact, seen her on some dodgy reality TV show about a health farm, and then subsequently on the front pages of a few not-so-reputable newspapers.

"I'm *not* D-list!" she told Jessica. "I have loads of offers of work."

"So do all the D-listers. It's quality, not quantity, that counts in this business. And you're clearly not getting much quality if this is the best you can do."

"I've been assured this programme will make prime-time viewing," she said. "And let's not forget we're working on the same show. You're the one directing the D-list celebrities in their crappy shows." She was loud and her voice piercing, but I felt she'd made a fair point.

"Speaking of work, I think we'd better get on." Jessica chose to rise above the insult – or maybe she just couldn't think of a good comeback. "Lucy, isn't it?"

I nodded.

"You need to run home and pack a bag. Whatever you think you might need. There's a driver waiting – he'll take you home and then to the airport. I'll meet you there with the others, and we can go through the paperwork then."

"So I'm going to Spain? Tonight?" This was

madness. I scanned the collection of TV crew and cameramen, noting the RDT logo splashed over everything. Realnet Direct TV was a big company, so this all seemed legitimate.

"You are indeed. We all are, and I'm sure we'll have a great time!"

I wasn't sure if she was being sarcastic, but she definitely didn't seem very convinced.

"Adam will go with you. We'll be filming everything."

One of the cameramen stepped forward and raised his camera to point it at me.

"Hi Adam," I said quietly, but got no response.

"Head for the road down there and you'll find the car waiting," Jessica directed me. "See you later for a trip to remember!" There was definitely a mocking ring to her voice.

Chapter 2

Adam and his camera were close on my heels as I walked in the direction Jessica had indicated. I looked at him when we got to the road and he motioned to a parked car opposite.

The cool metal of the car door brought me to my senses. That, and the fact that I knew better than to get into a car with a complete stranger. I snapped around, intent on telling Adam there was no way in the world I could actually go through with it.

"You know, I'm not sure—" The words caught in my mouth. A black sports car was travelling at speed towards us. Adam was too focused on his camera to notice. "Adam!" I screamed, lunging at him to pull him out of harm's way.

When his body crashed into mine, the force surprised me. The camera grazed my head. I heard a car horn blare and could smell Adam's aftershave. I took a deep breath.

I was sandwiched between Adam and the waiting car, Adam's face just inches from mine as he turned to watch the car race away.

"Thanks," he whispered, pulling away from me slightly. Our eyes met briefly before he dropped his gaze to my hand. It was still tucked into the waistband of his jeans – which had apparently been the easiest place for me to grab, to pull him from the jaws of death.

It felt like an eternity before the message got from my brain to my hand, telling it to get the hell out of the cute guy's trousers.

"S-sorry," I stuttered, my arm finally retreating. My hand jerked involuntarily to my head, which throbbed slightly. Adam brushed my hair off my face, inspecting the place where his camera had connected with my head. "It's fine," I told him, pushing his hand away and pulling my hair back around my face.

Adam reached around me to open the door. With all thoughts of making a quick exit gone from my mind, I slipped inside and scooted over for Adam to slide in after me.

"You got a death wish, Adam?" the driver said. "This stretch of road is a nightmare; people drive like lunatics. I'm Bill." He caught my eye in the rear-view mirror. "You're off on a little holiday, are you?"

"Er …" Was I seriously going to go through with this? "It seems like it. Maybe. I'm not sure." I looked at Adam but the camera obstructed my view of him and I couldn't make eye contact.

"Well, what's the worst that can happen?" Bill asked as he pulled away. I gave him my address and then sat quietly for the drive. What was the worst that could happen? The list was fairly endless actually, and I silently thanked Bill for putting the thoughts in my head.

I turned to Adam when I opened the door to the two-bedroom apartment I shared with my friend, Melissa. I silently thanked the heavens we were a pair of neat freaks. There definitely wouldn't be any underwear lying around or anything else I'd rather not have caught on camera.

"So you'll just follow me around the whole time?" I asked and held the door for him. He nodded.

"Can't you speak to me?" I asked and moved down the hallway and into the living room, where there was a bit more space.

He peeked out from behind the camera and shook his head.

"Not at all? Is it a rule? You're never allowed to speak to me even though you're following me around?"

"It's not a rule," he told me, his voice taking me by surprise. "I'm just concentrating on the camera."

"Well, I don't think you should give me the silent treatment after I just saved your life!"

I looked around the camera at him and he raised an eyebrow, the corners of his mouth twitching slightly. "Thank you for that," he said quickly. "Maybe you should pack …"

"Maybe," I replied, taking a seat on the couch. "I'm still not sure I can actually just go through with this TV holiday thing, though. Melissa! We've got company."

She appeared in the kitchen doorway, a cup of tea in her hand. "What's going on?"

"This is Adam," I said. "Adam, this is my flatmate, Melissa. Don't expect much chat from him," I told Melissa. "Apparently he's the strong, silent type."

She pushed her glasses up onto her nose. "Why is he filming us?"

I gave her a quick recap of the last hour and asked for her opinion on my current predicament. I was confident Melissa would talk some sense into me. I considered myself to be a level-headed person, but Melissa took being sensible to a completely different level.

"I think you've gone mad," she said. "You can't just waltz off to Spain. You've got no idea what you're getting yourself into. Anything could happen."

"My mum said I should throw caution to the wind."

"Since when do you take her advice?" Melissa asked, seating herself beside me. "Of course she would say that – she's crazy!"

"Not crazy," I corrected her. It always annoyed me when she talked about my mum and completely ignored the rule of families: I can complain about them, but I don't extend the privilege to anyone else. "She's just carefree, that's all."

"Well, whatever you want to call it, I don't think she's the best person to take advice from. What would you do about work if you fly off to Spain?"

"That won't be a problem." I found myself wincing as though I might be in trouble. "I got made redundant today."

"Are you serious? How did you get made redundant? They've been hiring people recently; you should talk to a lawyer."

"It's not so bad. Maybe I can get a job I actually enjoy." I noticed Adam moving out of the corner of my eye. "I forgot you were there." He held up his arm to look at his watch. "It's like charades. I take it you want me to hurry up and pack?"

"No!" Melissa jumped in. "You're not packing, because you're not going anywhere. Clearly you had a shock, losing your job. You shouldn't be making important decisions now. This is insane. What sort of reality show is this, anyway? What do you have to do? Do they film you everywhere? What about in the bathroom? When you're sleeping? You need to stop and think this through."

She was right; I had no idea what I was getting myself into, and normally I wouldn't have entertained the idea for a millisecond, but I wasn't quite feeling myself. In the space of a few hours I'd lost my job and had a lecture from my mum about being spontaneous. Then *voilà*, a camera crew appeared in the street to whisk me off to Spain. If I didn't believe in fate, I might have thought it was all planned.

"I might call my mum and see what she thinks."

"No! Not your mum," Melissa was adamant. "Ask someone sensible. Your dad's good with advice ..."

She was right; my dad would give me reasonable advice. I knew exactly what he would say. It would be the exact opposite of my mum's advice.

"I'll call Kerry," I compromised. Kerry is my stepmum. She's sensible and down to earth; fun, but without any hint of crazy. I looked at Melissa, who nodded her approval.

Adam subtly cleared his throat as the phone rang and I looked up at him. "Could you put it on speaker?" he asked.

I smiled at him as he retreated behind his camera, and switched to speakerphone, setting the phone down on the coffee table.

"Hi Kerry, it's me. I've got something random to ask you. I've been asked to do a reality TV show in Spain but I have to go *now*. It's for a week. I also got made redundant today, so getting time off isn't an issue. Melissa says it's crazy, but I know my mum would tell me to go and have fun, so I just need a third opinion before I make up my mind. There's a cameraman next to me recording everything and waiting for me to pack and go to the airport!"

"Wow!" I could hear the kids shouting in the background: my two little half-brothers, Max and Jacob. They're so full of energy that I can sit and watch them for ten minutes and feel like I've done a full body workout. Perhaps it's not the best approach to exercise, but it's as close to a workout as I ever get. "Sorry about the redundancy. How did the TV show come about?"

"They just came up to me in the street and asked. Chelsea Cartwright is the host, she was there. I can't decide what to do. It sounds crazy, doesn't it?"

"Completely! I think you should go."

"Oh." I paused, surprised by her definitive response. "Is this like a reverse psychology thing?"

"No. I really think you should go. Don't tell your dad I said that, though. He'd definitely agree with Melissa. I think it's about time you did something spontaneous. What's the worst that can happen?"

"I've thought about that," I told her, leaning back against the couch. "And there are a lot of really bad scenarios!"

"Oh, come on." She laughed at me. "You're sensible enough to know what you're doing. Just don't do anything you're uncomfortable with. You might even have fun."

I looked at Melissa, who was shaking her head in defeat. "This is not a good idea."

"Hi, Melissa," Kerry said. "Don't be such a killjoy.

Tell her to go and enjoy herself."

I sat up straight. "Okay, I've decided. I'm going!"

Kerry let out a short cheer. "Have a brilliant time and call if you need anything."

"I will. Thanks, Kerry. I have to go and pack. I love you!"

"Love you too. Take care."

"You're not serious?" Melissa asked.

"Very serious," I told her while I dashed across the living room. I looked at Adam, who took me by surprise by giving me a very cute smile.

Hannah Ellis

Chapter 3

The awkward thing about packing for a holiday with a stranger and a camera hovering over you is the underwear. I'm quite a private person, and the thought of Adam seeing my underwear was bad enough, never mind having it televised. I tried to keep my back to him as I pulled out a T-shirt from the drawer below and wrapped my knickers and bras in it before turning to pack it in the suitcase lying open on my bed. I glanced at Adam and wasn't sure if he was smirking or if I was paranoid.

I randomly grabbed at clothes, unsure of what I would need. I threw in my swimsuit, presuming it would be hot and I'd get at least a bit of beach time. Moving swiftly to the bathroom, I flung some toiletries in a bag and then went back to my room to look around for inspiration. I was sure to have forgotten something vital.

I looked to Adam. "I think I'm ready. Anything else I need?"

"Passport?" he prompted.

"Good job I've got you!" I told him and dug around in a drawer until I found my passport. "Let's go, then!"

I hugged Melissa goodbye. "This is a very bad idea," she warned me again.

"You can say 'I told you so' as soon as I'm back!" I

said, hurrying out of the door and back into the car. "I can't believe I'm doing this." I looked from Adam to Bill. "It's totally nuts!"

I had a sinking feeling in my gut. I was never impulsive and I wasn't sure why today was different. Maybe losing my job had made me a bit irrational. Melissa could be right: in fact, I was sure I'd heard somewhere that you shouldn't make important decisions after a trauma in your life. Was losing my job a trauma? Probably not. My mind whirred as we got nearer to the airport. I was surprised to find the camera on me as I turned to Adam. I'd almost forgotten about it. I looked past it to Adam. "Do you think this is really stupid? Should I just turn around and go home?"

He moved his head slightly and looked at me intently. I felt like I could trust him; he had kind eyes.

"I'm sure you'll have a great time." Bill's voice startled me, dragging my focus from Adam's blue eyes. (Eye, actually, since one was concealed by the camera.) "I hear they're putting you up in a nice place too. Sitting by the pool and drinking cocktails at someone else's expense sounds pretty good to me."

"You're right. I bet I'll enjoy it once I get there." I looked at Adam, but his attention was firmly on the camera.

"I just hope the other people aren't weird," Bill remarked. "I'm not sure what sort of people can fly off to Spain at the drop of a hat. Don't people have jobs?"

"I've not even thought about the others," I said, sighing. "You're right, though, what kind of people agree to fly out immediately for a bloody reality TV show? I'm going to be trapped in a foreign country with a load of nutters."

Bill's laughter became muffled as I dropped my head into my hands. I couldn't believe I was one of the nutters who had agreed to it.

I said goodbye to Bill and walked hesitantly into the airport. I heard Chelsea before I saw her and the mere sound of her voice made me want to run in the opposite direction. How would I cope with her for a week?

"Yoo-hoo! Lucy!" She was in the middle of a small crowd of people, with a few cameramen scattered around the perimeter. Detaching herself, she headed for me, her huge boobs bouncing ahead of her. Her long blonde locks flowed around her and she threw her arms up and did jazz hands as she got to me. It made me laugh and I indulged her by doing the same, albeit in a slightly sarcastic way.

"Are you ready for a trip to remember?" she screeched.

"I certainly am!" I decided I might as well get into the spirit of it, if I really was going to go along with this.

"Come and meet everyone …" She bounded back to the crowd and I turned to Adam.

"Is she on drugs or what? She's hyper. Off we go on a trip to remember!" I mocked her. "It's like her little catchphrase." Adam looked meaningfully at me.

"Is that the name of the show? Trip to remember? How cheesy!" He smirked and motioned the camera. I shrugged, not caring. If they wanted reality, they could bloody well have it.

"I'm going to assume you're on the show too?" A

girl with amazing ginger curls broke away from the group as I approached. She looked to be about my age, in her early twenties. Although, actually, at twenty-six I was definitely in my mid-twenties now, though I wasn't quite sure where the past five years had gone. "Or do you always have a cameraman following you?"

"Seems like I'm on the show," I told her. "You too?"

"Yes! Please tell me you're nice? I'm scared I'm going to be stuck with a load of horrible people for the week. I don't even know why I agreed to this!" She linked her arm through mine and pulled me in to whisper conspiratorially, "You look nice."

"I might be a bit crazy," I told her. "I used to think I was completely sane and rational but, as of today, I'm not so sure. I'm Lucy, by the way."

"Chrissie," she told me. "Nice to meet you." She had a pretty face, full of freckles, and gorgeous brown eyes.

"This is Adam." I turned but lost sight of him as the others in the group enveloped us.

"Yay! Another girl!" A blonde towered over us. I craned my neck to look up at her. *Please let her be called Barbie. That would just make my day.*

"I'm Kelly," she said. *No such luck!* She was a total Barbie, though: blonde hair, bright blue eyes, a face full of make-up, and a gorgeous figure.

"This is Lucy," Chrissie told her, still clutching my arm. I nodded like a fool. Apparently I couldn't even introduce myself any more.

"How exciting is this?" Kelly said. "I can't believe we're going to Spain! Do you think we'll share a room?"

Oh God, I hoped not. I'd not thought about that. They'd sold it to me as a holiday and I'd assumed I'd get my own fancy hotel room. *Please don't let us be sharing a dorm room.*

"Where's Margaret?" Kelly scanned the area. "Margaret, come and meet Lucy!"

A mature-looking woman joined us and gave me a hug. "Well, this is all very weird, isn't it, Lucy?"

"Definitely! Are you Australian?" I asked. Her accent gave her away but she also looked like the sort of person you could drop in the middle of the Outback and she'd be fine. Maybe it was her khaki shorts and hiking boots that made her look ready for anything. She had dark skin and dark hair, which had been twisted up and held in place with a large clip, though a fair amount had fallen free and framed her face haphazardly.

"Certainly am!" she told me. "I finally got my act together and came over this way to track down my long-lost relatives, and wouldn't you know it, some bloody sheila in the street asks me to go to Spain. You don't need to ask me twice!"

I smiled at her enthusiasm; maybe the trip would be fine after all.

"They seem okay," I whispered to Chrissie when Kelly and Margaret moved away from us.

"Wait until you see the boys." She peered into the crowd. "Look, there's Captain Caveman ..."

My eyes landed on the bearded man. I'm not sure how else to describe him. His unkempt brown beard took over his face, overshadowing his other features. He wore jogging bottoms with a grubby white T-shirt,

27

and I decided he was probably unemployed and that's why he could fly to Spain for a week without warning. Although perhaps I shouldn't be so judgemental, given my current employment status.

"The young guy is Ryan," Chrissie told me. I followed her gaze to a younger man who looked like he'd just stepped out of a boy band with his baby face, and hair gelled into a quiff. Even from a distance, energy radiated from him. At least *he* seemed excited about the trip; he was literally jumping up and down.

"Why did you agree to this?" I asked Chrissie, peeling my gaze away from Ryan. "Don't you have a job or anything?"

"I'm a student. Summer holidays! I was supposed to be studying this week. I threw a few books in my bag, but I'm not convinced it will be the most productive week of studying. It was good timing; I have to work for the rest of the summer. This is my last week of freedom, then I'll be slaving away in a supermarket until university starts again."

We were interrupted by Jessica, who clapped her hands and waved for us to move closer. She was tall and seemed to be constantly looking down at those around her. "I just need your attention for a minute," she told us. "This is the boring bit."

Moving into the middle of the group, she began handing out clipboards. "I need a signature from you all to say you agree to being filmed – theoretically 24/7, but I doubt it will be that much – and any footage can be televised. You will be given guidelines in Majorca about where you can go, and as long as you adhere to the guidelines and stay for seven days, then all your expenses will be covered. If you decide to leave early then you would have to arrange and cover the cost of the return flight." She talked fast and I looked down at my clipboard, which held numerous sheets of official-looking paper, headed with RDT's logo. "It's all pretty standard and straightforward, but feel free to take a moment to read through it all before you sign."

Chrissie's forehead crinkled as she flicked through the papers. I glanced over the documents, which were full of legal jargon I couldn't quite get my head around. I glanced up and saw Margaret and Kelly flip straight to the last page and sign their names, handing the clipboard back to Jessica. The bearded man and young guy did the same. There was someone else with them, who I'd only just noticed. He casually looked over the papers, as the corners of his mouth twitched into a smile.

"What does it mean by 'remaining within the required confines'?" I looked to Jessica and then down at the paper again. "It sounds like we'll be in prison or something. We are free to leave at any time, aren't we?"

"Of course." She looked at me like I was an idiot. "Your accommodation will be in a traditional Spanish finca, in the hills of Majorca. It has large grounds and a pool. I'm sure you'll love it. For filming purposes, we just need you to agree to stay where we can see you. If we arrive and you all disappear around the island, we have a slight problem."

"So we have to stay the whole week in this finca?" I asked.

"No. There will be group outings and organised activities, but we're just asking for your cooperation in order for us to capture your holiday on film."

"When will it be aired? And on what channel?" I was slightly nervous at the thought of being on TV. If it was just some random channel that hardly anyone would see then I could cope. If the programme would be aired on a mainstream channel at prime time then I might have a rethink.

I saw a look of impatience flash across Jessica's face. "We're about to launch a new channel, RealTV24, which will air different reality shows, 24/7. You've probably seen it advertised. RDT1 is airing a big new reality TV show next week to kick it off – you've no doubt heard about it. Anyway, we're currently filming a number of shows to see which formats work best for the new channel. There is a possibility this will never be aired. You'll be lucky if you get the 2am slot on a Tuesday. So anyone who's here in the hope of overnight fame might want to leave now."

Chrissie looked at me and shrugged before she signed the papers and handed over the clipboard.

"Any more questions?" Jessica hovered over me.

"No," I said hesitantly, flicking to the last page to sign my life away. I hoped I wouldn't regret it.

"Okay!" Jessica sounded relieved. "I also need all your mobile phones and any electronic devices. You'll get everything back at the end of the week." She passed around cards with a number for us to give to our families, in case of emergencies. I sent a quick message to Kerry before switching off my phone and handing it over. I noticed Margaret dig around under her shirt to pull her phone out of a security wallet tied around her waist.

"Let's get this show on the road," Jessica said. "Next stop, Majorca!" A weak cheer sounded around me, and I shuffled with the crowd through the airport, feeling decidedly unsure of myself.

***

"I'm Matt, one of your fellow inmates!" I'd just settled into my seat in the business class section of the plane when a tall, well-built guy took the seat next to me. I shook his hand.

"I'm Lucy," I told him and glanced around our section of the plane, which was bustling with TV crew, cameramen and us. "So, what's your story, then?" I asked Matt, aware of Adam in the aisle, a camera aimed at us. "How did you end up agreeing to this?"

"I'm a primary school teacher. School's just broken up for summer and I got stopped on my way home. Well, on the way to the pub, if I'm honest. The rest of the staff couldn't believe it when I rang and said I wouldn't make it to the pub because I was on the way to an all-expenses-paid trip to Spain."

I rooted underneath me for the seat belt, clicking it in place. "Wow."

"What? You're amazed one of us actually has a proper job?"

"To be honest, yes. Although I did have a job. I just got made redundant this morning."

"That sounds like fate," he said.

"Maybe. What are the rest of them like?" I asked, looking around at everyone settling in for the flight.

"The young guy's called Ryan," he leaned in and

whispered. "He seems to think he's a bit of a stud, so you'd better watch out."

"I'll bear it in mind. Thanks for the tip. What about Captain Caveman?" I asked. He smiled at the nickname.

"That's Dylan. He's a 'musician'," he told me with a wink. "Apparently he was busking when they found him. I think they were getting desperate at that stage." He looked around the plane. "Then there's Chrissie; she seems nice. A student, I think. Over there Aussie Margaret, the great traveller." He nodded across the aisle from us. "And Kelly's next to her. I'm not sure what Kelly does for a living but my guess would be either a lawyer or a doctor – what do you reckon?"

I snorted in response. "My bet would be a surgeon."

"Oh yeah, you could be right, surgeon would be more likely. Not just a plain old doctor." We both laughed before Matt glanced at the camera. "Aren't we mean? I hope she is a surgeon just so we have to eat our words. It's amazing how easy it is to forget about the cameras, isn't it?"

"Far too easy," I agreed.

Chapter 4

I felt the sun tingling blissfully on my skin as soon as we stepped out of the airport in Majorca. It was a long time since I'd had a holiday, and the heat was a delicious reminder of what I'd been missing out on. I hoped I would have time to relax and indulge in some rays.

We were ushered into a row of waiting minibuses. I stayed close to Matt. I'd enjoyed his company on the flight; he was easy to talk to and had a good sense of humour. Chrissie was on our minibus too, along with Adam and one other cameraman. A young guy climbed in behind Jessica, and I took him to be her assistant. Jessica sat in front of me, looking mildly flustered. There was an array of bags scattered among us, which shifted when we finally set off and drove away from the airport.

I'd been expecting to stay at some tacky accommodation in the heart of the tourist area but as we drove further into the arid countryside it became more apparent that wouldn't be the case.

Eventually the minibus pulled onto a dusty single-track road and we meandered along for a couple of miles before finally arriving at a gated driveway. We stopped momentarily before the gates juddered open and we drove through.

I peered out of the window but the track was overgrown, and the way it weaved meant we couldn't see the house until we were right in front of it. The convoy of minibuses used a fountain as a roundabout and came to a stop in the shade of what I would describe as a sand-coloured castle. We craned our necks once we exited the buses. The finca towered over us, set against the cloudless blue sky.

"Welcome to your home for the week," Jessica said, dwarfed by the huge front door. "Follow me and we'll get you settled."

We trailed behind her through the massive wooden doors which opened into a draughty entrance hall. The walls were adorned with random pictures and stuffed animal heads. Nothing seemed to quite fill the space. Large as it was, the room seemed to serve no purpose. I glanced through an open door at the far end, which appeared to lead to an inner courtyard.

We ascended wide stone steps into a huge living room. Again, the furniture and decorations seemed too small for the size of the place. Even the few windows were tiny.

"Come and see the best bit," Jessica instructed us. She led us outside through double doors into a little piece of paradise. At one side was a living area with comfy couches and a few scattered tables, and beyond that stood a long dining table with benches down either side. I walked across the beautifully kept lawn in front of us to look out over the low wall which lined it, and peered at the fountain and minibuses down below. There was a dog running between them. I followed the wall, stopping at the still water of the swimming pool, which glinted invitingly. The whole outside area was like something from a top hotel. I turned and marvelled at the sun loungers scattered around the lawn, each with its own grass sun umbrella. It seemed I might get time to sunbathe after all.

Chrissie appeared by my side. "How amazing is this?"

Matt squeezed between us and draped an arm around both our shoulders. "I think we might have a nice week here, girls!"

I had the feeling I had known these two for longer than a few hours, and a smile crept over my face. Matt might be right; this might just be a good week.

Then the three of us jumped back as a figure ran past and dive-bombed into the pool, causing a huge splash.

"Well, that's put me off using the pool," Chrissie said. "I wonder how long it is since Caveman last washed … Anyone know his name?"

"Dylan," Matt told her.

"I'll bet there were things living in his beard," she said.

"Hola!" A grey-haired lady in a pinafore dress and an apron offered us a tray of champagne. She was short and kept her head down, only occasionally glancing up, looking suspiciously at the cameras scattered around us. She whispered something in Spanish as we each accepted a drink from her. It seemed Matt and Chrissie had a similar level of Spanish to me, as we all thanked her in English, along with a lot of nodding and smiles.

"I'm going to check the rest of the house is set up for you." Jessica's voice broke the air as I took a sip of champagne. "Relax and get to know each other a bit. I'll be back shortly to give you a tour of the house." With that she made her way back inside, followed by her assistant and two other people. I was alone with my new housemates and a handful of cameramen.

I'd taken an instant liking to Chrissie and Matt but I hadn't even spoken to everyone else yet. Since I'd be living with them for the next week I decided I'd better introduce myself. Matt and Chrissie followed as I moved over to the lounge area.

"I'm Lucy." I reached out a hand, and the cocky-looking young guy sat up from the couch where he'd been lying flat on his back.

"Ryan," he told me.

I smiled at Kelly on the other couch, feeling suddenly awkward. The champagne tasted good and I hoped it would settle my sudden bout of nerves. I glanced at the camera as I raised the glass to my lips, aware that my every move was being watched.

"Looks like we're in for a good week, doesn't it?" Ryan picked up his champagne glass and clinked it against mine. I took another sip and worried I'd get drunk and make a fool of myself. Although I guess I could just as easily make a fool of myself sober ...

"I don't think we'll be sitting in the sun sipping champagne all week, will we?" Kelly asked. "There's got to be a catch somewhere."

"There will be a catch." Captain Caveman appeared and I took a seat. He loomed over me, dripping wet. "I'm Dylan," he told me.

"Lucy," I replied, self-conscious as he peeled his wet T-shirt off and then his jogging bottoms. I couldn't help but glance up at him. I registered his toned chest before I averted my eyes, noting that all the girls had their eyes on him.

"I'm sure they'll make us jump out of aeroplanes and eat raw snakes and things," Dylan said while he dried himself off. The aeroplane comment unsettled me. I could cope with anything but sky-diving. That would definitely be my cue to go home. "What kind of reality show would it be if we just sat around in the sun? No one would want to watch that."

"I don't know …" Kelly looked down and thrust her chest out before looking up at us with a mischievous smile.

"I'd watch *that* in a bikini for a week," Ryan commented with a raised eyebrow, successfully killing the atmosphere. We all threw frosty looks his way. "Sorry," he muttered.

"I just hope they feed us well," Margaret changed the subject. "I've seen shows where they ration your food to make you go a bit crazy. Makes for good television, I guess. I like my food – if it turns out like that, I'd struggle to stay calm for long."

"So what do you do, Lucy?" My eyes darted to Dylan at the sound of my name. He'd taken a seat on the floor opposite me and leaned against the couch.

"I'm currently unemployed." I was surprised to find I sounded quite proud of my statement. I toed my shoes off, then reached down to pull off my socks and stuff them into my shoes. "I had a job this morning … Isn't it funny how quickly things can change?"

I looked at Dylan, to find him staring at me intensely. I shifted in my seat and glanced around at the cameras, my eyes landing on Adam who was leaning against a pillar nearby.

"So you quit your job to come on the show?" Kelly asked.

"No." I pulled my gaze to her. "I was made redundant. I was on my way home when I bumped into Chelsea. If I hadn't lost my job, I wouldn't have even stopped for Chelsea; I'd have waved her off and kept walking. I'd be at home now watching a movie."

"Are you serious?" Kelly asked. "Just sitting at home on a Friday night?"

"I usually go out," I mumbled as I realised everyone was looking at me sympathetically. "But my flatmate, Melissa, has been having some cash-flow problems so I've been trying to be a good friend and stay in with her." That seemed to placate them. I went out with Melissa sometimes, but neither of us were big partygoers.

"What do you do, Ryan?" I attempted to draw the attention away from myself. Rooting in my pocket, I found a hair band and pulled my shoulder-length brown hair off my neck and tied it in a ponytail.

"I'm an electrician," Ryan told us. "Or I will be; I'm doing an apprenticeship."

"And you can just take a week off without any problem?" I said.

"I doubt it," he said, his voice light and jokey. "But I decided being rich and famous might be worth giving up my career as an electrician!"

"So, ladies and gentlemen," Jessica reappeared looking refreshed and cheerful. "Who's ready for the grand tour?" She moved over to us, followed by two more cameramen. "You've already familiarised yourselves with our outdoor area. I'm sure you'll spend most of your time here. We've tried to make it really comfortable for you and hope you'll take full advantage of that. Come on …" She moved into the house. "This is the living room." The furniture was old and mismatched, giving the room a dreary feel.

"This is the dining room."

It was a huge room with high ceilings, minimally furnished with a long solid table and matching chairs. "Maria, the housekeeper you met earlier, will provide all your meals. You can eat where you want but I guess you'll be most comfortable outside. Through here is the kitchen." She moved on and we followed her, taking in our surroundings. "A breakfast buffet will be set out for you here in the mornings, so just come and help yourselves. There are also soft drinks in the fridge, and tea, coffee and snacks, so make yourselves at home." I glanced at Margaret, who gave me a thumbs-up, happy to learn we'd be well fed.

"This leads down to Maria's apartment and is off-limits." Jessica motioned a door in a corner of the kitchen. "Please respect her privacy. The same is true of the rooms above the kitchen." She moved back the way she'd come and pointed out the staircase next to the kitchen. "That's where the crew are staying, so please stay out of that area. I'll show you where you're sleeping now." We followed her back through the dining room and up another staircase back near the entrance.

"You have another living room up here," she told us while we filed up the stairs to join her in a plain rectangular room. Our luggage was lined up against one wall. There was little else to see. Two small couches faced each other in the middle of the room with a small rectangular table between them. Long windows ran the length of the room, making it light and airy, but it had a musty feel to it, as did most of the house. I got the feeling they wanted to encourage us to be outside as much as possible.

"The boys' bedrooms are down that end." Jessica pointed back towards the staircase. "And the girls' rooms are over there." We automatically split up, the boys going to check out their rooms while we headed to the opposite end of the living room to find ours. Two doors opened to identical bedrooms, connected by a bathroom. They were basic, but nice enough. I felt Chrissie's eyes on me and she gave me a slight nod. I followed her through the bathroom and into the second bedroom, where she fell backwards onto one of the twin beds. I flopped onto the other, and that was how we decided where we would sleep.

We regrouped in the living room before heading back downstairs and outside. "I would really encourage you all to relax and enjoy your week here," Jessica addressed us again once we were seated. "Try to forget about the cameras; just be yourselves, and have a great time. You probably won't see much of me, but Chelsea will be around now and again to keep you informed of anything you need to know. Maria should be out shortly with some dinner for you. Enjoy your evening!" She gave a quick wave and left us.

"I'm still not sure what the catch is," Kelly said.

"Let's not look a gift horse in the mouth," Matt said. "It's a free holiday. I intend to do as I'm told and relax and enjoy it!"

"I think the catch is them," I pointed out the cameramen. "I'm not sure I'll be able to forget about them long enough to enjoy myself. I hate the thought that anything I say or do could be shown on TV. I feel like I'll be on edge all week."

"Just don't say or do anything embarrassing," Ryan told me plainly. "Then there's nothing to worry about, is there?"

"Surely no one sets out to embarrass themselves," Dylan said. "But you never know how you'll come across on TV. I think Lucy's got a point; the cameras are distracting."

"Why did you come then?" Ryan asked. "It's for a TV show. We'll all be famous. If you don't want to be on TV, why come?"

"Good question." Dylan looked distant. "I just got talked into it. I'm hoping it doesn't turn out to be a huge mistake."

"I'm not sure why I came either," I confessed. "I still can't believe I agreed to it. I don't want to be on TV. I'm hoping I can just hide behind the rest of you and barely be noticed."

"That's if this even gets on TV," Matt put in. "It didn't seem definite to me."

"I'd love to be a celebrity," Kelly told us. "I think I'd be great at it." Her eyes twinkled and she had us all laughing when Maria arrived with a huge tray containing plates and tableware.

"Thank goodness they're not starving us," Margaret sighed when we sat down to a huge pan of paella, an assortment of breads and an olive oil dip. "There's even wine. Now I can relax!"

"Of course there's wine," Ryan said. "We'll be drunk and embarrassing ourselves in no time. It'll make great TV!"

"Not me," I commented under my breath while I pulled out a chair to sit down. I was confident the rest of them were big enough personalities that I would be able to fade into the background. I could sit in the sun for a week and then get back to my real life.

Chapter 5

"What do you think of Dylan?" Chrissie asked me in the darkness. I was glad I was sharing a room with her. Kelly and Margaret seemed nice too, but I felt really comfortable with Chrissie.

"He seems nice enough, once you get past the beard."

"It's off-putting, isn't it? So much facial hair on such a young guy. How old do you think he is, anyway?"

"I'm not sure," I told her quietly. "Late twenties? Maybe younger?"

"Can't be younger," she whispered. "How many years would it take to grow a beard like that?"

"It's not so long, really," I mused. "It's just unruly. I bet he'd be really cute without it."

"No way!" I could just make out Chrissie's silhouette as she sat up in bed. "How can you say that? He looks like he's probably flea-infested."

"He's got nice eyes, though."

"You don't mess around, do you?" She lay down again, wriggling to get comfy. "Looking into the boys' eyes on the first day?"

"It wasn't like that," I told her, chuckling. "Anyway, what do you think about Matt? I think he was flirting with you."

"Now Matt is definitely cute. Was he flirting with me? How did I miss that?"

I plumped my lumpy pillow. "I thought so. Maybe."

"Don't put ideas in my head. You'll make me self-conscious around him. I just came for a holiday. I don't want a TV romance."

"You really think this will end up on TV?" I asked.

"Probably not. But we'd better get some beauty sleep just in case."

"Goodnight, Chrissie," I whispered and turned onto my side. The room was uncomfortably hot, and I was certain I'd find it hard to fall asleep.

I was feeling surprisingly relaxed, though. I didn't usually drink much, so it might have been the champagne that had an effect on me, but I was really calm about this bizarre situation. So far it had been fun, and I was happy my fellow housemates were so pleasant.

I decided a break from reality might be just what I needed. I smiled to myself, realising the irony of this; that I was currently taking part in a reality TV show. This was an entirely different kind of *reality* to what I was used to, though.

***

The sunlight woke me early, and I showered while Chrissie slept on. In the upstairs living room, I was surprised to find Adam dozing on a couch, his camera by his side. I moved to the window and looked out over the back of the finca.

Maria walked out of a door far below me and

started to hang washing on a rickety washing stand. A dog circled around her legs, and chickens wandered nearby. I crossed the room to look through the opposite window, but I was distracted by Adam and paused to look down at him.

I'd not managed to get a good look at him yesterday as he was always partially hidden by his camera. I knew he had kind eyes. If he didn't, I might not be here; there was something reassuring about him and he'd quietly put me at ease about the whole situation. He had sandy brown hair, classically cut, which was now ruffled into a 'slept on the couch' style. I wondered how long he'd been on guard up here.

His eyes opened so suddenly that I didn't have time to move or look away, and his hand darted for the camera as though he was reaching for a weapon.

"Sorry," I told him quickly, banging my leg on the table when I took a step back. "I wasn't watching you sleep, I promise. I only just came in here. I wasn't being creepy or anything."

There was a brief flash of amusement in his eyes before he stood and brought the camera to his face, while simultaneously pressing a button, making the red light appear beside the camera lens.

"Looks like a nice day anyway," I muttered awkwardly, moving to the window at the front of the room to look out over the driveway and rolling hills. "I wonder what we'll be doing today. Are you coming downstairs?" I turned to look at him as I headed for the stairs. It was weird to talk to someone and not have them say anything back. The silence was unsettling, so I just kept talking.

"Did you sleep okay? It can't have been comfy on

45

the couch. You weren't there all night, were you? Were you supposed to be awake? Am I getting you into trouble now by saying you were asleep?" I realised I needed to learn to avoid asking questions. If you're going to talk to a wall, at least don't be crazy enough to ask it questions. I looked into the camera. "He wasn't really sleeping. Just having a rest. He jumped up as soon as I came in. He's doing a great job." I beamed into the camera and then gave Adam a discreet thumbs-up, out of shot.

I made my way through the dining room and into the cosy kitchen. It was one of the only rooms that felt lived in. I found Maria taking orange juice from the fridge to add to the breakfast buffet.

"Morning," I said, making her jump. She looked at me cheerfully, and started chattering in Spanish. I looked at her blankly and took the plate she offered me. She opened the door in the corner of the kitchen and disappeared down the stone staircase.

I exchanged the plate for a bowl, helping myself to cereal and a glass of orange juice, and almost bumped into Adam when I turned to leave the kitchen. "Sorry. Do you want anything?"

He shook his head.

It was nice to sit outside and eat in the glorious sunshine, The camera aimed at me was slightly unnerving but I kept my head down and did my best to ignore it.

I'd just set my bowl down on the table in front of me when another cameraman appeared and moved into Adam's spot, leaning on the pillar ahead of me. He wore cargo shorts and a plain green T-shirt: the same ensemble as Adam, only in slightly different colours. A cameraman's uniform, perhaps. Adam lowered his camera and gave me a quick salute before he headed inside.

"I don't think we've been introduced," I told my new cameraman. "I'm Lucy."

"Carl," he told me with a smile. He looked older than Adam – maybe around forty. He had a shaved head and a pot belly. There was an air of calm about him, and I thought that perhaps they'd chosen the cameramen purposely to be the sort of people who you'd happily chat away to even though they stayed quiet. Although I would have thought they would choose people who blended in with the background and didn't draw inane chatter from us. It was actually slightly strange they had cameramen at all. Surely hidden cameras were all the rage these days?

"You're much chattier than Adam already," I told him. "What do you do for a living, Carl?"

He rolled his eyes before putting his hand to his belly while he mimed an over-the-top laugh.

"I can't help the jokes," I told him with a grin. "It's just something you'll have to get used to."

"Morning."

I turned, to see Matt walking out to join me with a plate piled high with food, and another cameraman behind him.

"Morning," I replied. "How did you sleep?"

"Not great. It's so hot up there – and Dylan snores. You probably heard him from your room …"

"I slept like a log," I told him and sipped my orange juice.

He shook his head and loaded a piece of bread with ham and cheese, taking a huge bite.

"What do you think we'll be doing today?" I asked.

"Lying in the sun, with any luck," he said through a mouthful of food.

"Hey, Lucy!" I turned to see Chrissie hanging out of an upstairs window. "Get your bikini on and we'll have a morning swim."

"I'm all ready." I smiled up at her and pulled my T-shirt off one shoulder to reveal my striped blue swimsuit.

"Brilliant! I'll be down in a minute." She disappeared from view and I heard some grumbling in the background.

"Is that your room?" I asked Matt.

"Yeah. I guess she finally put a stop to the snoring."

Chrissie arrived and headed straight for the pool in her tiny bikini. I noticed Matt's eyes following her. He was smirking.

"Come on, Lucy," she beckoned me over.

I slipped out of my shorts and T-shirt and moved to join her.

"What's that?" Chrissie asked as I walked down the steps into the pool.

"What?"

"What are you wearing?" She whispered and glanced at Carl over my shoulder.

"It's a tankini," I told her. "It's great because it covers my tummy."

"What's great about that? We're being filmed."

"Exactly." I set off to do some laps and Chrissie shook her head at me. "What's wrong with it?" I asked.

"Nothing." She sighed and turned on her back to float around the pool.

I actually didn't have a problem with my stomach; I was a naturally slim size ten and was happy with my body. I just didn't like the thought of having too much flesh on display, especially in front of a bunch of strangers and several guys with cameras. It felt too exposed.

I swam a few laps while Chrissie relaxed on the pool steps. "If we can just swim in the pool and lie in the sun all week, I'll be very happy," I told her.

"They told me I would have time to study, so we obviously don't have a packed schedule. I should get my books out later."

"What are you studying?"

"Social work. I'm finishing my second year – just got one year left. I probably don't need to get the books out on the first day, do I? I should give myself some time to relax."

"Maybe."

"I'll do some work tomorrow. It would make really boring viewing anyway, me with my head in my books."

I waved to Margaret, Kelly, Ryan and Dylan as they trickled outside over the next half hour. I was floating on my back, savouring the warmth of the sun on my face, when Chelsea arrived, her annoying smile plastered to her face.

I got out of the pool, wrapped a towel around myself and took a seat next to Ryan, drops of water falling from my hair and rolling down my face while I stared at Chelsea.

"Great to see you're all settling in and making yourselves at home," she said.

No one reacted. I'm not sure what it was about her

– maybe it was that she seemed so fake. It made people ignore her.

"Over the next week, we have a number of activities for you – some just for fun and others where you will have the chance to win a prize!" She sounded so scripted it was painful. How she'd got a job as a presenter I'd never know. "Your first challenge will take place this morning, and the winner will receive a cash prize!"

That gained her everyone's full attention, and we looked at her eagerly.

"What do we have to do?" Matt asked.

Chelsea looked at us coyly. "Follow me and all will be revealed!"

Chapter 6

We congregated by the fountain. Three quad bikes were parked in front of the finca.

"Your first challenge of the week," Chelsea said as we stood around the quads, "is our quad bike time trial, and there is £500 up for grabs for one lucky winner!"

It was difficult to be excited about the cash prize anymore, since the chances of me winning such a race seemed minuscule. Matt's face lit up, though, and he exchanged an excited look with Dylan before directing his attention back to Chelsea.

"See the flagpoles along the driveway?" she asked us. "Each pole has a flag stuck to the top. All you have to do is drive to the gate and back, collecting the flags as you go. Any missed flags will incur a ten-second penalty. The person with the fastest time wins!"

Ryan rubbed his hands together and looked at Matt. "This should be fun."

"I've never driven a quad," I told Chelsea nervously.

"Don't worry, you'll get a lesson first. Why don't you jump on?"

Cautiously, I climbed on to the nearest quad bike. A man approached me with a helmet and gave me brief instructions in broken English. Chrissie sat on the bike next to me, looking just as apprehensive as I felt. Margaret had confidently driven away already.

The quad lurched slightly when I first pressed the accelerator, but I quickly got a feel for it and drove slowly down the dusty driveway, taking care to avoid the many potholes. Margaret looked like she was having a great time when she whizzed past me.

As well as the flagpoles and trees that lined the path, I also noticed the cameramen dotted around the place. I gave Adam a wave when I passed him on my way back towards the house.

I stood in the shade of the finca and watched as everyone took turns having a test drive. The boys all shot off at top speed and I was surprised to see that Kelly was fairly confident too.

"I think that's enough practice," Chelsea announced half an hour later when we'd all had a turn. "Time to start the competition! Ryan, would you like to go first? Drive up to the line and wait for my signal, please."

Chelsea stood on the starting line – a line of green paint – holding out a white hanky. There was a man beside her with a stopwatch and a clipboard, and when she lifted the hanky Ryan put his foot down and took off towards the first flag.

He seemed to make great time, and was back with all ten flags in no time.

Chrissie went next and missed three of the flags. Chelsea told her immediately that she hadn't beaten Ryan's time. I think it was fairly obvious anyway. Dylan managed to get all the flags, but Chelsea told him he was three seconds slower than Ryan.

Ryan was looking thoroughly pleased with himself and not at all worried when I set off down the drive. My slow and steady approach meant that I got all the flags, but it didn't prove to be a winning tactic. I didn't even ask what my time was. I knew I hadn't beaten Ryan's time.

Kelly also didn't manage to knock Ryan off the top spot, but did provide some entertainment when she overshot a flagpole and sent a cameraman diving out of her way.

Ryan looked nervous when Matt drove up to the start line. Matt gave Ryan a wink before he set off at speed along the path. He collected all ten flags with ease and looked expectantly at Chelsea when he returned.

"You made good time," she told him, glancing at the clipboard. "But …"

Ryan's face broke into a grin.

"There's still a chance for Margaret to knock you off the top spot, Matt!"

Matt pulled off his helmet and cheered.

"Don't get too excited," Margaret told him seriously. "You'll only be disappointed when I beat you!"

"Go, Margaret!" Chrissie cheered when she climbed onto the quad and manoeuvred it to the start line.

She took off quickly and seemed to maintain a good pace as Chrissie, Kelly and I cheered her on.

"She's doing really well," Dylan commented to Matt, who was starting to look worried.

We got more animated as Margaret returned with the ten flags. She looked full of confidence when she pulled off her helmet.

"Sorry, Matt," she said. "I think that money's mine!"

"Hang on a minute," Matt replied, looking at Chelsea for confirmation.

"And the winner is …" Chelsea's voice rang out. "Margaret!"

Margaret looked very smug. Matt hung his head for a moment before congratulating her, along with the rest of us.

We moved slowly back through the finca and found lunch laid out for us.

"That was fun," Chrissie said as we sat down together and tucked in to the delicious food. "Now we get a lovely lunch and an afternoon by the pool. It's not bad really, is it?"

"Not bad at all!" Margaret said, still on a high from her win.

"If I had a beer, it would be like a proper holiday," Matt said grumpily.

"Hola!" Maria appeared with jugs of iced water and placed them on the table.

"Don't suppose you've got a beer for me, have you?" Matt asked. "I'd love you forever …"

She stared at him, with clearly no idea of what he'd said.

"*Cerveza?*" Dylan added, looking at Maria, who beamed at him and started chatting away in Spanish. He shook his head nervously. "Sorry, I only know the word for beer. That's the extent of my Spanish."

Maria carried on talking, and when we all looked blankly back at her she grabbed Matt's hand and pulled him away from us. I followed them, and saw a door which I'd not registered before.

"I think I've pulled," Matt shouted over his shoulder as Maria opened the door and dragged him inside. Chrissie and I watched from the doorway as Maria led Matt into the bare room and showed him a huge fridge filled with assorted drinks, including plenty of beer.

"Wow!" Ryan followed them into the room and peered into the fridge with Matt. "Heaven."

Maria shook her head and left us alone.

"There're pool inflatables in here too," Ryan said as he surveyed the room, "Now it's like a proper holiday!"

We dumped the inflatables into the pool and I settled myself in an inflatable armchair. It felt like we were in slow-motion bumper cars as we filled the pool and bobbed around, bumping into each other before pushing off, only to bump into someone else.

"Now this is the life," Margaret said with a sigh, lying on a lilo.

"We need to explore later," Ryan suggested. "If there was a room full of beer and toys we didn't know about, what else are we missing?"

"Don't really care!" Matt told him as he nudged over and splashed me before pushing away again.

When I finally left the pool to dry off in the sun I noticed Adam sitting on the low wall at the edge of the lawn, camera pointed at me.

"There you are," I stated, choosing the sun lounger nearest to him to spread my towel over. "Is it weird that I missed you?"

I watched a smile creep over his face.

"Can you do me a favour and not sit on that wall?

There's a huge drop at the other side and I'm concerned for your safety."

He rolled his eyes and stretched out his legs with a grimace.

"I don't care how much your legs ache; I can't relax thinking you might fall to your death at any moment. I'll find you a chair, if you like …" I ignored his silent headshake and wandered off in search of a chair. I found a pile in the little room with the beer fridge and took one back to Adam. "Here, sit there and I'll feel much better." He moved into the chair, smiling at me the whole time. I settled on my sun lounger and turned, to find him still looking at me.

"Thank you," he whispered.

"You're welcome!" He finally averted his gaze, though his smile stayed fixed, creating lines around his eyes and I found it suddenly difficult to take my eyes off him.

Chapter 7

The afternoon passed amiably by, and I sat with Chrissie and Kelly on the couch, taking a break from the sun and tucking into a fruit platter. We watched Ryan and Matt kicking a ball over the pool to each other. They seemed to be getting on better since they'd found the beer and pool toys.

My eyes wandered to Dylan, who'd been swinging quietly on the hammock most of the day.

"Who needs beer?" Matt shouted as he moved to get a fresh one.

"Everyone!" Chrissie called back to him.

"Ryan," I shouted when I saw him going inside the house. "Can you grab some more snacks from the kitchen if you're going that way?"

"Good idea," Chrissie said. "Fruit and beer isn't the best combo, is it?"

"No," I agreed. "I want some junk. I don't think Ryan heard me though." I got up and followed him, Adam behind me. I was surprised to find Carl on his own in the kitchen. "Where's Ryan?" I asked.

I couldn't read Carl's expression as he looked at Adam. "I lost him."

"How could you lose him?" I said.

"Oh my God!" Ryan burst through the door in the corner. He looked at me with big eyes. "You won't believe what I just found!"

"What were you doing down there?" I asked, looking beyond him to the stone stairs which descended into darkness. They led to Maria's apartment, and we'd been told not to go down there.

"I heard a scream," he told me quickly, shaking his head. "It was just Maria, she'd burnt herself on a pan, no big deal. Anyway, you won't believe what's down there ..."

"Ryan!" Chelsea appeared in the kitchen. "It's time for your interview now!" She linked her arm through his and marched him out of the kitchen.

"Ryan!" I hurried after them, and he turned while Chelsea took him up to the rooms designated for the crew.

"I'll tell you later," he called down to me before he disappeared with Chelsea.

Back in the kitchen, I looked from Carl to Adam. "That was weird."

They avoided looking at me, and Carl closed the door to Maria's flat before walking away.

"What's down there?" I asked Adam, moving closer to him and ignoring the camera, which he was using as a shield. I glared at him for a moment, but with no effect.

I headed back outside empty-handed, forgetting all about the snacks until Chrissie asked me.

"Where's Ryan?" Matt asked.

"Chelsea took him for an interview."

"We have to do interviews?" Chrissie asked.

"It seems like it," I replied, taking a seat on the couch to wait for Ryan to return, wondering what he'd seen that he would be so excited about.

It didn't take long - maybe ten minutes - and then Ryan was back with a sly smile on his face. He went to the fridge to get himself a fresh beer.

"So?" I looked at him.

"They just wanted to ask me a few questions. I talked into a camera about my life and stuff. No stress."

"What about Maria's apartment?"

He took a seat opposite me and placed his beer on the table between us. "It's a really cool apartment." He looked around at the others, who were lying around on sun loungers or floating in the pool.

"That's it?"

He didn't look at me. "Yeah."

"Why were you so excited? You said there was something down there …"

"It's just a really nice apartment," he told me again. "Hey, Matt," he called, standing up. "Move out of the way. I want to see if I can use the inflatables as stepping stones to run across the pool."

"I'd like to see that too," Matt said as he pulled himself out of the pool.

Ryan ran and splashed into the pool, making the rest of us laugh. "It's not as easy as it looks," he told us as he came up laughing. I was sure there was something he wasn't telling me about Maria's apartment, but he obviously didn't want to talk to me about it. Maybe I'd ask him again another time.

We spent an amusing half hour taking turns at Ryan's silly game, with varying levels of success.

"Come on, Dylan," Margaret called. "I know you're dying to have a go. Let's have a race." He moved beside her and gave her a nod before they set off across the pool. Margaret lost her balance and dived at Dylan as she fell, taking him down with her. They came up laughing and moved out of the way as Ryan announced he was having yet another try.

As the rest of us got bored and went back to our sunbathing and relaxing, Ryan continued his attempts to get all the way across the pool. He got funnier the more often he failed.

"Just give up, please!" Dylan groaned when Ryan dragged himself out of the pool for about the hundredth time.

"But I can do it," Ryan replied.

"You clearly can't, though!" Dylan said as Maria arrived to set the table.

Ryan was still obsessing about his pool challenge when we sat down to a table laden with chicken, homemade potato wedges and a big bowl of salad, along with a couple of bottles of wine.

"Maybe more alcohol would help you," Matt suggested.

"Worth a try, I guess!" Ryan lifted his beer bottle to us, before taking a swig.

"I wonder why it was only Ryan who had an interview," I said, taking a second helping of salad.

"Maybe they just do one a day," Kelly suggested.

Dylan looked at Ryan. "What did they ask you?"

"Just stuff about my life and my job."

"Well, that sounds boring," Matt said with a smile. Ryan gave him a dirty look and focused on his food while Margaret launched into a story about her long-lost relatives who she'd been visiting in England.

I enjoyed the banter as we ate and couldn't help but think this was how it would be to have a big family.

Growing up, it had only been Mum and me sitting down to dinner, and most of the time we ate in front of the TV. Meals at Dad's house were livelier these days, but it was a different kind of chaos with two small children at the table.

"Do you want more wine?" Chrissie asked as she refilled her glass.

"No, I'm fine with this, thanks." I was making my way slowly through a glass of red, carefully avoiding getting drunk. The conversation was getting more and more raucous. I laughed when Kelly challenged Ryan to an arm wrestle, and the others cheered at the suggestion.

I joined Dylan, who'd gone to sit on a couch.

"Hey." He smiled at me as I plonked myself down beside him. "They're such a bunch of kids!"

"Yeah. They're fun," I said. "Why are you sitting over here on your own?"

"I don't want to be a TV star," he whispered. "I figure if they show anything, it will be Kelly making Ryan cry over an arm wrestle, not me sitting here doing nothing."

"Really?"

"Makes sense, doesn't it?"

"Yes, but is that really why you're keeping your distance from everyone?"

"I'm not a big people person," he said, shifting his gaze to the action at the dinner table. Kelly had beaten Ryan and was moving on to wrestle Matt.

"I think I might sneak off to bed while they're preoccupied," I told Dylan.

"Not such a big people person yourself?"

"It's the fun I'm not so good at!"

"I don't believe you," he said with a grin.

"You're following me again!" I told Adam when he trailed me up the stairs. "Nothing to say for yourself?" I asked when I reached my bedroom door. "You've walked me to my door, you could at least say goodnight."

No response.

"Come on, give me a smile?" I poked him in the ribs and laughed as he took a step back. His face softened with amusement.

"Goodnight, Lucy."

"Goodnight, Adam!" I closed the bedroom door on him and decided that a glass of wine with dinner was probably my limit.

Chapter 8

"You're keen," I said when I almost bumped into Adam the next morning, walking out of the bedroom. "I don't think I can talk to you any more." I squinted in the bright light of the living room. "All this one-sided chat is getting me down. We'll go for a comfortable silence from now on."

As we walked through the house, I kept glancing at Adam, who was being very professional and ignoring my looks. "This isn't a comfortable silence, is it?" I grinned at him. "You're missing my wit and scintillating conversation already, aren't you? I can read you like a book! Let's go back to the awkward one-sided conversations then, shall we?" He kept a straight face but his sparkling blue eyes betrayed his amusement.

"Morning, Maria!" I said when we reached the kitchen. "How are you today?"

She touched my arm and said something to me before looking at Adam and attempting to shoo him away, as though warding off evil.

"Don't look at me," I said to Adam while he backed away from Maria. "I've already saved you twice this week: once from a potential car accident, once from a potentially fatal fall … I draw the line at little old ladies. You'll need to learn to take care of yourself at some point. I won't always be around to rescue you."

Maria appeared at my side as I reached for breakfast, chatting relentlessly. She took my plate and loaded it with food before handing it back to me, tutting at me and pinching my stomach. I took a step back and she rolled her eyes before scurrying away to her apartment. My eyes stayed on the door for a moment, wondering what was down there. I shot Adam a look as I moved past him to eat outside.

"Do you feel as bad as you look?" I asked Matt when he joined me outside just as I finished my breakfast.

"Yes! I think we emptied the beer fridge." He deposited his breakfast on the table and moved away from me. "It's full again!" he told me on his return. "It's a magic beer fridge. Life doesn't get any better than this!" He relayed the information with great enthusiasm to the rest of the group as they arrived for breakfast. Only Ryan seemed excited by the revelation, hurrying away to see for himself.

"Maybe she's not coming this morning," I said while we waited for Chelsea to arrive. We were all sitting around on the couches after breakfast, wondering what our activity would be for the day.

"I'm going to work on my tan," Kelly told us, striding over to a sun lounger on the lawn.

"If we're not doing anything, I should probably do a couple of hours of studying this morning," Chrissie said. "I'll just read a few chapters and make some notes for my essay, and that'll be enough for today."

"Great idea," I said. "Are you coming for a swim first?"

"You're a bad influence," she told me, putting

down her coffee and stripping to her bikini. "A quick swim and then I'll study!"

The morning passed quickly, with no sign of Chrissie leaving to study. We'd just eaten lunch and settled down on sun loungers when the unmistakable voice of Chelsea Cartwright broke through the relaxed atmosphere. "Hello, beautiful people!"

I groaned as I turned to see her bouncing over to us with a huge grin on her face.

"I feel like I'm not going to get my nap now," Chrissie commented beside me. "I knew it was all too easy."

"Do you think there's a reason she's dressed like Lara Croft?" I asked, making Matt sit up for a better look.

"I'm so happy to see you all settling in so well," she said and beamed her horrific fake smile. "But I'm afraid I'm going to spoil your peace now! Who's interested in a little outing?"

"Do we have a choice?" Kelly asked from the couch.

Matt pulled himself out of the hammock and stretched his arms. "Is there a prize?"

"No prize today!" Chelsea told us in her annoying sing-song voice.

"Where are we going?" I asked.

"What a great question, Lucy!" she said, looking at me, her eyes huge. I was positive she must be on drugs. "And you'll find out when you reach your destination! You have five minutes to get changed into some comfortable clothing. You'll need closed shoes – no heels please, girls. I'll see you all down by the fountain in ten minutes! Go!"

Her enthusiasm infected absolutely no one, but we slowly got up to move upstairs. "It's definitely okay if I wear my heels, isn't it?" Matt asked on the way inside. "She only said you girls couldn't wear heels."

"I think everyone would love to see you in a pair of stilettos," Chrissie laughed. "That would be sure to attract a few more viewers."

We went our separate ways at the top of the stairs and Adam lingered in the doorway to our room while Chrissie and I debated what to wear. I opted for knee-length shorts and a plain V-neck T-shirt with a pair of trainers. We took it in turns to use the bathroom to dress away from Adam and his camera.

We congregated outside by the fountain and climbed into the bus when it pulled up. It was refreshing to get out and see some of the countryside around us, although I was slightly apprehensive about where we were going. I still had the skydiving comment floating around my head.

"Shall we have a sing-song?" Matt said.

"You're such a teacher!" Chrissie told him as the driver turned the radio up in the front. He'd chatted to us in Spanish when we were getting on the bus and I'd presumed he couldn't speak English, but it seemed like he understood enough, and was unimpressed by the idea of us serenading him.

"What do you teach, anyway?" I asked Matt, as the driver turned the radio down again.

"Eight-year-olds," he replied with a cheeky grin. "At least, I try to!"

"I thought about becoming a teacher after uni," I told him. "I was only supposed to keep that boring office job for a year while I paid off some of my loan.

But my little brothers are such a handful, I can't imagine teaching thirty kids at the same time."

"The kids aren't so bad once you get to know them," Matt said. "It's the parents that drive me nuts."

"I bet all the mums love you," Margaret said. He smiled coyly back at her without commenting.

Hannah Ellis

Chapter 9

After half an hour we pulled into a car park beside a forest and disembarked the minibus into the heat of the midday sun. I could feel beads of sweat forming on me, and was glad to follow Chelsea under the shade of the trees.

"I hope no one's afraid of heights," Ryan said. I followed his gaze to the tops of the trees, where I could just make out wires and rickety rope bridges connecting them.

"At least we're not skydiving," I commented. The thought of climbing trees didn't fill me with too much dread. I was fairly confident I could manage it.

Jessica and Chelsea hovered around us as Carl and another cameraman attached microphones to us all. A little black box hung from the waistband of my shorts with a wire leading to a small microphone that was clipped to my T-shirt. We were then fitted with climbing harnesses and helmets with cameras on them, before being given brief safety instructions and sent to a ladder which extended up a tree.

I lingered on the ground chatting to Matt and Chrissie while Dylan took off up the tree with Margaret, Ryan and a cameraman close behind them. Kelly followed them with surprising speed, and Carl went after her.

"I guess it's our turn," Chrissie announced and started slowly up the ladder. "Catch me if you can, Matt!" She looked down at us with a grin before upping her pace and disappearing out of sight.

"See you up there," Matt told us as he went after her.

"This could take a while," I told Adam quietly. "I think Matt's scared of heights."

"Really?"

"He definitely went a bit white when we got here. And he's looking pretty cautious going up there."

"What about you?" he asked. "Feeling confident?"

"Yeah." I grinned at him as I realised this was the most he'd even spoken to me. "It's strange seeing you without your camera."

"I've still got a camera," he reminded me, pointing to his helmet.

"That's not the same. Plus, it's the talking that's really weird. I was just getting used to you being mute."

"It's hard to get a word in with you around." He smiled at me.

"Hey!" I gave him a friendly nudge. "I'm not usually chatty at all. It just seems weird to have someone constantly watching you and nobody talking."

"Careful – you're making me sound like a creepy stalker."

"Well, you do seem to follow me around a lot!"

The instructor hooked me up to the rope and I turned back to Adam as I put my foot on the first rung of the ladder. "Don't stare at my bum the whole way up, will you?"

"I can't promise anything," he shouted back at me and I scrambled up the ladder as fast as I could, wondering what on earth had possessed me to make that comment.

"What took you so long?" Chrissie asked as I reached the platform at the top of the tall tree. She was halfway across a rope bridge which led to the next tree and looked pretty pleased with herself.

"You okay, Matt?" I asked while I moved my carabiners over to the next set of ropes as we'd been instructed.

"I'm not sure why we couldn't have had an afternoon at the beach," he said, staring straight ahead and gripping the tree branch beside him.

"Not a fan of heights?"

"Not really. Have you seen those?" Matt nodded to a small camera perched in a tree a little way from us. I scanned the trees and saw more scattered around. It made sense, I guess. Surely the cameras on our helmets wouldn't capture everything.

"Do you think they're always there or are they just for us?" I asked.

"No idea." Matt shrugged.

"Maybe they have to have them so when someone falls to their death, they can prove it was because they didn't clip themselves on to the ropes properly, and not because of faulty equipment."

Matt laughed sarcastically.

"Come on, Matt." Chrissie called as she reached the platform of the next tree. "You can do it. Just don't look down. It's easy!"

"Yeah, right," he muttered and moved cautiously to the bridge. "These are attached properly, aren't they?"

he asked when he clipped himself onto the next rope.

"Perfect," I told him. I had to bite my tongue to stop myself from teasing him. It didn't seem that he'd appreciate it much at the moment.

"There you are," I said to Adam as he made it up the ladder. "I thought I'd lost my shadow. I was starting to miss you!"

"Here I am," he said. "How's everyone doing?"

"Fine. Just Matt who's a bit slow." We turned to look at him. "Almost there, Matt!" I called.

"Just another thirty trees to get through!" Adam shouted.

"Don't be mean," I said. "He's really scared."

"Why? What's the worst that can happen?" He looked down and when I followed his gaze he gave me a shove, pulling me back just as I felt I would tumble to my death. I let out a girly shriek and clutched his arm while he laughed.

"You almost gave me a heart attack," I told him.

His walkie-talkie crackled with static then we heard Jessica's annoyed voice travel up to us.

"You realise you're not part of the show, Adam? What's with all the chat?"

He grimaced as he pushed the button on the side of the walkie-talkie. "Sorry!"

"Leave Lucy to talk to the others." Jessica's voice was harsh and authoritative.

"Copy that." He turned and rolled his eyes at me. I grinned.

Static filled the air again before Jessica's voice reached us. "And if you roll your eyes, I'm going to see that on Lucy's camera."

Adam raised his eyebrows. "Told you I'm not

supposed to talk!" he said, pointing at the rope bridge before us.

"See you at the other side," I said before setting off across the bridge. I decided not to look down and took it at a good pace. I was beside Matt in seconds.

"That was fast," he commented while we looked at the next challenge. This time it was a single rope to walk across. There were more ropes dangling, to be used as hand grips, and the distance from this tree to the next was much shorter, but it still looked pretty tough.

Chrissie let out a cheer when she made it to the next tree and shouted for Matt to follow her.

"Good luck," I told him as he set off, with wobbly legs, across the rope. I looked ahead and saw the rest of our group spread out across the forest before us. I just caught a glimpse of Dylan who swung from one tree to the next, Tarzan style.

"Hi," I said to Adam when he appeared by my side. I turned when he didn't reply and he shrugged at me. When Matt was safely at the other side I set off across the taut rope between the trees. I was almost at the other side, and was smiling at Matt, who'd been cheering me on, when my foot slipped and I fell. There was a moment of panic before I felt the safety rope catch me. I dangled at a funny angle until I remembered how to breathe and think again. I kicked around until I was upright and grabbed for the rope beside me.

"You all right?" Matt called to me.

"Yep." I grinned up at him. "Just hanging around!"

I vaguely heard Chrissie shouting something at me and there were cheers and catcalls as the others turned to watch me scrabbling around pathetically in mid-air. I managed to get hold of the rope, but didn't have the strength in my arms to pull myself up.

"Can you help me?" I asked Matt as I inched closer to the platform he was standing on.

"Maybe." He held out his hand but didn't move nearer the edge of the platform, so it wasn't particularly helpful.

"Come closer," I instructed him.

He made a pathetic attempt to reach out to me. "I don't want to end up dangling down there with you."

"You're attached to that tree. You can't go anywhere!" I shouted up at him as I swung for the edge of the platform.

"Almost!" Chrissie encouraged me from somewhere nearby. I tried again and managed to get a hand to the wooden edge, but my arms didn't have the strength to pull me up.

"Lucy's stuck," Adam said into his walkie-talkie. I dangled helplessly, abandoning my efforts to climb back up.

"We can see." Jessica's voice crackled up to us. "They're sending someone up."

I looked down and saw figures on the ground way below. There was a ladder running up the side of a tree and someone was roping up at the bottom.

Adam's voice drew my gaze up to him. "I could just get her."

"There's not supposed to be two people on the rope at the same time," Jessica reminded him.

He looked at me and then down at the people on the ground before clipping on his carabiners and setting off across the rope. I was stunned when he moved quickly and confidently across, stopping to move his carabiners across mine and reaching down to pull me up when he got to Matt and the next platform.

Jessica's voice reached us again while I stood beside Adam, catching my breath. "You've just made a Spanish man very angry," she told Adam flatly.

We leaned over and could just make out the safety instructor, shouting and gesticulating wildly.

I looked up and met Adam's gaze. "Thank you," I said, suddenly shy.

He shrugged in reply, and it was Chrissie's voice that broke the silence.

"Aww! Adam to the rescue. What a hero!" she called, making me blush.

Hannah Ellis

Chapter 10

We made steady progress through the trees and ended our treetop adventure by taking a zip wire across the valley, landing at the edge of another forest at the other side. I wasn't sure Matt was going to manage it, but after threatening to push him, he finally stepped off the platform to sail across the valley, his eyes firmly closed.

We regrouped at a clearing in the forest and set off together for the walk back to the bus.

"I actually quite enjoyed that," I told Adam as I dropped to the back of the group and walked with him. I unclipped my helmet and took it off, noticing the rest of the group had done the same. I was slightly surprised to see Adam take his off too. Then he reached for my microphone, unclipped it from my T-shirt and pushed it into my pocket.

"There's going to be some lovely footage of the ground," he told me, looking down at my helmet which swung by my side. "I did warn them there was no way we could film this part with these crappy helmet cameras."

"I saw the cameras in the trees," I said.

"Yeah, the climbing part will be fine, it's just the walk back that's not going to come out."

"So we're free for a while?"

"Looks like it."

"Go on then," I prompted. "Tell me all about yourself, now that you can talk to me."

"I didn't realise you were going to ask about me," he said, smiling. "Maybe we should put the microphones back on and walk in silence."

"It's only fair. You get to hear everything about me and I know nothing about you."

"Fine," he sighed. "My name's Adam and I'm a camera operator. I'm currently working on some dodgy reality TV show in Majorca …"

"Hey," I bumped his shoulder. "Tell me something else."

"What do you want to know?"

"How old are you?" I blurted.

"Thirty."

"What do you do in your spare time?"

He hesitated briefly. "I take photos."

I shot him a puzzled look.

"The TV camera work pays the bills, but still photography is my hobby. If I could earn a living from that, then I'd give all this up …" He indicated the helmet camera and smiled.

"What else?" I asked.

"I hang out with Carl," he told me, glancing ahead to where Carl was walking with the rest of the group.

"Oh! Are you two …?" I held up my hand with my fingers crossed.

"No!" he laughed. "Carl's married. And I'm not that way inclined. He's my best friend. I live in his garage. Any more questions?"

"Yeah. What's so exciting about Maria's apartment?"

His gaze shifted to the forest beside us, his eyes roaming as though searching for something. "I don't know."

"That sounds like a lie."

He looked at me seriously and I thought he was going to say something, but instead he reached into his pocket for his microphone. "We should put these back on. I'll get into trouble otherwise."

I stopped walking and put my hand over his, enclosing his microphone in his palm. I was about to quiz him further before deciding it would be a waste of time.

"I like it when you can chat," I told him and then moved away when I felt the heat rise in my cheeks.

"Me too," he told me before clipping his microphone to his T-shirt and motioning for me to do the same.

We drove back in silence, everyone worn out from the climbing. Sitting on the bus, I thought about everyone around me. I'd been pleasantly surprised by the group. I was amazed to find that I genuinely liked all of them. I felt especially close to Chrissie and Matt, and somehow Adam and Carl too, which was weird considering the circumstances. My gaze travelled to the front of the bus and I watched Adam fiddle with his camera, which pointed back at us. When he looked up, I quickly shifted my gaze back out of the window, ignoring the fact that my heart had speeded up like a galloping horse.

***

I lost track of Adam when we got back to the finca.

By the time I got out of the shower, another cameraman had replaced him, and when we'd finished dinner it was obvious he had the evening off, but I found myself looking for him regardless.

"I wish we had some music," Matt said when we moved to sit on the couches with full stomachs.

"I don't really like music," Ryan said, sipping his beer.

"What?" Matt sat upright to shake his head and squint at Ryan. I smiled, already amused.

"How can you not like music?" Kelly asked.

"I just don't like it."

"*No* music? You don't like *any* music?" Matt looked like utterly perplexed.

"Not really," Ryan replied.

"I don't think I've ever met anyone who didn't like music," Margaret said.

"It's weird," Matt said. "I can't believe you admit that."

"Why not?"

"I'm fairly sure it makes you a sociopath or something," Matt told him.

"Calm down," Ryan laughed. "I don't hate music. I'd just rather sit in silence."

"It's weird," Matt sighed and sank back into the couch.

"Dylan's got a guitar." Ryan took another swig of his beer. "If you want music, ask him."

"That's true." Matt sat up and looked at Dylan, who was lying on a couch away from the rest of us. "You were busking, weren't you?"

"I'm not going to be the evening entertainment," Dylan said.

"Come on!" Matt nudged Ryan. "Run and fetch his guitar …"

"No." Ryan smiled. "I don't like music."

"Don't touch my guitar," Dylan shouted Matt when he strode inside.

"Here." Matt returned and handed the guitar to Dylan. "I barely touched it."

"I'm not playing," Dylan told him, taking the guitar and setting it down next to him.

"Please?" Matt grinned at him.

"No!"

"Fine. I'll get you another beer and we'll sit here and drink until you play me a tune!"

I smiled at Dylan as Matt disappeared to get beers. "Are you going to play something? Because I really want to go to bed but I don't want to miss a performance."

"You won't miss anything, I promise!"

"Okay, then." I stretched when I stood, fairly sure I would ache tomorrow after the climbing.

"Don't listen to him," Matt said as he deposited more beers on the table and put an arm around my shoulder. "You don't want to miss the music man!" He winked at Dylan.

"I'm done in," I said, wriggling away from Matt. "Night!"

I was vaguely aware of a cameraman following me upstairs but I didn't look at him, just went up to my room and closed the door behind me.

Hannah Ellis

Chapter 11

I woke to the sound of Matt clapping his hands and cheerfully wishing us a good morning before the end of my bed sank under his weight.

"Come on!" He shook my leg. "Time to get up! It's a beautiful day."

I propped myself up on an elbow and watched him reach over to Chrissie's bed to give her a shake.

"Get off me," she groaned and pulled a pillow over her head.

"Come on, ladies! Rise and shine!" He flashed his boyish smile at me and I registered Adam standing in the doorway, filming us.

"I'll get dressed," I said, adjusting my pyjamas as I pulled back the sheet and stood up.

"You missed Dylan giving us a little show last night," Matt told me.

"No! Really?"

"He's got a good voice," Chrissie said, emerging from under the pillow.

"I can't believe I missed it." I picked up my swimsuit and moved towards the bathroom.

"Wait!" Chrissie was suddenly animated. I stopped and watched her push Matt and Adam out of the door, claiming we needed a private girls' talk. She closed the door on them and turned to me. "We need to talk swimwear."

"What about it?"

"Please don't wear that coverall thing again," she said with an awkward smile.

"What?"

"Don't be offended," she said. "I'm not trying to be mean. It's just that you have a really nice body and … Well – here, have this." She pulled a skimpy bikini out of her drawer and handed it to me.

"It's a nice colour," I told her. "I just think I'll feel a bit exposed." It was a lovely teal colour but there wasn't much to it.

"Just try it," she pleaded with me. "It'll look great on you, I promise."

I ducked into the bathroom to try it and then returned to show Chrissie.

"Hot!" she announced with a grin.

"I'm not sure." I pulled at the bikini bottoms, trying to stretch the fabric to cover more of my rear end.

"You look amazing. Trust me. Let's bin the old-lady one!"

Chrissie disappeared into the bathroom as I adjusted the bikini top. I pulled on a pair of shorts and a T-shirt and then looked up to find Chrissie smiling at me from the bathroom doorway. "I guess we'll work on the rest of your look later. Baby steps, hey?"

"What now?" I looked down at myself.

"The shorts could be a bit shorter," she said.

"I like to keep my thighs hidden."

"Don't be silly – there's nothing to hide. Come on, let's get some breakfast."

Adam followed us through the house and we were almost at the kitchen when we met Matt coming the other way with a plate piled high with food. I was about to tease him about how much he ate when I heard raised voices. The three of us paused and looked up at the staircase that led to the rooms the crew used. Jessica's voice drifted down, loud and clear.

"This whole show is a joke; I may as well kiss goodbye to my career now." It sounded like she was pacing. Then another voice said something I couldn't make out, but clearly annoyed Jessica as her voice got louder still. "This is not the idea I pitched ... I don't have enough camera operators. The way we're filming is a joke. The house was supposed to be rigged with hidden cameras, for goodness' sake. We should be recording at all times, in every part of the house. And how did we end up with seven people who actually seem to like each other? They're the most boring bunch of people I've ever met."

We exchanged glances and stifled our laughter as Jessica continued. "We need to shake things up a bit. I need cat-fights and sex in bathrooms! Climbing trees and splashing around in a pool is not going to cut it. Somehow we need to make them look interesting, or we're all wasting our time. If I don't end up with something that will bring in viewers, I'm done for."

We didn't move for a moment after her voice trailed off.

"I'll meet you outside for breakfast then," Matt broke the silence, his eyebrows raised, and we slowly continued what we were doing. Chrissie and I got breakfast and moved outside without a word. Silently, Adam shadowed us.

"Shall we have a quick swim before we eat?"

Chrissie asked as we set our breakfast on the table outside. "It'll get the metabolism going."

"Okay." I shrugged.

"Come on, Matt," she instructed.

"I'm eating," he mumbled with his mouth full.

"Come for a swim," she said again and glanced fleetingly at Carl, who had his camera on Matt.

Matt looked sadly at his plate of food before standing and pulling off his T-shirt. I stripped down to my bikini, feeling self-conscious as I headed for the water.

"Have you seen today's activity?" Matt said, nodding towards the other side of the lawn. There was a round blue mat with two sumo suits lying on top of it.

"That's going to get sweaty!" Chrissie commented, walking slowly down the steps into the pool.

We formed a little huddle in the middle of the pool and spoke in low whispers so our voices couldn't be picked up. Carl and Adam walked along the poolside, aiming their cameras at us.

"What do you make of Jessica's little rant?" Chrissie asked.

"Sounds like we're not entertaining enough," Matt said.

"So if we continue to be the most boring people on earth then we're probably not going to make it onto TV at all?" I suggested. "It sounds good to me."

"I was quite excited about being a minor celebrity," Matt told us. "My school kids would be very impressed!"

"I just wanted a free holiday," Chrissie told us. "I'm not bothered about fame. I think Ryan is going to be disappointed, though. Let's not tell him or he might start pulling stunts to make us TV-worthy!"

"Something's going on with Ryan," I told them. "Why did they interview him and not the rest of us?"

"That was odd," Chrissie agreed. "It's all a bit of a weird setup, isn't it? With the cameramen coming and going, and poor old Maria waiting on us."

"It doesn't seem very well organised," I said, my arms beginning to tire from treading water. I moved to the edge of the pool.

"Morning." Ryan appeared when we got out of the pool. "I reckon that will give the ratings a boost, Lucy." He looked me up and down in my skimpy bikini, and I reached for a towel to cover myself up.

"I wonder if we're on live TV now …" Ryan ran a hand through his hair and posed into the camera.

"I doubt it," Matt told him. "But get away from the camera, just in case. People don't want to see your scrawny body."

"I think you're jealous," Ryan told him with a grin as he sat down and tucked into his breakfast. I glanced at Adam, who was standing at the edge of our breakfast gathering. I waved without thinking but got nothing back.

"It's too hot," Kelly complained when she and Margaret joined us. "I'm melting!"

"It's not that hot," Margaret said, used to a warmer climate than us. Dylan followed them outside and sat slightly away from the rest of to tuck into his breakfast.

"It's going to get much hotter when we're wearing those," Matt said, pointing at the fat suits.

Ryan jumped up and went to check them out.

"They're pretty heavy," he commented, picking one up.

"Good morning!" Chelsea greeted us. "I see you've found today's activity. Today is a test of strength and agility, and there's another £500 to be won."

Once again, I didn't think it was worth getting excited about the money. It seemed very unlikely that I could beat Matt or Dylan at this challenge. Or Margaret, come to think of it. I might have a chance against Chrissie, and Ryan was fairly scrawny – I think I could take him.

As it turned out, Kelly was the only person I managed to beat, and only because I moved at the right moment and she fell past me and off the mat. It was hilarious, though, and after two hours my face ached from laughing so much. Ryan was right: the sumo suits weighed a ton, and they were so hot. It was entertaining just trying to get in and out of them.

Dylan won in the end, but no one was very competitive about it, even Ryan. It was too much fun to worry about winning.

Since my facial muscles had got a good workout from all the laughing, I had a quick swim after lunch to exercise the rest of my body. I was thoroughly relaxed when I joined everyone on the couches, where they were drinking beers.

"Does anyone else think this is all a bit weird?" Dylan said, looking shiftily at the cameraman nearest him. "How can they record everything with so few cameras?"

"Dylan's got a point," Margaret agreed. "It all seems a bit amateur. It seems far too easy to escape the cameras."

"I just don't think this is going to be a big show," Chrissie said. "I think they're doing a trial run to figure out the logistics. If it *was* a real show, they'd pick the participants to make sure they got an interesting bunch. They'd get extroverts who would argue and fight or wander around naked. Stuff that makes good viewing. They'd be more organised, not just pick people an hour before the plane left."

"I don't really care," Matt told us. "I'm having a great time. I'm not going to ruin it by overthinking things. I'm quite happy to relax and enjoy myself."

"Dylan's right about the cameras, though," Kelly said, pausing to take a swig of beer. "There's been a few times when I don't think there was a camera pointed at me at all. It worries me. They might miss something good. What if I have a bikini malfunction and no one sees it?" She flashed her mischievous grin at us.

"I could probably keep an eye on that situation for you if you want …" Ryan offered, killing the atmosphere.

"I think you have a problem with your delivery," Matt told him, one eyebrow cocked. "You need to stop staring at boobs and loose the creepy little smirk."

I bit my lip to stop myself from laughing at the look on Ryan's face. Chrissie snorted beside me.

Ryan seemed to be attempting to kill Matt with a look. Matt took the hint and stepped away from him. "I think I'll have a dip," he told us. "If you ladies could do me a favour and avoid having any bikini malfunctions while I'm not around to monitor the situation, I'd really appreciate it!" He winked at Ryan before continuing his path to the pool, taking a run up then diving in.

"Oh my God!" Ryan jumped up from his seat and headed into the living room at lightning speed. I looked around, confused.

"What's wrong?" Chrissie asked as we watched Ryan huddle in the doorway. "What?" she snapped, when he just stood there, frozen to the spot.

"Look!" He pointed, looking like he'd seen a ghost. We all shifted our gaze to the far side of the pool. There was a little wooden fence separating us from the overgrown bushes which ran up the hill beyond. Wandering on the other side of the fence was a large brown chicken.

"Yeah," Chrissie said slowly as we looked back at Ryan, who was clutching the doorframe. "It's a chicken."

"It's creepy," Ryan told us, shaking his head. "They freak me out."

"Are you serious?" Kelly asked.

"Yeah, they're horrible."

I saw the mischief in Matt's eyes as he pulled himself out of the pool and leaned over the fence to pick up the chicken. When he turned to goad Ryan with it, Ryan was nowhere to be seen, and it was an hour before he cautiously returned to join us outside.

Matt corralled us into a game of water polo in the afternoon, but it didn't last long before we gave up in favour of splashing and dunking each other. I was laughing hard when I pulled myself out of the pool to catch my breath.

"I need a rest," I told Chrissie as she stood laughing at the side of the pool. We ducked to avoid the ball that Matt threw at us and, as I went to throw it back at him, Chrissie shoved me into the pool.

"I'll get you back for that!" I told her when I came up laughing.

Hannah Ellis

Chapter 12

Silence fell as everyone settled down for a siesta. I smiled at Matt when he walked past me with a finger to his lips. I watched him walk inside. When he reappeared a few minutes later, he had a chicken under his arm. I sat up and watched him place it on the floor next to Ryan and then come to perch on the edge of my sun lounger.

"Ryan," Matt called gently. "Hey, Ryan!"

Ryan slowly opened his eyes and looked over at us.

"I think there's finally a bird interested in you," Matt told him and nodded at the chicken.

It felt a bit mean, but I couldn't help laughing as Ryan fell out of his seat in a bid to escape from the chicken. He managed to scramble to his feet and shot inside at top speed.

"I think you enjoy teasing him a little bit too much," I told Matt.

"I know," he sighed. "But it's just too easy."

"It's not funny!" Ryan's voice drifted down from above us and we looked up to the bedroom window. "Can you please get rid of it?" He looked genuinely upset and I felt sorry for him.

"Take it away," I encouraged Matt.

"It's just a chicken," Matt told him.

"It's a real fear," Ryan replied.

"Sorry," Matt shouted up sincerely. "But maybe you should face your fear. It's not going to hurt you."

"It might …" Ryan hesitated as though he couldn't quite bring himself to say the words. "It might … peck me."

"How about I keep hold of it and you just come and have a look at it?"

"I don't trust you," Ryan shouted down.

"I'll hold it," Margaret offered. "I'll keep it still and you can come and stroke it."

"I'm not touching it!"

"Come down," Margaret told him as she moved to pick up the chicken. "I promise I won't let go of it."

Ryan hesitated for a minute before moving away from the window. He arrived at the living room doorway moments later. "Don't move," he warned Margaret.

"Let's call it Matilda," Matt suggested. "It's difficult to be scared of anything called Matilda, isn't it?"

Ryan's eyes moved from Matt to the chicken. He looked as though he might turn and flee at any moment.

"Matilda is a lovely chicken who wouldn't hurt a fly," Matt told Ryan in soothing tones. "She just wants to be friends."

Ryan took a few steps towards Margaret and the chicken, as Matt kept talking. "Matilda is the nicest chicken in the whole world. She's shy around people and insecure. She just wants to be loved."

Ryan inched closer.

"She'd really love it if you stroked her soft feathers." Matt stopped talking and Ryan took a deep breath before backtracking the way he'd come.

"Can you take her away now, please?" Ryan called as he retreated. "I can't touch it."

"Okay," Matt told him while he scooped Matilda up out of Margaret's grasp.

"That was nice of you," I commented when Matt returned without the chicken a few minutes later.

"She's gone," he shouted to Ryan, then lay down on my sun lounger, nudging me off it.

"Hey!" I laughed from the grass and automatically held my hand out for Adam to pull me up. He'd been standing not far from me for the last hour, and I decided he could make himself useful. He hesitated before reaching out and pulling me up.

"Thank you!" I grinned at him and got the briefest flash of a smile in reply.

Aimlessly, I wandered inside. I was restless, and needed to get out of the sun for a while. Adam followed me and when I found myself in the kitchen I was drawn to Maria's door, which was slightly ajar. I moved over and pulled it wide. Adam coughed. I looked back at him before walking down the stone steps.

The steps turned a corner, and I followed the dim light to the passageway at the bottom. It was creepy, but blissfully cool, and I called for Maria as I moved towards a door that was slightly open off the cramped passageway. I glanced back, surprised that Adam hadn't followed me, and when I continued, I let out a short scream at the sight of a man, looming in front of me.

"You're not supposed to be down here," he told me, pulling the door beside him and banging it into the frame.

"I know. I was just looking for Maria. Who are you?"

"The catering assistant," he told me gruffly.

Then Maria appeared from the other end of the passage. She was chattering as she went, and pushed the huge guy out of her way as she came towards me. I didn't resist when she turned me around and escorted me back up to the kitchen, where I found Adam waiting for me. He lifted his camera to his shoulder when I walked in but said nothing. Maria patted my arm and disappeared back the way she'd come, leaving me more confused than ever.

Chapter 13

I counted five cameramen spread around us when Chelsea sauntered out the next morning in hot pants, sequinned tank top and a pair of sandals with stiletto heels.

"Good morning, boys and girls!" she addressed us in her usual grating voice. "And isn't it a beautiful morning?"

We stared at her and she barely managed to conceal her contempt for us as she cleared her throat. "I'm sure you're excited to find out what's in store for you today!"

"I'm so excited I might just wee my pants." Matt told her sarcastically. "Please, tell us quickly, before the anticipation kills us." He grinned at her and my mouth twitched while I fought to contain my giggles. I didn't dare look at anyone else, sure that if I caught someone's eye the laughter would take over.

"Well, Matt!" Chelsea glared at him, a huge fake smile plastered on her face. "This activity should be right up your street. It's a test of fitness, stamina and good old-fashioned map-reading skills!"

She turned to the doorway, where a big cardboard box had appeared. "In the box you'll find everything you need for today's adventure. There's a backpack for each of you, filled with essential supplies to get you through the day, and you'll also find a compass and a local map marked with places you need to find. At each of the points marked on the map, you will find a flag. Collect all the flags and get back home to claim your reward!"

I managed to smile at her. I felt pretty sorry for her really; we weren't making her job easy.

"I'll see you back here later. Good luck!" She sauntered back into the house, leaving us to explore our box of supplies.

Ryan opened it up and passed around backpacks, which were tagged with our names.

"I just want to sit by the pool, not hike around the countryside," Kelly complained as she peered into her backpack. "They've even supplied awful clothes for us to wear." She took out a pair of hiking boots and a camouflage-patterned baseball cap. Somehow, when she pulled the cap on and threaded her long blonde ponytail out of the back of it she still looked stunning. I left my cap in the backpack, certain that I couldn't pull it off in quite the same way.

"It looks pretty straightforward," Matt told us while he pored over the map. "We start out along the road and then veer off into the hills. Let's meet down at the fountain in ten minutes." He was clearly happy to take the lead in organising us, and no one complained. Having a teacher around might just come in useful.

***

Adam and Carl got to work attaching microphones to us when we gathered at the fountain, and then we set off down the driveway and walked along the road, before turning off onto a dirt track through the barren countryside. We reached the first flag in just under an hour, and half an hour after that we had to stop for another break. We were out in the open, and the heat was becoming unbearable. As I returned the bottle of water to my backpack, I pulled the cap onto my head, hoping to keep the sun off my face a bit. I could feel sweat trickling down my neck and the backs of my legs.

"Isn't there a way to stay in the shade?" Ryan asked Matt, looking towards the trees farther to our left. "I really think we need to try and keep out of the sun."

"Yeah, we need to go that way," Matt told us, looking at the map and then pointing to the trees. "But first we need to find the flag, which is over there …" He pointed in the opposite direction. "It's just in that next field."

"I'm dying," Chrissie told me. She was sitting beside me, slumped against a rock and leaned in to rest her head on my shoulder.

"You all head over to the trees," Dylan said, peering at the map over Matt's shoulder. "I'll get the flag and meet you over there."

"My hero!" Kelly announced, looking slightly revived by the suggestion. She seemed to have been coping the worst with the heat, and I was starting to wonder whether she could manage much more hiking. To be fair, she was doing her best to stay positive, but she was clearly struggling. I thought about the conversation we'd overheard the previous morning, and wondered whether this task was designed to push us to breaking point and have us fighting among ourselves. So far, it wasn't working very well.

"I'm not sure you should go alone," I shouted to Dylan who had set off across the field.

"I very much doubt I'll have the luxury of being alone." He turned and grinned at me and then shifted his gaze to Adam, who was following behind him. We also had Carl hanging around us and another guy whose name I didn't know. I had asked him, but he was taking his job rather seriously and had completely ignored me. I think there were seven or eight cameramen altogether, and I'd only managed to get any communication out of Adam and Carl.

We made it to the trees and then sat down to wait for Dylan. It was still hot but it was infinitely more comfortable under the shade of the trees.

"Can we stay in the shade for a while?" I asked Matt.

"Yeah, mostly. There are a couple of places where we'll be out in the open again, but not too much."

"Great," Ryan groaned, leaning back against the tree.

I opened my backpack, pulled out the envelope with my name on it, and turned it over in my hands before taking out the photo that was inside. It was of an elegant ladies Rolex watch. The watch was silver with a pale pink face and looked beautifully simple in its design. It was exactly what I would choose for myself if I were ever going to spend a small fortune on a watch. I had never owned anything so extravagant, and was unsure that I would ever dare to wear something so expensive. Apparently it was mine, though.

The first flag we'd found had flapped gently in the breeze above a small wooden box which contained an envelope for each of us. On the back of the photos were instructions to bring the picture back with us and exchange it for the real thing. Needless to say, we had abandoned any thoughts of opting out of the task, and were now intent on making sure we found all the flags before returning to our temporary home. A clever move on the part of the producers.

"What did we get this time?" Ryan asked excitedly when Dylan and Adam re-joined us.

"I need a drink." Dylan slumped down on the ground and pulled his water out of his backpack. We watched him gulp down the water before reaching into his bag and pulling out a bunch of large brown envelopes. "I haven't looked yet," he told us and handed them out to us.

I felt the envelope, which seemed to be empty apart from one lumpy object. I heard Kelly gasp and Ryan swear just as I upended my envelope and caught the car key that fell out. I stared at it for a moment, spotting Chrissie jumping up and down somewhere in my peripheral vision. I shook the envelope and a piece of paper fluttered out. It read: *Stay for the week and your prize will be parked outside your house on your return home.*

"Is this real?" I asked Dylan, who was sitting on the floor in front of me while the others danced around us. "We really get a car?"

He shrugged. "It seems like it." I tried to gauge the look on his face. I was desperate to know what he was thinking as he casually slipped the key into his backpack and reached for the map, which Matt had abandoned in all the excitement. "Are you okay?" he asked when he looked up and caught me staring at him.

"Yeah, just a bit surprised by how the day is going," I told him.

"Crazy, huh?"

"You can say that again."

At that point the rest of the group bounced over and drew me into their rowdy group hug. We walked on through the shade of the trees and had a great time chatting and joking as we went. I could feel the anticipation building as we neared the next flag, and we increased our pace when the blue flag came into view in a little clearing in the wood. Two wicker picnic hampers and two cool boxes stood under the flag.

"Not quite a car or a Rolex, but I'll settle for a picnic," Margaret told us. "I'm famished!"

The rest of the group seemed to be in agreement as we went to work spreading out picnic blankets and setting out a lovely selection of picnic foods complete with champagne. There'd been sandwiches and cereal bars in our backpacks, but I think everyone had devoured them early in the hike, and were glad of the extra sustenance.

We were tipsy thanks to the champagne when we packed up the picnic. Matt and Ryan were fooling around like school kids and seemed to be playing a game of tag, running between the rest of us. When we continued our treasure hunt, I dropped to the back of the group and ambled along beside Dylan.

"Are you okay?" I asked, slowing to put some distance between us and Margaret, who was just ahead.

"Fine," he told me with a fixed smile. I glanced

back at Adam, who was a little way behind us, and then unclipped my microphone to shove it in my pocket. Dylan copied me.

"Where did you learn that trick?" he asked.

"From Adam."

"Ah." He smiled coyly and glanced back in Adam's direction. "I see!"

"No," I told him defensively. "Not like that. He just … Never mind. Is everything okay?"

"Yeah," he said uncertainly. "I'm just a bit suspicious of all this, I guess."

"Me too. But then, what's the worst that can happen? We end up on TV? It's not like anyone is doing anything embarrassing. I actually think Chrissie is right and we won't make it on to TV at all. We are pretty boring."

"You're probably right. But I don't think I should have come …"

"Why did you?"

"I'd just had a big argument with my dad and then Chelsea appeared and asked me to come here. Seemed like a great idea in my angry, irrational state of mind."

"Matt said you were busking …"

"It was a bit of a misunderstanding," he said and laughed. "My dad owns a bar and I work there with him. I'd been trying to persuade him we should have an open mic night, but he argued that I just wanted to play myself and would drive all the customers away if I did! I was sitting outside playing my guitar to annoy him. I feel bad that I just left. I was really pissed off, and this seemed like the perfect opportunity to get away. I live in an apartment above the pub. I sneaked in the back door and threw some things in a bag and left. I didn't even tell him I was going. He'll be going crazy."

"So he has no idea where you are?" I asked, worried on his dad's behalf. "He might have reported you missing. We could try and contact him … ask to use a phone, tell them it's an emergency …"

"When they took our phones, I sent a quick message to my mum so they know I'm okay. He's just going to be really mad at me."

"Don't you get on?" I asked.

"We do, but …" He tilted his head and appeared to be searching for a way to explain. "We have different ideas about how the pub should be run. We've been struggling to stay afloat for a while, and Dad won't listen to my ideas. He's pretty stuck in his ways. So if we didn't work together, I think we'd get on great. We used to. Now we just argue a lot."

"Have you got siblings?"

"No, it's just me and Mum and Dad. I worry about my dad: his health isn't great and all the stress of the business seems to be wearing him down. I worry he'll have a heart attack while I'm over here playing in the sun. I'd never forgive myself."

"I'm sure he'll be okay. It's just a few more days. And maybe a bit of time apart will be good for both of you."

"Maybe," he said. "Anyway, what about you? Out of everyone here, you're a bit of a mystery to me. You just don't seem like someone who would drop everything to jet off on a holiday with a bunch of strangers and a TV crew …"

"I'm not," I laughed. "But I was at a loose end. I'd just lost my job and my mum told me I should try something new … so here I am."

"Do you think this is what your mum had in mind?" he asked, smiling.

"Oh, I think I will have exceeded my mother's expectations this time. She'll be delighted! She's always encouraging me to be spontaneous and have adventures. I don't think she's ever been able to believe she ended up with such a straight-laced, sensible daughter."

"She sounds pretty cool."

"She's good fun," I agreed. Not that I'd ever seen that as a positive thing before.

"It's not turned out too badly, has it? Following your mum's advice and doing something you wouldn't normally do …"

"Amazingly, it seems to be working out okay," I agreed. "Maybe we should put these back on …" I pulled the microphone clip out of my pocket and attached it to my T-shirt again. Dylan reluctantly did the same and we picked up the pace to catch up with the rest of the group.

The energy levels in the group dropped as we left the shade of the trees and meandered along a dusty path in the blazing sunshine. The gradient got steadily steeper as the trail led us uphill. We stopped for a break and huddled under the shade of a lone tree as we gulped down water.

"I'm almost out of water," I commented and the others informed me they were in the same position.

"I'm not quite sure what happens when we reach the top of this hill," Matt told us, holding up the map. "It looks like someone has cut the edge of the map off."

I looked over his shoulder and saw that he was right; the map ended abruptly and appeared to have been cut. The top corner was missing completely and the edge wasn't straight.

"So where's the next flag?" I asked, wiping sweat from my face with the sleeve of my T-shirt.

"The map ends at the top of the hill," Matt told me. "And there's an arrow pointing to the edge. It feels like it might be the end of the world. Anyway, I'm guessing there'll be a clue of some sort at the top of the hill."

"Let's hope so," Kelly said.

"I'm hoping for an ice-cream van at the next flag," Ryan told us.

Margaret shook the drips of her water bottle into her mouth. "A tap dispensing ice-cold water would suit me fine."

"Let's find out," I suggested, moving out from the pathetic patch of shade under the tree.

I wasn't sure we'd make it up the hill. Silence hung over us as we put all our energy into trudging slowly up the rocky path in the blazing heat. Matt and I reached the top of the hill first, and I smiled as I plonked myself down at the edge of the path. Matt came over to high-five me and we marvelled at the glorious blue sea that stretched out below us. We turned to grin at the others as they drew nearer.

"Come on," Matt encouraged them. "It's all worth it. The view's fantastic!"

Chapter 14

The view was amazing; the water down below was crystal clear and utterly inviting, and the secluded beach looked like no one had ever set foot on it. We hadn't realised we were approaching the coast. The path ahead snaked steeply down to the sandy cove below. A yellow flag flapped in the breeze on the beach and I could see a mound of some new treasure waiting beneath it.

The mood of the group lifted again as we stood atop the hill, taking it all in. We set off down the path and reached the flag in no time. I lifted the lid of a large cool box and was relieved to find it full of bottled water chilling in ice.

"You got your wish, Margaret," I said while I handed out bottles of water.

There was a stack of rolled-up towels, which were individually embroidered with our names.

Without a word we all stripped down to our swimwear and headed for the water. It felt like utter bliss. I walked quickly into the water and then lay floating on my back, my eyes closed. I smiled at the sound of the boys splashing around me, and laughed wryly as I thought of my initial reluctance to travel to a foreign country, with a bunch of strangers, for a TV show. It seemed like a great decision now.

I lowered my feet to stand in the shallow water as Matt splashed water over my face. When I splashed him back he reached out to push me playfully under the water. I came up spluttering and Chrissie appeared at my side to help me get him back. It was fun, playing around in the water with my new friends, and I completely forgot about the cameras until I left the water. Then I was suddenly aware of the tiny bikini I was wearing as I walked towards Adam and his camera. He followed me and I wrapped my towel protectively around myself.

Kelly and Margaret were chatting as they lay nearby on their towels, and I was about to join them when I noticed Adam's sweat-soaked T-shirt. It hadn't really occurred to me that our cameramen were as uncomfortable as we were in the heat, and they weren't even able to cool off as we had. I had a sudden idea.

I walked quickly past Adam and put my hand on his camera arm to keep him from turning to follow me. He flinched at my touch and automatically tried to move away from me until I caught his gaze and our eyes locked. I pointed at him and then the sea and made a brief swimming motion. Ignoring his look of uncertainty, I moved my hand cautiously over his, and he allowed me to take the camera from him. He pointed into the viewfinder and positioned me so I could see Kelly and Margaret in it.

Carl caught what was going on and moved away from the girls to film the others, who were emerging from the water. The unknown cameraman was filming Dylan, who was staring out to sea a little way away from the rest of us. I held the camera steady and glanced out of the corner of my eye at Adam, who stripped down to his boxer shorts and headed into the sea, away from the rest of our crowd.

The girls glanced up at me and I put a finger to my lips as we exchanged smiles. They briefly looked over to Adam and we watched him dive under the water and reappear a moment later. The girls went back to chatting about Margaret's travels, and I enjoyed watching them through the camera.

I didn't notice Adam returning until he was beside me. He grinned his thanks at me and tugged at the corner of my towel, which I'd been struggling to keep around me with my free hand. I was determined to keep the camera steady, and felt helpless as Adam unwound my towel and used it to pat himself dry and rub his dripping wet hair. I felt self-conscious as I stood next to him in the tiny bikini, and was glad when he draped the towel over my shoulders and picked up his clothes.

He gave me another warm smile when he carefully took the camera from me. I got myself another bottle of water, then turned at the sound of someone clearing their throat loudly. Carl was staring at me. His camera was directed at Ryan and Matt, who were lying in the sun, but his eyes bored into me. He pointed at the sea and then his camera, and I realised what he was asking me. I looked back at Adam, who made sure I was out of his shot when I walked over and took the camera from Carl. Matt and Ryan glanced up but didn't react as they went back to sunbathing.

Carl took a dip in the sea and I looked over at Adam, who smiled back at me. Ryan made me jump when he suddenly leapt up to waft a bee away from him. He was really pathetic about it, and I had to bite my tongue not to shout at him to stay still. I took a few steps backwards to try and keep him in the shot and almost bumped into Adam, who skilfully adjusted the zoom on Carl's camera while keeping his own camera on the girls on his other side.

Luckily, Carl returned and I was relieved of my camera duties. I think we got away with it. The producers would never know. I looked towards the third cameraman and, as though reading my mind, Carl touched my arm and shook his head, rolling his eyes dramatically.

Suddenly tired, I moved over to the girls and spread out my towel next to Chrissie's to lie down for a bit of sunbathing.

I awoke to the sound of static crackling down a nearby walkie-talkie and looked up to find Adam sitting on a rock close to me. He told whoever it was that we were still at the beach, and then all was quiet again. The girls were snoozing next to me, and Matt and Ryan were standing at the water's edge skimming stones. It was idyllic.

I felt Adam's eyes on me.

"Sunscreen," he said when I turned to look at him. My gaze shot down to my shoulder and I saw it was red. Getting up, I retrieved a bottle of sunscreen from my backpack and got to work smearing it all over me. The girls slept on as I haphazardly rubbed the lotion into my shoulders.

Ryan and Matt walked up the beach towards me. "Need some help?" they asked at once.

"Please," I replied and threw the bottle to Matt before turning my back to him and pulling my hair off my neck.

"Do you have to?" I asked Carl as he appeared in front of me. He grinned in reply and I thought that being a yes person wasn't such a great idea. How did I end up on a secluded beach, being filmed as some guy rubbed sunscreen into my shoulders? And what was taking him so long? I looked over my shoulder impatiently as Matt's hands ran up and down my back and over my shoulders. There was a smirk on Carl's face and Adam was sporting a similar look. Clearly my discomfort was very entertaining.

"Thanks," I said curtly and moved away from Matt.

"My turn next." Chrissie looked up at Matt. She was lying on her front and Matt cheerfully knelt beside her to smear sunscreen over her back.

"If anyone else needs any assistance …" Ryan offered.

"I think Matt's got it covered, thanks!" Chrissie told him.

"I'll wait for Matt," Kelly grinned. "He looks like he knows what he's doing with his hands!"

I laughed and sat down on my towel, shuffling over to make space for Ryan, who was hovering awkwardly over us. I felt slightly sorry for him.

"How long do you want to stay here?" Matt asked no one in particular.

"Forever," Chrissie breathed.

"I would definitely be fine with that plan if we had food," Matt replied.

"We've only just had lunch," I told him with a slight shake of the head.

"That was nearly four hours ago," he told me.

"Really? I've not got a watch. How long was I

asleep?" I paused before adding, "Oh, actually, I do have a watch. It's a Rolex! I've not got it with me but I can show you a picture if you don't believe me!"

"I think my Rolex is bigger than yours," Matt said. "I've got a picture if you don't believe me!"

There was a round of daft jokes about whose Rolex was bigger and whose Rolex had the most diamonds before we finally settled down and Matt brought the conversation back to leaving the beach.

"You're such a party pooper, Matt," Kelly declared. "We're sitting in paradise and you want us to leave."

"There's still one more flag to find," he said.

"One more swim," Margaret stated. "And then we get moving again?"

We murmured our agreement and started to get up as Dylan joined us.

"What's going on?" he asked.

"We're going for another swim before we go in search of the final flag," I told him. "You coming?"

"Sounds good," he said.

We set off down the beach, breaking into a run and splashing into the water together.

Chapter 15

The last flag stood over a cooler containing seven bottles of beer and a note telling us to hurry back to the finca and get ready to party.

The double doors to our outdoor paradise were closed when we returned, tired and dirty. We trooped upstairs and took turns in the shower.

"I don't know what to wear," Chrissie told me when I came out of the bathroom.

"I'd really like to just go to bed," I told her.

"Liven up, it'll be fun. All we need are some cocktails and music and we're sorted. I really hope they've got cocktails!"

"I presume you're not going to let me wear shorts and a T-shirt?"

"No." She smiled. "I'm not. What do you think?" She held up a long flowing yellow dress to show me, and I nodded my approval.

"You look amazing," I told her as she slipped it over her head and tugged it into place. "I didn't really bring anything very dressy."

"This is nice." She pulled out my trusty navy blue dress from the wardrobe. It was sleeveless and stopped just above the knee. An old favourite.

"Thanks." I took it from her and put it on before looking at myself in the mirror. "I guess that'll do."

"We're not finished," Chrissie told me. "What about accessories?"

"I don't really accessorise much. I tend to just wear it like this …"

"Hang on …" She trawled through her things, pulled out a wide brown belt and slipped it around my waist. "That's better. Now we can see your shape."

I turned to the mirror again and was amazed by the difference. It cinched my waist and made the dress slightly shorter so more of my legs were on show. "I like it," I told her.

"What size are your feet?" Chrissie asked.

"Six."

"Try these …" She threw a pair of strappy sandals at me and I frowned at the chunky wedge heel.

"I don't usually wear heels …"

"I guessed." She grinned at me. "Just try them."

I slipped my feet into them and admired my reflection in the mirror. "I like them," I admitted hesitantly. "I'm not sure I can walk in them, though."

"Walk around the room a few times. You'll get the hang of it."

Chrissie sat in front of the oval mirror at the dressing table while I walked around the room. "Why are you frowning?" she asked when I took a seat on the edge of the bed.

"I'm just tired," I told her vaguely. Actually I'd been thinking about Adam, but I couldn't bring myself to tell her that. Looking at myself in the mirror, my first thought was that Adam wouldn't see me dressed up. The cameramen seemed to take shifts and, since he'd been with us all day, I presumed he'd be off until the morning. Why was I thinking about

Adam anyway? I wondered.

"Should I do something with my hair?" I asked as Chrissie smoothed serum into her gorgeous ginger locks and scrunched up her curls with her fingers.

"No, never," she snapped. "You have the silkiest, smoothest hair I've ever seen. Don't mess with that."

"It's boring, though," I complained. "I'd love to have your hair."

"Don't say that," she said. "No one wants ginger curls."

"I think your hair's amazing."

"You have no idea how much work it is," she told me. "I wouldn't wish this on anyone. I would kill for your hair." She raised her eyebrows when I laughed at her. "You think I'm joking," she said with a grin, "but I would actually commit murder for that hair. Then I'd spent the rest of my life locked in a cell, happily stroking my beautiful silky hair!"

The bedroom door opened a crack and Matt's voice drifted in. "Are you decent?"

"Yeah," Chrissie called back.

"Never mind, then!" he replied. Chrissie and I exchanged a look as Matt's mischievous smile greeted us around the door. "Are you coming? I've got a cameraman and I'm ready to party." When he opened the door wide, I was surprised to see Adam behind him. It caught me off guard. I wasn't expecting him to be around this evening, and I wasn't sure why I suddenly had a stomach full of energetic butterflies.

"I thought you'd get the evening off," I said, realising I was staring at him. I got the usual shrug in response.

"Apparently, some of the cameramen have come

down with food poisoning so we get more of Adam and Carl this evening," Matt filled us in. "Although I guess there's a chance Adam has Tourette's syndrome and randomly shouted 'food poisoning' at me for no reason."

I caught the smile on Adam's face and was happy he would be around for the evening.

"Anyway, ladies," Matt addressed us, moving further into our room. "I forgot my manners. You're both looking cracking tonight! Come on, give me a twirl."

Chrissie came to stand beside me and we did a slow turn for Matt, who gave a low whistle.

"Yeah," he said. "You'll do. I'll take you both." He moved to stand between us and offered us an arm each. I linked my arm through his and we all fell about laughing when we reached the doorway and bumped into each other in our attempt to squeeze through side by side.

Carl was standing in the middle of the upstairs living room, his camera pointing at a guy sitting quietly on the couch. He was staring at us and I smiled politely.

"All ready to party?" he asked and my eyes went wide at the sound of his voice.

"Oh my God!" I let go of Matt and moved quickly across the room. "Wow!" I was staring, but I couldn't help it. "What happened?"

"I decided it was too hot for a beard! You didn't recognise me, did you?" he asked with a cheeky smile.

"Not at all!" Chrissie joined in with the staring and we both parked ourselves on the coffee table in front of Dylan to gaze at his lovely clean-shaven face.

"Go on," he offered, sticking his chin out. We both ran a hand over his silky-smooth jaw.

"Oh, come on," Matt threw his hands up dramatically. "I shaved, too … I'm as smooth as a baby's bum." He put his hands to his face. "I'll let you have a feel!"

There was a screech as Kelly appeared and caught sight of Dylan. "You look amazing," she told him, sweeping over, looking stunning in a long white dress.

"It really suits you," Margaret chimed in when she joined us to huddle around a grinning Dylan.

"Well, I think I'll just go and cry myself to sleep," Matt told us. "I'm sure no one will miss me. But, just in case, that's where I'll be … just crying myself to sleep while you all fawn over Mr Smooth there." He stuck his bottom lip out. "Now I know how Ryan feels!"

"What are you saying about me?" Ryan appeared from the bedroom wearing a crisp white shirt, his hair slicked into place with gel.

"I think we need to go and drown our sorrows, buddy," Matt sighed. "We've been cast aside!" He wore a boyish grin as he moved to put an arm around Ryan and led him to the stairs. "At least we've got each other …" He turned and gave a dramatic sniff before they disappeared down the stairs. Carl followed behind, and the rest of us were laughing when Matt shouted up the stairs. "Well, at least come down here to flirt with him! A party with two people is just awkward."

We joined them downstairs and found the tables elegantly dressed with white tablecloths and candles.

In fact, there seemed to be candles everywhere.

"Yes! We've got a bar." Matt rubbed his hands together and moved to the other side of the pool – which was now covered – where a bar had appeared, complete with a barman in a suit. He introduced himself as Phil when we flocked over to him.

"Do you do cocktails?" Chrissie asked as she approached.

"Yes."

"And there's a dance floor too!" Chrissie beamed at me and I followed her gaze to the makeshift dance floor, lit with coloured lights. "It's everything I wanted!"

"Can I get you all a glass of champagne to kick things off?" the barman asked.

"I really want a cocktail," Chrissie whined at the same time as Matt requested a beer.

"You TV stars," Phil commented with a chuckle. "You're all divas!" He got to work making us drinks, and soon I was sipping on something called a Red Velvet alongside Chrissie.

"I don't usually drink cocktails," I whispered to Chrissie, suddenly conscious of Adam, who was hovering in front of us.

"That doesn't surprise me," she whispered back.

"Look!" Kelly's high-pitched voice reached us and we turned to see her jumping up and down excitedly at the other side of the room. We joined her and found a table laid out with a row of Rolex watches, all standing in front of photos of us. We reached to retrieve our prizes and I spent a few minutes admiring mine. I've never been very interested in material things, but I loved the watch, and it felt nice to own something so extravagant. I strapped it onto my wrist and gazed down at it.

"I love it!" Chrissie told me, holding her arm out.

"I thought this was all low-budget?" I commented, realising that seven Rolex watches and cars would add up to a fair amount.

"Yeah, right!" Ryan said. "I reckon we'll be aired at prime time and they'll flick straight to a Rolex advert in the break."

"I need another cocktail," Chrissie declared as she slurped the last of her drink through a straw. "Drink up! I need you to dance the night away with me."

"I don't really dance …" I told her and caught the glint in her eye. "You guessed that, didn't you?" I sighed and smiled back at her. "Am I really so predictable?"

"Yeah," she told me happily. "But it's not really a bad thing. Plus, you could always surprise me!"

I rolled my eyes and drained the rest of my drink.

"You see!" she said. Chrissie skipped over to visit Phil at the bar. She returned with a green cocktail for me this time and I eyed it with contempt before taking a sip and deciding it was nicer than it looked.

Moving away from our little huddle, I joined Dylan on one of the couches. "How does it feel to ditch the beard?"

He rubbed his chin. "A bit exposed."

"I think it might be good for the busking," I told him cheekily.

"I might actually have to take it up when my dad fires me!"

"I'm sure it will all be okay," I said.

"At least he'll be happy the beard's gone. He's

always telling me I have to look presentable at work, and somehow that always made me want to look as scruffy as possible. It seems ridiculous now, but being around my parents makes me act like a child."

"I think that's normal. Although it was never really like that with my mum and me! There's not much point worrying about things at home, though. You may as well just make the most of the holiday."

"I guess so. I should take a leaf out of your book and relax and see what happens."

"Why not? I'm having a great time," I told him while I scanned the room. "And these cocktails are going down far too easily. Can you get your guitar out again sometime? I missed your show."

"No! I'm not sure how Matt talked me into that. Anyway, we have music tonight. You're right, these are pretty good." He picked up his bright blue cocktail and clinked his glass against mine before finishing it off. "In fact, I think I need another one, since Chrissie is insisting I dance with her later."

"Yeah, I think she's determined to get us all making fools of ourselves on the dance floor."

"Do you want another?" he asked, standing up with his empty glass.

I desperately wanted to say no but I suddenly heard my mum's voice in my head telling me to be a yes person. "Yes, please!" I replied and he looked amused by my laughter. He shook his head and chuckled as he headed for the bar. It was a moment before I noticed Adam, who moved in front of me.

"Oh, go away, will you?" I said. He smiled at me from behind the camera and I sank back into the couch as I took in everything around me.

The atmosphere was relaxed. We spent the evening chatting and laughing in our beautiful surroundings. As we sipped cocktails in the fading light, I felt that I didn't have a care in the world.

"You were right about Dylan," Chrissie told me when we found ourselves alone for a moment. "He looks so different."

"I think we did well with the guys here. They're all pretty nice."

"Ooh, who are you interested in?" She giggled and leaned closer to me, wobbling slightly.

"No one," I told her, too quickly. "I just think they're all good guys. Everyone's nice, aren't they?"

"Yes." She sighed and linked her arm through mine. "I'm really glad you're here!"

She leaned her head against mine and I realised she was pretty drunk. In fact, everyone seemed quite merry. "I'm glad too," I told her and squeezed her arm lightly.

"I think it's time to dance," she declared.

"I think you're right!"

We headed to the dance floor and Chrissie shouted for the others to join us. After a couple of songs I went inside to the bathroom, wobbling as I made my way across the lawn. I squinted while my eyes adjusted to the dim light of the living room, and I smiled at Margaret and Ryan who were laughing on the couch. When I made my way back outside a few minutes later, Kelly shouted from the bar that we were doing shots.

"No way," I told them when I joined them. "I don't do shots ... and I'm already drunk!" Matt ignored my protests and handed me a shot. I winced as I swallowed it and turned to Carl, who was standing just outside our circle. "I think you're missing some action inside," I told him with a hiccup. He raised an eyebrow and glanced at Adam who was standing at the other side of us.

"What's happening inside?" Chrissie asked, craning her neck in the direction of the living room.

"Margaret and Ryan are kissing!" I informed her.

"No!" Matt said. He walked quickly across the lawn and the rest of us followed to peek in the living room to spy on them. Carl crept inside and aimed his camera at them from behind the couch.

"I can't believe that!" Kelly said when we moved back towards the bar and fell about laughing.

Matt seemed fairly traumatised by the sight. "That's just wrong!"

"She must be old enough to be his mother …" Chrissie commented.

"She's forty," Kelly told us. "And Ryan's twenty, I think."

"I need another shot," Matt declared. "I'm in shock!"

"I have to go to bed." Dylan saluted us and walked back towards the house.

"Dylan!" I called. "You work in a bar; you should have more stamina!"

He ignored me and continued on his way.

"I think I need a lie down," Kelly told us and we watched her stumble over to the hammock at the edge of the lawn. She dropped down to sit on it and, as she attempted to manoeuvre herself to lie down, she wobbled and fell out the other side, cackling with laughter before getting up to try again. "I made it!"

she finally called before giggling quietly to herself. Soon she was quiet.

"Who wants to dance again?" Chrissie asked.

"Not me!" I told her. "My feet are killing me." I kicked off Chrissie's wedges and walked over to one of the couches.

"Go on, then!" I heard Matt relent when Chrissie tugged on his arm and pulled him to the dance floor. The music slowed and I saw Matt and Chrissie put their arms around each other and sway to the music.

"That's nice," I told Adam, who took a seat at the other end of the couch. The cameras were becoming a familiar sight and, after all the alcohol, I don't think I really registered Adam's camera at all. "Everyone's getting cosy."

I leaned on the arm of the couch and felt my eyelids start to droop. Adam shuffled along the couch and nudged me gently. "Bed," he mouthed as I focused on him.

"That's a bit forward," I said, chuckling to myself. "I barely know you!" I couldn't stop giggling and I moved towards Adam, reaching for his hand. "I don't know if I can get to bed," I confessed. "Can I just sleep here?" He shook his head and I felt my eyes getting heavier. "Just stay here with me a minute …" I said to him as my eyes closed. "Just for a minute."

Hannah Ellis

Chapter 16

When my eyes fluttered open, my head was resting on Adam's shoulder. I glanced at the camera lying beside him and didn't dare move. Taking a deep breath, I lifted my head slightly, hoping I'd be able to creep away without disturbing him. He stirred when I moved and stretched out, before putting his arm around my shoulders, drawing me to him before he settled back into a deep sleep.

Part of me wanted to cuddle up and stay in his embrace, while another part of me was screaming to get up and run. I allowed myself a moment to relax and rest my head on his chest, listening to the steady beat of his heart. Then I moved my hand to his and ran my thumb over the back of his hand.

I managed to extract myself without waking him and crept across the lawn in the moonlight. The house was still when I tiptoed up the stairs and slipped quietly into the bedroom.

I woke not long later to the sun streaming through the windows, and turned towards Chrissie's bed to find her looking in my direction. "Well, that was an interesting night," she said.

"Yeah," I groaned. "What happened with you and Matt?"

"Nothing," she said with a sigh. "Well, okay, I

kissed him!" A smile lit up her face before fading again. "I really like him," she told me.

"What's the face for?" I asked. "That's good, isn't it?"

"I don't know. I'm not sure if he likes me or if it was just a drunken snog ... Plus, it seems a bit embarrassing, drunkenly kissing some guy on a reality TV show. I don't know what to think."

"I think he likes you," I said. "I don't think you need to worry about it. Matt's a nice guy."

"He is, isn't he? And what about you? Last I saw, you were draped over Adam!"

"This is why I don't usually drink much," I told her. "I fell asleep on him. I'm really embarrassed."

"Was he still there when you woke up?"

"Yeah." I remembered the feel of his arm around me and the warmth of his body next to mine. "I crept away and left him sleeping."

"Sneaky." A slow smile spread across her face. "I think Adam's lovely."

"I was just drunk," I said. "I'm so embarrassed."

"Don't worry about it. There's nothing to be embarrassed about. And anyway, he didn't look too concerned." She paused. "Anyway, there will be people with worse hangovers than us this morning ..."

"Ryan and Margaret!" A laugh escaped me as I remembered them kissing in the dark. "Alcohol is bad!"

"So bad!" She laughed with me. "Do you think we can get away with staying in bed all day?"

"I doubt it. Anyway, it's already too hot to stay here. Maybe that's why they didn't bother with air conditioning, so we at least have to get up and move down to the pool."

"I think a swim might fix my hangover," Chrissie told me.

"I need to eat," I told her as I sat up on the bed. "And I need water. And possibly painkillers!" My head was starting to throb. I forced myself to stand up, and opened a drawer to find some clothes.

"Borrow another bikini from me," Chrissie offered. "Just take whatever you want."

"I feel bad, borrowing your clothes all the time."

"Why? I brought far too much for a week anyway. And you can't wear your swimsuit … not when you're trying to impress Adam!"

"I am not trying to impress anyone!" I said before catching her sly smile.

"Here, try the spotty one." She appeared next to me and pulled a bikini out of her drawer. "It'll look cute."

"Okay," I agreed. "Thanks."

"Hey!" I was taken aback by Chrissie's tone – until I realised she wasn't talking to me. "Get out, you pervert!" she shouted at the cameraman who had just stuck the lens of his camera around the doorway. She went over and slammed the door on him, leaving us in peace. "I guess we're not allowed to hide in our bedrooms all day," she told me.

I went into the bathroom to change into Chrissie's bikini and brushed my teeth furiously in a bid to remove the smell of the alcoholic rodent that had apparently died on my tongue. The door of Kelly and Margaret's bedroom opened suddenly, making me jump.

"Sorry." Kelly was pale and her cheeks were streaked with last night's eye make-up. "I think I'm going to throw up."

"I'm finished in here!" I told her as I put my toothbrush away and hurried back into the bedroom.

"Wear this skirt," Chrissie instructed me as she stood holding my denim mini skirt.

"It's very short. I'm not sure why I brought it. I was in a rush when I packed."

"I like it. Put it on." She threw it at me and I noticed my T-shirt that she had in her other hand.

"I just wear that one for bed," I told her quickly.

"Thank goodness! No offence, but it's awful!" Her eyes twinkled when she asked, "Do you trust me?"

"Yeah …" I replied slowly.

"And this T-shirt holds no sentimental value? It's just an ugly T-shirt that you happen to have?"

"It's just for bed," I repeated.

"Good. Here goes, then …" she picked up a pair of scissors from the bed and proceeded to cut the arms off my old baby-blue T-shirt and then slashed it across the neckline. "Ta-dah!" she sang, handing it to me.

"Thanks," I said cautiously and slipped it over my head before pulling my skirt on. I jerked at the T-shirt when it slipped off my shoulder. Chrissie slapped my hand away and tugged the T-shirt back off my shoulder before turning me to the mirror.

"Oh!" I was pleasantly surprised. "How did you do that?"

"It's just my thing!" She grinned and picked up a hair slide with a white flower on it.

"No …" I shook my head when she approached me. She ignored me and slid it into my hair.

"Okay," I agreed as I looked at my reflection again.

"Don't ever doubt me," she told me. "Now, I'll get ready and we can go and get breakfast."

"Kelly's throwing up in the bathroom," I warned her.

"Oh no!" She put an ear to the bathroom door and grimaced. "You go ahead. I'll meet you down there."

I walked out of the bedroom and straight into a cameraman. "Morning." I got no reply so I moved around him and went for the stairs. I was thankful it wasn't Adam. I wasn't sure I wanted to be alone with him. Hopefully my embarrassment would be diluted in a group.

The door to the boys' bedroom opened and Matt walked out looking half asleep. We met at the top of the stairs and he smiled at me.

"Morning," he mumbled and motioned for me to go ahead of him.

"How are you feeling?" I asked.

"The cocktails were pretty lethal, weren't they?"

"The shots probably weren't necessary either," I said.

"I forgot about the shots," he groaned. "They were completely unnecessary."

"Shall we stop talking about alcohol?" I asked.

"Good plan."

We reached the kitchen and found Maria waiting nervously at the foot of the stairs which led up to the crew's rooms.

"Morning!" I smiled at her. She pointed up the stairs and put a finger to her lips. In the silence I could just make out Jessica's voice. She was shouting again. Apparently she was upset about half the cameramen being ill and missing out on a good portion of last night's antics as a result. Again she was worrying about her job and her career. I shrugged at Matt and couldn't even be bothered to eavesdrop. I guessed we'd all be happy that the previous night's recordings were limited. The fact that it seemed more and more likely that whatever recordings they did have would never see the light of day was not a problem for me at all.

"Amazing." Matt sighed and held up a box of painkillers to me. "Found these in the fruit bowl. Someone is very thoughtful."

"I'll take some of those."

"If I just had a full English breakfast, that would be my hangover taken care of." He opened the fridge and peered in. Maria chatted away to him in Spanish, presumably asking what he was looking for. "Any idea how you say 'bacon' in Spanish?"

"Sorry," I said. "No idea."

"Pig?"

"No," I chuckled.

"I could probably act that out …" He grinned at me.

"Please, don't. I can already envision it … Just don't." He ignored me and snorted like a pig. I immediately got the giggles, which seemed to spur him on, and he did it again. Poor Maria was getting more and more agitated, determined to figure out what Matt was trying to tell her.

"It's fine." He waved her away. "Don't worry about it."

She snorted a pig noise back at him and mimed out an eating motion.

"Yes!" He gave her a thumbs-up. "I want to eat pig," he mimed back. "And eggs!" he added.

"That's helpful," I told him.

"Eggs," he repeated slowly and attempted to illustrate the point with his hands. Maria pulled out a little notepad and pencil from her apron and handed it to Matt, who proceeded to draw a plate of bacon and eggs. He then added sausages and toast for good measure. Maria peered over his shoulder and clicked her tongue while he drew. When he handed her his artwork, she raised her voice and threw her hands in the air before flinging open her door and disappearing down the cramped staircase.

"Do you think that's a no, then?" Matt asked.

"I can't believe you just did that," I said. "Couldn't you just have bread with cheese and ham like every other morning? Or cereal?" I looked around at the food spread out on the table. "Yoghurt? Fruit? It's not as though there's nothing to eat."

"I wanted hangover food, that's all. I feel bad now, though."

I put some bread and cheese on a plate and wondered whether my stomach could even cope with that. I grabbed an apple too and a glass of orange juice. Matt loaded up his plate and we headed back through the house.

"So, you and Adam?" Matt said, distancing himself from me as we walked, as though expecting a punch.

"We're not talking about that." I took a breath. "And unless you want to talk about you and Chrissie, you'll shut up now …"

"Fair enough." He grinned as we stepped out into the sun, and then winced at the brightness. The sun loungers had been moved off the lawn and an elaborate crazy golf course had taken over. We stood for a minute, looking at the castle, windmill, loops and ramps. It looked like fun.

"I could actually win this one," I said confidently. My dad couldn't walk past a crazy golf course without having a go. He was a bit obsessed, and I was suddenly thankful for all the time he'd forced me to spend hitting a ball around miniature courses.

"Sorry," Matt said. "This one's mine!"

"Don't count your chickens …"

He sat down to eat breakfast. "Did you see Margaret this morning?"

"No," I said, the corners of my mouth twitching upwards as I sat opposite him. "Did you see Ryan?"

"No sign of him yet."

"Good morning!" Margaret suddenly appeared behind us and I felt like we'd been caught out.

"Morning," we greeted her.

"Let's get it over with, then …" She looked at us each in turn, once she'd spent a moment checking out the golf course. "Who's got something to say about last night?"

Matt and I attempted to look puzzled, but she laughed at us. "Oh come on … out with it. I'm old enough to be his mother and whatever else you're saying …" She grinned as though she was genuinely amused by the situation.

"Oh, you mean you and Ryan?" Matt asked innocently. "I say go for it. You're only as old as the guy you're snogging, isn't that the saying?" He looked at me.

"I don't think that's it," I mused. "But we are all adults …" I attempted to sound serious, but when Margaret started laughing I struggled to keep the smile from my face.

"Oh, you're very sweet, both of you," she said. "I feel rough. I'm not even sure I can eat," she went on as she took a piece of ham from Matt's plate and gingerly put it in her mouth. "Were there cameras around, by the way? My memory is slightly hazy …"

"I think there was one … maybe …" I thought about Carl standing next to the couch while Ryan and Margaret played tonsil tennis. "I'm not sure."

"It was Carl," Matt announced.

"I just hope this never gets shown in Australia. My daughter would disown me."

"You've got a daughter?" I asked.

"Yeah, she's sixteen, and I'd say Ryan is just her type …" I lost it at that point and Matt and I both gave up on being polite and fell about laughing. I looked up to see Ryan walking in, and quickly got myself under control.

"Morning, Ryan!" Matt and I greeted him simultaneously.

"Morning," he mumbled and nodded at Margaret. I started giggling when Matt snorted with laughter.

"I forgot coffee." Matt's voice came out as a squeak as he stifled his laughter. "I'll be back in a minute."

"Me too," I said, following him. Carl came with us and we just made it into the dining room before we let our laughter out. I was holding my sides as I laughed uncontrollably. Eventually I had to drop to my knees, gasping for breath.

"That …" Matt kept saying but couldn't get any further with his sentence. I lay down on my back and stared at the ceiling while I held my stomach and tried to take deep breaths.

I calmed down pretty quickly when Adam moved into my vision. "Hi," I said.

"I might just get that coffee …" Matt grinned at me before wandering back to the kitchen with Carl in tow.

"Sorry about last night," I blurted. "I might have been a bit drunk." Of course, he said nothing so I just lay on the floor, looking up at him, feeling like the biggest fool who ever lived. "Anyway, I'm a bit embarrassed and I wanted to say something so it's not awkward, but I think it might just be more awkward now." He reached out and pulled me up from the floor. I looked right into his eyes. And he winked at me.

"I had to use the boys' bathroom," Chrissie told us loudly when she descended the stairs at the other side of the room. "Kelly has the hangover from hell. Bless her. Sorry, did I interrupt something?"

"Nope," I replied and moved in her direction.

"You look hot," Chrissie commented, as though she hadn't chosen my clothes and admired my new look ten minutes ago. "Doesn't she look hot, Adam?"

I gave her a quick death stare before walking past her and back outside to join Ryan and Margaret. I kept hoping the ground would open up and swallow me, but I wasn't that lucky.

"I'm glad they're not making us do anything energetic today," Matt commented, handing me a cup of coffee. He glanced at Chrissie and gave her a quick nod before sitting down to the remainder of his breakfast. "Sorry about before," he told Margaret. "I think I swallowed something funny by mistake."

"It seemed like it," Margaret smiled at him. "I hope

you're okay now?"

"Fully recovered, thanks!"

"You're a sorry-looking bunch," Dylan told us when he walked past and dived into the pool, looking annoyingly sprightly.

I glanced at Ryan and felt worse just looking at him. He looked like he had the ultimate hangover: nausea and a headache mixed with embarrassment and shame. It was painful to look at him, and he was the quietest he'd been since we arrived.

Chelsea arrived five minutes later, and I could've sworn she enjoyed the fact that we all looked and felt terrible. "As I'm sure you have all realised, we're having a few technical problems …" She trailed off as Maria's voice drifted through to us, her Spanish accent unmistakable. She walked purposefully in with a tray and deposited a full English breakfast in front of Matt.

I swear I saw Matt's eyes well up. He stared at Maria for a moment before standing to envelop her in a hug. She squeezed his cheek as he released her, never stopping chattering. He kissed her cheek and then she disappeared as quickly as she'd appeared.

I smiled as I looked at Matt and saw there really were tears in his eyes. "Bloody hell," he sniffed. "I think that's the nicest thing anyone's ever done for me." He picked up a sausage and took a bite before glancing up at Chelsea, who was looking fairly dumbstruck. "Sorry, what were you saying?"

"Erm … technical problems …" she began again. "There's a temporary shortage of cameramen so the producers have asked that you try to spend the bulk of your time out here in the communal area, to help with

135

filming. They would really appreciate your cooperation. Enjoy your breakfast, and I'll see you shortly for a round of golf!"

Chapter 17

It was a lovely, relaxed morning. Chelsea returned half an hour after she left us, wearing a quirky pink golf outfit, and was as flamboyant as ever while she refereed our golf tournament. I thought it was great fun and, with another £500 at stake, I began to be a little competitive. Ryan, on the other hand, was not handling his hangover well and spent the whole time complaining and asking if he could just go to bed and forfeit his chance of winning the money. It wasn't worth it, he told us; he was dying!

Matt and I were in the lead the whole time. At the last hole, he was heckling me as we stood side by side. Our scores were tied.

"You shouldn't even bother," he told me. "I can get this in one. With my eyes closed!"

"Feel free to take it with your eyes closed," I replied as I set my ball down and lined up my club. Looking up, I surveyed the ramp which led up to the windmill with its rotating sails. The hole was just at the other side of the windmill, and beyond that was Adam. He moved and caught my eye.

Chrissie's voice broke the silence. "You can do it!"

My short swing was confident and the ball raced up the ramp. It flew through the gap in the sails and I held my breath. Plop! Straight into the hole. Kelly squealed and I turned to smile at Matt, my eyebrows raised. "Beat that!"

I cheered when his ball hit the windmill sail and bounced back to him.

"No need to be smug," he told me while I danced around him.

"I never win anything," I told him. "I can't believe it! Plus I've got no job; I can use the money."

My excitement remained and I teased Matt about his poor shot over lunch. Winning a game of crazy golf had never felt so good.

Lunch – and a beer! – perked Ryan up and he was full of energy again when he suggested we play a game.

"Like what?" Kelly asked. "More golf?"

"No. Something else." He looked around for a moment before chuckling and moving over to stand beside Carl, who took a step back. "I'm inventing a new game," he told us proudly. "It's called 'stand behind the cameraman'." He moved quickly behind Carl, who turned with his camera to follow him. Ryan moved around behind him and Carl looked like a dog chasing his tail before standing still and letting out a sarcastic laugh. He nodded at the other cameraman, who walked over to film Ryan while Matt ran over to stand behind the cameraman by the house.

"I've got Adam!" I shouted while Kelly, Chrissie and Margaret spread out to annoy the other cameramen. There were only four of them, so we had them well covered.

"Go away!" Adam flashed a cheeky grin when I moved to stand directly behind him. He turned and grabbed my arm to pull me in front of him. I laughed and ducked behind him again, my arms naturally wrapping around his waist as I stood behind him.

"What are you going to do now?" I asked, expecting him to wriggle away.

"Nothing," he whispered. My heart raced when his hand brushed briefly against my arm. I enjoyed the feel of his body against mine, and was reluctant to move away. I stood on my tiptoes to look over his shoulder and watch the others playing around. The mute cameraman who Matt was messing with looked completely unamused. Dylan was leaning out of his hammock to watch the entertainment.

"Look," I whispered in Adam's ear. "Dylan's cracked a smile – make sure you get that on camera." He moved around and I moved with him.

"New game," Matt suddenly shouted. "Tickle the cameraman!"

I spat out a laugh when I saw Matt tickling the guy, who looked like he might punch him at any moment. "That sounds like a great game," I told Adam, "and I already know where you're ticklish."

He wriggled away from me when my hands moved over his ribs.

"No!" He tried to look serious but laughed while I tickled him. "Stop it!" he told me. "If the camera ends up broken, we're both in trouble."

"Maybe you should put it down, then." I continued to tickle him and he grabbed my wrist with his free hand.

"Seriously! Stop it now," he said with a laugh. "Right, that's it …" He put his camera on the table and grabbed me around the waist.

"Get off!" I squealed.

He lifted me off the ground and I squirmed as he moved towards the pool.

"Okay, I'll leave you alone," I promised. "Let's just stop it now. Game over. Put me down!"

"Fine," he agreed, setting me down next to the pool. "But no more tickling, okay?"

"Promise!" I told him, just as I caught sight of Matt as he ran past, giving Adam and me a quick shove as he went. I grabbed at Adam's arm to steady myself, tightening my grip when we toppled into the water together.

When I emerged from the water I gasped and smiled as I heard the laughter around me.

"Oh, great," Adam said beside me. "There goes my job." He attempted to look annoyed, but his eyes sparkled and his mouth twitched into a smirk. "The pool's nice," he quipped as he splashed water over my face and swam to the steps. "I'll be right back … if I don't get fired!" He gave Matt a friendly shove and shook water from his walkie-talkie while he headed into the house.

Chrissie gave me a look when I got out of the pool, her eyes sparkling with amusement. She opened her mouth and sang, "Lucy and Ad—" I cut her off with a quick shove and she landed with a splash in the pool.

She was laughing when she swam up to the side of the pool. I stripped off my dripping wet clothes to reveal my bikini underneath, deciding a proper swim would be nice. I'd just spread out my clothes to dry when Ryan jumped up from the couch and ran inside.

"The bloody chicken's back," he shouted when he

reached the safety of the living room. I saw the golden-brown bird bobbing around on the other side of the fence.

"Don't call her that," Matt said. "It's sweet, gentle Matilda. She's come for your therapy session."

"Just get rid of her, will you?" Ryan said.

"I've got an idea." Matt moved into the storeroom and came back with a bottle of beer. "If you can get to me, you get the beer." He stood halfway between Ryan and Matilda.

"Or I could just get myself a beer," Ryan told him.

"If you go in that room, I'll bring Matilda in and lock the door," Matt told him. "Just come and get the beer. Matilda's behind a fence; you're safe."

I sat with my legs dangling in the pool and watched Ryan edge slowly outside. Silence settled over us while he took small steps towards Matt, taking deep breaths as he went. He was reaching for the beer when Matt took a step back in Matilda's direction. Ryan glared at Matt and took another step. They moved closer and closer to Matilda until Ryan came to a halt a few steps before the fence.

"Just give me the beer now."

Matt handed it over and Ryan didn't take his eyes from Matilda as he took long swigs of beer.

Matt slapped Ryan on the back. "Well done!"

"So have you conquered your fear?" I asked when Ryan joined me by the pool.

"No. But I don't think Matilda is as evil as the other chickens. She's a nicer colour."

I smiled to myself and turned to find Adam hovering over my shoulder. "Hi." I looked up at him. His hair was still damp and ruffled. He returned my smile.

***

"I don't know what's going on," I told Chrissie as we lay in bed that night. "Adam winked at me. What on earth does that mean?"

"I have no idea," she said. "But maybe it means he loves you."

I rolled my eyes. "I really like him."

"That's good, isn't it?"

"No, it's confusing," I told her. "I don't know if he likes me and this is a really weird situation. How can I have a crush on someone who barely speaks? I still can't believe I fell asleep on him!"

"To be honest, I don't think it's a big deal that you got drunk and fell asleep on him. But I do think it's a big deal that you're obsessing about it."

"I'm not obsessing about it."

"Okay, you're obsessing about *him*!"

"No, I'm not!" I protested, turning on my side to face Chrissie. "Okay, maybe I am! I really don't want to like him."

She sat up, removing her hairband and shaking out her hair. "I think he's nice."

"You're not helping me! Let's talk about Matt instead …"

"Do you think he likes me?" she asked sheepishly.

"Definitely."

"I think so too," she told me, lying down. "I hope so. You're right, though, it's a weird situation."

"We're already halfway through the week, you know? It'll be over before we know it." I turned onto my back and stared up at the ceiling. I was surprised by how much I was enjoying myself, and the thought of it all being over in a few days was strange. I'd been convinced I'd have an awful time and would be able to tell my mum that her approach to life just led to trouble. So far, however, things couldn't have gone better. "As soon as this is over, you, me and Matt should go for a night out at Dylan's bar."

"Definitely," Chrissie said as she reached to turn out the bedside lamp.

Hannah Ellis

Chapter 18

We were tucking into our continental breakfast the next day when Maria placed another full English breakfast in front of Matt.

"I think I'm a little bit in love with this lady," he told us as he stood to give her a big kiss. She squeezed his cheeks before leaving us.

"That's not fair," Ryan complained, stealing a sausage from Matt's plate. I'd been amused to find Ryan chatting to Matilda when I'd arrived downstairs. He was at a safe distance, with the fence between him and the chicken, and he swore he wasn't talking to her – but I knew what I'd seen.

"I can't help it if Maria's got a soft spot for me." Matt grinned and moved his plate away from Ryan.

I swam for a while and then lay sunbathing while we waited for Chelsea to make her morning appearance. The crazy golf had disappeared overnight and the sun loungers had been returned to their rightful place, spread out evenly around the lawn. There were seven loungers under seven umbrellas as usual – but each umbrella had a small wooden box under it too. If it hadn't been for the fact that they had only just appeared, I would have thought they were little tables and thought no more about them.

"Do you think she's forgotten about us?" Kelly

asked. She was lying on the sun lounger nearest me, turning frequently to ensure an even tan.

"I hope so," I told her. "I'd quite like to relax here all day."

"Me too. I think I'd like Chelsea's job …"

"Really?"

"Yeah. I think if I could have any job I wanted, I'd be a TV presenter."

"What do you do now?" I realised I didn't really know much about Kelly.

"I work in an Italian restaurant at the moment, waitressing. Well, I did anyway. I'll probably get fired for this." She gestured at our surroundings.

"You deciding it was worth risking your job for?"

"Yeah. I like my job but life's short, isn't it? I can get another job easily enough. People like pretty waitresses."

I smiled at her lack of modesty.

"This seemed like it would be a fun adventure. Plus we'll be on TV and who knows what opportunities will come from that?"

"You sound a bit like my mum," I told her. "She thinks life's too short to do anything remotely boring. She hated me working in an office."

"She's right. Why do a job that you don't enjoy?"

"Money! I have bills to pay. And a student loan to pay off."

"What did you study?"

"Psychology." I always felt I needed to explain my choice. "My dad always wanted me to get a degree but since I didn't know what I wanted to do with my life, I just picked anything. My dad thinks a degree creates opportunities."

"No offence, but your dad sounds annoying."

"He's not so bad," I said. "But after three years at university, I ended up with a degree in psychology and a student loan to pay back. Of course, I still didn't know what I wanted to do. I thought about teaching, but that meant another year of studying and I decided I had enough debt, so I got an office job to pay the bills and pay back the loan. It was supposed to be temporary, but I just sort of got stuck in it."

"Couldn't your dad have helped you out with the loan, since it was his idea for you to go to uni?"

"No, I think it was supposed to be a life lesson for me. Money management and all that."

"Why did you listen to him? If I was you I'd be taking advice from my mum, not my dad."

"I think it was because my mum's life always seemed such a mess. They were never really together and I grew up with my mum." I registered Dylan hovering around us.

"Coming for a swim?" he asked as I looked up at him. I shook my head and continued chatting to Kelly.

"My dad can be a bit boring, but he always provided for his family and never had any financial worries. He's an architect and his life always seemed so ordered; I guess that made sense to me. I was always the one trying to create order for my mum and me, and I wished she was more like my dad so I didn't have to worry so much. But—" I spluttered in shock as water suddenly sprayed all over me. I pushed my wet hair off my face and glared at Dylan, who was treading water in the pool in front of me.

"What was that for?" Chrissie demanded on my behalf. She was swimming laps beside Dylan.

147

His gaze bore into me and he had a look on his face that I couldn't read. "Come for a dip."

"I'm talking," I told him impatiently. "I'll come in a bit. What was I saying?" I asked Kelly.

"Come on," Dylan coaxed. "Don't make me drag you in." He splashed me again and I grew increasingly irritated. I'd been enjoying chatting with Kelly. Dylan stared at me with wide eyes and then tipped his head in the direction of the nearest camera.

"I'll be back in a minute," I told Kelly and lowered myself into the pool.

I swam to the middle and Dylan followed me. "You should watch what you say," he told me under his breath. I turned to look at him and we treaded water. "Don't talk about your family. Imagine how you'll feel if they watch that on TV."

"You really think this will end up on TV?" I asked him.

"It could."

"I don't even think there was a camera near me," I told him, glancing round at Adam, who was standing a good distance from where I'd been chatting to Kelly.

"Just be careful. Don't forget you're being watched. And you've no idea what the reach is for the microphones on those things." He glanced at Carl who was walking along the poolside. "Modern technology is pretty impressive."

"You realise you sound paranoid?" Chrissie said, floating on her back beside me.

"Maybe," he replied without taking his eyes off me.

"We overheard Jessica saying everything was going wrong and this probably wouldn't end up on TV at all," I told him.

"Okay," he said. "Maybe it won't be on TV. But maybe it will. We have no idea what will happen."

Chrissie sighed. "Lighten up, will you?"

"I just don't want you to do or say anything you'll regret," he told me.

My head jerked around as Chelsea's voice rang out. "Good morning, boys and girls!" She beckoned us over to the couches and we moved slowly to gather around her. "You will be excited to hear that there is a whopping £1000 up for grabs in today's test of endurance!"

I was fairly sure I knew what the challenge was going to be, and was disappointed at the producers' lack of imagination. This had all been done before.

"You've probably noticed the boxes under the sun umbrellas," Chelsea continued. "The challenge is simple: whoever stays on their box the longest is the winner! And I'm sorry to rush you but the challenge will start in ten seconds, so please position yourself on a box immediately."

Ryan took off at a run and hopped up onto the nearest box. The rest of us were less enthusiastic.

"I think I might be at a disadvantage," Matt shouted. He had to bend so his head didn't hit the grass umbrella.

"You're welcome to sit," Chelsea said as she walked among us. "Just make sure you don't touch the ground or you'll be out."

"I can't sit on it," Matt told her. "I don't fit!"

Kelly was also too tall to stand comfortably under the umbrella, but she managed to sit cross-legged on the box.

"This is really stupid," I said, looking at Adam who was standing near me and then turning my attention to the others. "We could all give up now and share the money …"

"I'm up for that," Matt said.

"There can only be one winner, I'm afraid," Chelsea informed us.

"Okay," Margaret said. "But the winner would be free to share the money."

Chelsea was starting to look flustered. "I suppose so, but …"

"I'm not sharing," Ryan said. "And you've all just proved that you've got no stamina. It's not been five minutes yet. I could stay here all day."

"Oh, Ryan," Matt said on a sigh. "Didn't your parents teach you about sharing?"

"This is a competition," Ryan told him. "And I intend to win."

Matt looked at Dylan and with a nod they stepped off their boxes and walked over to stand in front of Ryan.

"Do you want to get off yet?" Dylan asked. "Or shall we help you?"

Ryan's words came out fast and laced with panic. "You can't touch me. Surely that's not allowed!" He turned to Chelsea, who looked confused.

When Matt and Dylan took another step towards Ryan, he held up his hands and stepped down. "I was only joking," he said with a nervous smile. "Of course I'll share the money. Who wants to stand on a box all day?"

Margaret and I got down from the boxes and Kelly blew Chrissie a kiss as she uncrossed her legs and put her feet on the ground.

"Am I the winner?" Chrissie asked Chelsea excitedly.

"I'm not sure this is allowed," she said.

"I'm the last one on a box," Chrissie told her. "Surely the money is mine."

Chelsea looked around at us all. At that moment, I'm fairly sure she hated us. "Congratulations, Chrissie!" she said, adopting a cheerful tone.

Chrissie stepped down from her box. "Yes! We're all winners; I'll share the money and no one has to waste the day standing around on a box!"

We watched Chelsea walk across the lawn. "Have a great day!" she called over her shoulder and disappeared inside.

Hannah Ellis

Chapter 19

"I'm twenty-six years old and I'm playing hide and seek," I mumbled to myself while I skipped down the stairs. Admittedly, I play hide and seek fairly regularly – but usually with a couple of five-year-olds, not a group of adults. It was Ryan's idea, of course.

"Hey, Matilda," I greeted the golden chicken, which was wandering around down in the huge entrance hall. The door leading to the back of the finca was open and I watched Matilda stalk outside and wander across the courtyard to Maria, who was sitting on a bench outside the door to her apartment. It was a drab and dusty area, littered with tools and rusting parts of machinery. A scruffy dog lay in the shade of a washing rack near Maria, its wiry black hair matted in places.

I smiled at Maria, who didn't notice me. Matilda clucked happily over to her and Maria gently picked up the fluffy bird and tenderly stroked its head – before abruptly snapping its neck.

She turned at my gasp, waving cheerfully while she laid the lifeless chicken on the small wooden table next to her. My eyes were like saucers, but I managed to keep a smile on my face when Maria called out to me. By her hand gestures, I concluded that Matilda was on the menu for dinner.

I waved and took a step back, bumping into Adam. "She just killed Matilda," I whispered, stepping away from him and closing the door to the courtyard of death.

"Coming!" I heard Ryan's voice ring out around the finca, and remembered I was supposed to be hiding. I opened a door at the foot of the stairs and slipped into the cramped, musty-smelling cupboard. There were floor-to-ceiling shelves on the three walls and each shelf held piles of blankets and bedding.

"You'll have to come in too," I told Adam, pulling him inside before closing the door and shutting out the light. "Ouch!" I bumped into the camera and we shuffled awkwardly in the tight space.

"Sorry," he said and put a hand on my face before running it down to my shoulder, making me catch my breath. "Sorry," he repeated. "Just trying to figure out where you are so I don't knock you out with the camera."

"The light's gone out," I told him when the red light from the camera disappeared.

"I switched it off," he told me and I could just make out him setting the camera on top of a pile of blankets. "I don't think it's much use in here."

"What about the microphone?" I asked.

"Do you want me to switch the camera on again?" he asked, amusement in his voice.

"No," I told him quickly. "I just thought you might get into trouble …"

"Possibly. But it's a freelance job, and it's almost over. I don't think I'll get fired at this stage. Plus, no one batted an eyelid when I drowned a walkie-talkie yesterday."

"That was Matt's fault." My eyes started to adjust, and the sliver of light from under the door was enough for me to make out Adam's face. "The week's gone fast, hasn't it?"

"Yeah." His walkie-talkie suddenly crackled into life, making me jump, and I reached out a hand to steady myself. "I'm hiding in a cupboard with Lucy," he told Jessica casually. "Be quiet or you'll give us away!" He turned his walkie-talkie off and sighed. "They probably won't be in a hurry to employ me again …"

We stopped talking at the sound of footsteps on the stairs, and I held my breath as I waited to be discovered, trying to ignore my proximity to Adam and the fact that my heart rate was rising steadily. Then there was a sudden shriek from somewhere nearby and the footsteps returned when whoever it was headed quickly back upstairs.

"I think Ryan just uncovered Maria and her murderous ways," Adam said quietly.

"I can't believe that sweet little old lady just killed poor Matilda with her bare hands."

"She's funny," Adam said. "She reminds me of my gran."

"Yeah?"

"My gran kept chickens too. Mostly for the eggs, but I remember seeing her plucking one of them when I was a kid and I was traumatised for a while."

"I think I might be traumatised for a while too," I told him.

In the silence I was acutely aware of my heartbeat. I was sure that Adam must be able to hear it. It felt like wild horses were stampeding through my chest. I was only wearing a bikini and there was so little space that, if either of us moved, we bumped into each other.

"Sorry," I said when I shifted my weight and stood on his foot. "I should probably have found somewhere more spacious to hide." My voice sounded strange and I almost felt like opening the door and walking away. "And why on earth are we playing hide and seek anyway?"

"I think it's a nice cupboard." He was so close that I could feel the warmth of his breath on my face, his voice so soft it was barely audible. "And it might be the best idea Ryan's had all week."

I shivered when he ran his hand down my arm and lingered over my hand. My brain shut off and I entwined my fingers with his, pulling him to me until his lips brushed mine. My breath caught in my throat. His hand rested on my lower back, and when he hesitated, I moved my hands into his hair and pushed my lips to his. His arms tightened around me and I felt my feet leave the ground as I kissed him.

"There you are …" Light filled the tiny space around us and I squinted at Kelly, who was standing in the doorway. "Or not!" she said, pushing the door shut again. I untangled myself from Adam and reached for the door while he grabbed at his camera.

"You found us!" I called after Kelly, who was halfway up the stairs.

"Oh, great." She grinned at me. "It was really dark in there; I almost missed you!"

Chrissie appeared at the top of the staircase, a big smile on her face. "You found them?"

"Yep, we're here," I told her, feeling like I'd run a marathon and hoping no one noticed my breathlessness. Adam was pointing his camera up at us, his face blank. I struggled to get my breathing under control as I smiled at Kelly and Chrissie.

"You have to come and see this," Chrissie told me. "Ryan is freaking out about Maria plucking a chicken. I think he's going to be scarred for life!"

"Okay." I ran up the stairs and we went back outside.

"I'm not eating dinner tonight if it's chicken," Ryan was telling Matt, who suppressed a smile and patted him reassuringly on the knee. "What if it was Matilda?" he asked. "Can someone go and look for Matilda?" His breathing was even more erratic than mine, and his face was pale when he looked up at us and took a swig of beer.

"It was Matilda," I told him. "Sorry, I saw Maria snap her neck."

"Oh no," Ryan sighed dramatically and dropped his head to the table. "Why did you let me get so attached?" he asked sadly.

"I don't mean to sound insensitive," Dylan chimed in. "But when you buy chicken in the shop, what exactly do you think you're getting?"

"That's different, isn't it?" Ryan snapped.

"These ones are well looked after before they're killed," Dylan retorted. "That's about the only difference I can see."

"He's right," Matt said. "Matilda had a nice life. Who's coming for a swim?"

Kelly and Margaret were left to console Ryan, when Dylan bagged the hammock and I submerged myself in the pool with Chrissie and Matt. I looked over at Adam, but he was focused on the camera. I was happy he was filming Ryan and the girls while one of the other cameramen covered the pool area. My mind raced as I swam lengths. I couldn't believe I'd kissed Adam. And he kissed me back! My stomach did a flip at the thought of it. I would never normally do something like that, but when I'd been so close to him I couldn't resist.

"You're energetic today," Matt commented, floating next to me on an inflatable armchair.

"Yeah, but that's enough exercise for one day. I'm going to lie in the sun again."

"Good – you were making me feel really lazy."

Refreshed by the pool, I made myself comfortable lying face down on a sun lounger. I caught Adam's eye and he gave me a quick smile before I closed my eyes.

Seconds later a shadow fell over me and I looked up. "Hi," I said to Kelly, who was pulling another sun lounger next to me.

"Hi," she whispered, lying down beside me, facing me. "I saw you kissing Adam!"

I smiled widely at her, and opened my mouth to say something – but all that came out was a laugh. Being in Spain, surrounded by cameras was very surreal. And I'd just kissed a cameraman in a cupboard! Kelly laughed too and it took us a minute to calm down again. "Well?" she demanded. "Tell me everything!"

"There's nothing to tell," I whispered, trying not to move my lips when I spoke. Carl was nearby. "I just kissed him in the cupboard and then you came in." I put a hand over my face in embarrassment.

"I've seen you looking at him all week," she told me. "You really like him, don't you?"

"You've seen me looking at him? That's embarrassing. Am I that obvious?"

"No, not really. I don't think anyone else has noticed."

"I really like him," I told her, so quietly I wasn't sure it was even audible.

"Thought so!" she said, glancing in his direction. "He's really cute. And I've seen him looking at you too, by the way."

"Really?" I needed some reassurance that this wasn't just infatuation on my part.

"Yep. He definitely likes you."

Silence settled over us. Kelly had just closed her eyes. Then I felt myself getting emotional. "Kelly," I whispered, and waited for her to look at me. "I don't want to go home."

"It's nice here, isn't it?" She pushed my hair behind my ear and laid her hand over mine.

"It's the best holiday I've ever had," I told her. "I can't believe we've only got one more day."

"We can all meet up and hang out when we're back home," she told me.

"I hope so." That was what was bothering me, really. It wasn't the place or lying in the sun all day; it was the people I was going to miss. I had never expected to get so close to them in such a short time.

"Who needs cooling off?" Matt suddenly loomed over us, dripping wet.

"No thanks!" Kelly told him before seeing the mischief in his eyes and getting up to run away. He chased her, finally catching her and wrapping his arms around her, shaking his head like a wet dog, sending drips flying everywhere.

He moved towards me. "I don't know what *you're* laughing at!"

I ignored him and closed my eyes to continue sunbathing. Suddenly, his wet body covered mine and I squealed when he lay on top of me.

"Get off," I shouted through my laughter. "I can't breathe!"

He rubbed his wet hair over my face and I wriggled out from under him, shoving him onto the ground as I went.

"You're stronger than you look," he said. I walked quickly to the magic fridge and grabbed a bottle of Coke before heading back to Matt, shaking it as I went.

"No!" He shook his head wildly when I approached him. I ignored his protests and opened the lid slightly, spraying him with Coke and chasing him around the pool. He finally gave up trying to escape and stood still while I poured the dregs over his head. He sprayed me by blowing a raspberry while the Coke ran down his face. "That was a bit naughty," he told me flatly, taking my hand and falling backwards into the pool, pulling me with him.

"You're an idiot!" I told him, spluttering in the shallow end. "I'm going to get showered before dinner," I announced, pulling myself out of the pool and smiling at the array of amused faces. Adam's expression was blank when I passed him, which annoyed me, though I wasn't quite sure why. He followed me upstairs and I completely forgot about the camera. As soon as we were in the upstairs living room and away from everyone, I turned to him.

"Adam, I—" The look of panic on his face stopped me in my tracks, and I suddenly remembered that the little piece of equipment by his face was recording my every move. And my every word. I stared at him for a moment and he shook his head almost imperceptibly. I wasn't quite sure what I was going to say to him, anyway. Hastily, I walked away and into my room, closing the door behind me and lying on the bed to stare at the ceiling.

I turned to the door, and thought of Adam at the other side of it. I think getting so comfortable with the cameras had also made me forget he was working. I'd found myself getting irritated by his lack of communication and by the fact that sometimes he didn't even acknowledge me. It annoyed me that every time I turned around he was there, watching me. Sometimes it felt like he was judging me. I even felt guilty for playing around with Matt. It was such a bizarre situation, I felt like I was going mad.

The sound of static from Adam's walkie-talkie broke into my thoughts. I heard a muffled voice, then the door opened and he walked in. I really wanted to be on my own but I knew I didn't have much choice in the matter. Why couldn't Carl or one of the others have followed me?

I stared at the ceiling, my attempt to blink back tears futile. Adam took a seat on Chrissie's bed and faced me. "You okay?" he whispered.

"Yeah," I managed, and felt a tear roll down my face. He looked concerned and I felt pathetic. I wasn't even sure why I was upset. "I need a shower," I told him, standing up. He kept the camera aimed at the bed, and took my hand when I moved past him, squeezing it for the briefest moment before standing and moving the camera back to me.

***

"Come on," Dylan coaxed Ryan when Maria brought chicken and chips to the table at dinnertime. "We can't let Matilda die in vain."

"I might turn vegetarian," Ryan declared as he wandered over to us and piled some delicious garlic chips on his plate.

"Here's to Matilda," Matt said, raising his glass. "The happiest chicken I've ever known. She had a great life and a quick death. She'll live on in our memories."

I couldn't help myself. When I went to drink in honour of Matilda I choked on a giggle. "Sorry," I said through a cough. My body shook while I tried my best to contain my laughter. I'd given myself a little pep talk in the shower, telling myself to stop being weird about Adam and focus on enjoying the rest of the holiday, but enjoying myself had meant drinking wine with the girls before dinner – and it had gone straight to my head.

"It's not really a laughing matter, Lucy," Matt said. "I didn't have you down as being so cold-hearted."

"Sorry." I tried to maintain my composure, but when I reached for a chicken leg I had to give in to my laughter. "Sorry, Ryan," I spluttered and looked up to find everyone smiling and laughing while they tucked into the chicken.

It was another beautiful evening. We sat around

drinking and chatting as the sky darkened and filled with stars. I'd slowed down on the alcohol but still felt fairly tipsy when I went to lie on the lawn.

"It's amazing, isn't it?" Dylan commented when he joined me. The others came too and I was perfectly content as I lay in the silence with my new friends, looking up at the brilliant star-studded blanket stretching out above us.

Chapter 20

"Oh no!" I heard Chrissie groan as I woke and turned over in bed to face her. "It's the last day." She pouted.

"Why did you have to remind me? Let's just pretend it's not the last day, okay?"

"Good plan! I really don't want to go home."

"Shush!"

"Oh, yeah, sorry. I really have to do some studying today, though …"

"Yeah, right!" I threw my pillow at her, then stood up and headed for the bathroom. I was amused to find Chrissie had laid clothes out for me when I returned.

"What are you going to do when you've not got me around to help you get dressed?" she asked with a cheeky grin.

"Are you going to make depressing comments all day? I thought we were going to pretend we're not going home tomorrow …"

"I know. I'm not doing very well, am I? I can't get it out of my mind."

"Hot pants?" I asked, ignoring her and holding up the tiny shorts.

"Just try them!" she told me as she skipped off to the bathroom.

We went through the usual routine of getting

breakfast and having a morning chat with Maria, in which neither of us understood the other party. When we first arrived I found it uncomfortable, but now it seemed normal and even quite comforting. I could have told her all my secrets – if there hadn't been a camera in the room.

We were outside eating breakfast when I registered Adam's absence. Most mornings he'd been the one to silently greet me when I opened the bedroom door, but this morning it had been someone else. I didn't think much about it, but everyone had arrived down for breakfast and there was still no sign of him. I glanced around, stupidly checking I'd not missed him somewhere, but he was definitely nowhere to be seen. Maybe he got some time off, I thought.

I didn't recognise one of the cameramen at all. Maybe he was one of the ones who had food poisoning and was giving the others a break now he was well again. It seemed strange, though, that he would appear on the last day. I didn't like the idea of not seeing Adam all day, and I was uncomfortable with the thought of spending the day waiting to see if he turned up.

"Where's Adam?" I whispered to Carl, who was standing just behind me.

"Ask Matt."

I looked at Matt, who was merrily eating his cooked breakfast. I saw the guilt on his face as soon as Carl mentioned his name.

"Where's Adam?" I asked him.

"Aww. Are you missing him?" he asked, deflecting the question. I glared at him until he kept talking. "Okay! Ryan and I did a few shots after everyone had gone to bed last night. Adam might have got drunk with us and be sleeping off a killer hangover."

"Really?" It seemed unlikely. Adam could have a laugh with us, but I didn't think he'd get drunk while he was working. Carl cleared his throat loudly and I turned to see him raising his eyebrows at Matt.

"Okay, maybe *he* wasn't drunk," Matt corrected himself. "But I was, and it was an accident. Just bear that in mind. Plus I heard there's no lasting damage, so let's not all freak out."

"What did you do?" Chrissie asked sternly.

"Are we talking about Adam?" Ryan came over, dripping wet from the pool. "Matt stabbed him!"

"*What?*" I shrieked as everyone gathered around to listen.

"I didn't *stab* him," Matt rolled his eyes at Ryan. "Don't be so dramatic."

We all glared at Matt and he pushed his plate away, leaning back against the couch. "I accidentally slashed him with a sword," Matt told us slowly. "It's not as bad as it sounds, though ..."

"He was pretending to be a Samurai!" Ryan jumped in.

"Shut up!" Matt snapped before continuing. "As I said, I was a bit drunk and I was looking at those swords that were hanging in the big dining room ..." Dylan nodded but the rest of us looked blank. I guess it was a guy thing. There were so many random ornaments and decorations around the place that I hadn't registered a sword.

"So I took them off the wall and was pretending to be a Samurai ... but I honestly had no idea those things are sharp, and I think Adam moved at the wrong moment … and I just cut the back of his hand a little bit …"

"Slashed it open!" Ryan elaborated. "Blood everywhere!"

"Stop being dramatic," Matt glared at him. "He'll be fine. Won't he?" He looked to Carl for reassurance and the rest of us did the same.

"He'll survive," Carl agreed reluctantly.

"Poor Adam," Margaret commented.

"I can't believe you stabbed him!" Kelly swatted the back of Matt's head when she walked past and headed for the pool with Margaret.

"Ouch," Matt rubbed the back of his head. I stared at him while Dylan moved away to sunbathe and Ryan headed inside to get more breakfast.

"Don't look at me like that," Matt said to me.

"You really stabbed him?" Chrissie asked.

"Yes! Slashed him really, but whatever. Can we stop going on about it? I feel bad enough without you two giving me evil looks … and him." He pointed at Carl. "I honestly didn't know they were sharp, or I wouldn't have been messing about with them. I feel terrible." His bravado had disappeared now that everyone had gone, and he looked genuinely concerned.

"He is okay, though, isn't he?" I asked.

"Yeah. There was a lot of blood, but he was still trying to take a swing at me with the other hand, so that was a good sign! He had to go to the hospital to get stitches but they said he'll be fine. He might have a small scar. Shit, I feel really bad." I watched Matt turn pale, and felt sick myself. I really wanted to see Adam and check he was okay. I was also panicking at not knowing when I would see him. Maybe they would fly him home and I'd never see him again. I tried to push the thought from my mind, and resisted the urge to march up into the rooms above the kitchen to find him.

Everyone gathered around the couches when Chelsea arrived, but there was no challenge for us. Instead we were being treated to dinner in a traditional Majorcan restaurant. Chelsea told us to be ready at 7.30pm and left before I had a chance to ask her about Adam. Truthfully, I hadn't dared ask her in front of everyone. They would definitely tease me, and I was feeling too emotionally fragile to deal with it.

I couldn't relax, and spent the morning flitting between sunbathing, swimming and nervously wandering the house. I pushed my pasta salad around my plate at lunchtime and decided I would just have to ask Carl what was going on. Then Adam appeared outside just when I'd plucked up the courage to approach Carl. He smiled at me, but then the rest of the gang noticed him and rushed over to surround him.

"It's fine," I heard him say as I got nearer to him. "Back off, will you? I'm supposed to be working." Everyone was talking at once, asking him if he was okay and making sympathetic noises. "Honestly, it's just a scratch," he insisted before looking at Matt. "Just don't let this clown near any sharp objects!"

"Sorry, mate," Matt told him sincerely, holding out a hand to him as the others dispersed. Adam laughed and waved his bandaged hand, the other hand holding the camera.

"Shit, sorry!" Matt frowned.

"It's fine. Don't worry about it," Adam assured him. "Getting stabbed is pretty much an occupational hazard." He raised his eyebrows and flashed a sly smile.

"If it's any consolation," Matt smirked and glanced at me. "Lucy said she'd kiss it better for you …"

"Go away!" I told Matt, unable to suppress a blush. "Is it really okay?" I asked once Matt had wandered off. I moved closer to Adam and felt those wild horses set off around my chest again.

"Yeah," he told me softly. "It's okay."

"Good," I replied awkwardly, resisting the urge to fling my arms around him.

"Can you believe they're still making me work?" he asked with a boyish smile.

"I'm glad they did," I told him before heading to the nearest sun lounger and settling down to a peaceful nap.

I smiled at Adam when I woke up and he quickly jumped up from his seat on the wall and mouthed an apology at me. I laughed. Checking the time, I was annoyed to find I'd slept for two hours. I felt like I'd missed out on precious time on our last day. Matt handed me a beer and I moved to the couches to spend a couple more hours enjoying the company of my new friends in a beautiful setting. I couldn't believe it was our last evening together.

Chapter 21

The restaurant was half an hour's drive from the finca. It was a beautiful old building, full of charm. The terracotta walls and marble pillars lent an air of elegance to the quaint building, which overlooked the crystal clear waters of the Mediterranean.

We were led to a terrace at the back of the building, the focal point of which was a water feature consisting of a woman holding a jug. Water trickled out of the jug and over her body, making an eye-catching piece. Wrought iron tables were set simply with white tablecloths and tea lights.

Our table was situated away from the other diners. A waiter poured water when we took our seats, and there was silence as we took in our tranquil surroundings. White lanterns hung from the trees around us. The setting was stunning.

I caught sight of Adam standing opposite me, and butterflies took flight in my stomach. I reached for a menu to hide behind while memories of kissing him danced in my head, making me blush.

"Don't tell us you're a wine connoisseur now?" Matt gave me a cheeky look from his place opposite me.

"I might be," I told him, realising I was holding the wine list. "I've drunk more wine this week than the entire rest of my life."

"It's been fun, hasn't it?" Chrissie sighed. She was sitting next to Matt. I couldn't see, but I guessed they were holding hands under the table.

"So much fun," I agreed. My chest tightened at the thought of going home the next day – home to my sad little life with no job, no plan, no fun and, most of all, none of these people around me. I glanced along the table, and thought of how fond I'd become of each of them. "We'll keep in touch, won't we?" I looked at Chrissie and Matt, and heard the hint of panic in my voice.

"Yep," Matt told me definitely as Chrissie smiled her answer at me.

The waiter poured wine and brought bread baskets to the table, with an array of flavoured oils for dipping and little pots of black and green olives. He told us in broken English that he would bring out a selection of traditional tapas.

The food was delicious, and the wine made my head fuzzy. I watched the sun set slowly over the water behind Adam. Though the view was stunning, my eyes strayed frequently to Adam, who was standing casually against a pillar at the edge of our group. Behind him the jagged rocks tumbled into the ocean. Adam's white T-shirt showed off his bronzed skin, which glowed with the tan that had developed over the week.

"Lucy …" I brought my gaze to Chrissie who was offering me the last triangle of tortilla.

I shook my head. "No, thanks."

"Great view, isn't it?" Matt quipped, looking over his shoulder at the sunset – and Adam. I felt myself blush again when he turned back to look at me with a cheeky grin, and Chrissie elbowed him in the ribs.

"Let's have a dance." Dylan was suddenly standing beside me, offering me his hand. He led me to the open space beside our table and I noted the looks from the other diners, intrigued by our camera crew and impromptu dancing. Dylan placed a hand on my waist and took my hand in his, to sway me gently to the subdued music.

Someone turned the volume up slightly as Matt and Chrissie joined us, followed by Ryan and Kelly. Not to be left out, Margaret grabbed a waiter and dragged him over for a dance.

"Do you think the restaurant always has so many cameras?" Dylan asked me quietly. I was taken aback by his words, and followed his gaze to cameras, which were concealed by plants, at the top of several pillars.

"Some restaurants have security cameras, don't they?" I reasoned. "They probably aren't even switched on."

"They're only in this section, around our table."

"There's one over there by the door too," I told him, scanning the room.

"That's a standard security camera. That one belongs to the restaurant. These ones are different."

"So?" I asked, suddenly not caring. "We agreed to go on a TV show. Cameras shouldn't be a surprise."

"But why are they hiding them?" he asked. "Why have cameramen *and* hidden cameras?" He raised his eyebrows at me and I shrugged in response. "So we don't look for hidden cameras," he suggested. "So we think we're not being watched all the time."

"We agreed to be on a TV show," I reminded him again. "We knew we'd be filmed. Why are you worrying about it so much?" I was annoyed with him for trying to dampen my spirits and ruin our last night.

"Because we leave tomorrow and I'm wondering what kind of a show it is," he told me. "I think there's something going on that we have no idea about. I don't trust them."

"I don't care," I told him, pulling my hand from his and standing still. "It doesn't really matter now, does it? Like you said, we leave tomorrow. It's too late to worry about it."

"My turn!" Matt stepped in and pulled me into his arms while Chrissie went to dance with Dylan. "You okay?"

"Yeah," I told him, pushing the conversation with Dylan from my mind. "I don't think I want to go home, though."

"Me neither." He lifted his arm to twirl me under it. I grinned at him while he spun me around the dance floor. The locals gradually got up to join us, and the atmosphere was light-hearted as we swapped partners frequently to dance the night away.

Taking a break from the dancing, I headed back to the table, becoming irrationally annoyed when I looked at Adam and once again got no response. He stared straight past me as though he couldn't even see me. I sat with my back to him and watched the dancing.

A moment later I saw him walk slowly towards the dancers, place his camera on a table and look through the viewfinder to make sure it was in position.

"It doesn't really seem fair that everyone else got to

dance with you and I only got to watch," he told me, offering his good hand. I let him lead me to the edge of the restaurant, away from everyone.

"How's the hand?" I asked.

"It hurts!" he confessed, holding it up to show me the bandage before returning it to rest on my lower back.

"I can't believe Matt did that."

"I think he feels pretty bad about it," Adam said.

"Are we out of camera shot here?" I asked, changing the subject and looking up at the small black cameras balanced above our table.

He looked nervous when he nodded. "I hope so."

I eyed him seriously. "I convinced myself that this would never be aired because that's what I wanted to believe. I can't think of anything worse than being recognised in the street, but even if we do end up having five minutes of fame, it was all worth it."

When he didn't say anything I briefly thought of telling him about Dylan's suspicions and asking what he knew. I hesitated, not wanting to ruin the moment.

"I'm sorry about yesterday," he said, breaking the silence.

"Which part of yesterday?" I asked playfully.

"Well, not the cupboard, obviously! I'm sorry you were upset when I came into your room."

"It's fine," I told him. "I was just a bit emotional."

"It's really annoying that I can't talk to you properly. It's all been a bit crazy, hasn't it?"

"Yeah." I laughed.

"Can I see you again?"

"Huh?" I moved back to look at his face.

"Will you go out with me when we're home?"

"Like a date?" I asked, my heart racing.

"Yes," he grinned. "Exactly like a date."

"Yeah," I told him, and moved closer to him again, resting my head on his shoulder and breathing in his scent. I listened to the waves breaking against the rocks and swayed to the music with Adam, wishing I could pause the moment and stay in it forever.

Chapter 22

"The last meal." Matt looked up from his full English breakfast when Chrissie and I joined him outside. "Annoyingly, I seem to have lost my appetite," he told us.

"Really?" Ryan asked eagerly.

"Go for it." Matt slid the plate over to Ryan, snatching a sausage from it before relinquishing it.

"I can't believe it's all over," Ryan commented while he shoved bacon and eggs into his mouth. I pushed my plate away and leaned back. My appetite had disappeared too.

"Could we just refuse to leave?" Chrissie said.

"I'd love to," I told her, moving to make space for Kelly and Margaret.

I'd had a strange feeling since Dylan had told me his fears the previous evening. I'd been paranoid and even found myself searching for hidden cameras. My worry about the tiny bikinis was fairly ironic if there were cameras in the shower. I didn't find anything but I still couldn't shake the feeling that something wasn't right. I hadn't mentioned the cameras in the restaurant to Chrissie – or anyone else. I'm not sure why. I think I just didn't want us to spend our last evening speculating about hidden cameras and whether or not we'd end up on TV.

"I'd stay here with you guys forever," Kelly announced. "You're my new family. I love you all!"

"Oh my God! Stop it," Matt told her. "I'm struggling to keep it together as it is." He put his arm around Chrissie and she snuggled into him.

"*I'm* even going to miss you," Dylan told us, perching on the arm of the couch next to Chrissie.

"Well, that's tipped me over the edge!" Matt's face crumpled into a look of mock grief. He pushed Chrissie away and patted the space next to him in an invitation for Dylan. "Come on …" Matt coaxed him.

"My boys!" Matt laughed putting an arm around Ryan and Dylan and pulling them to him, giving them each a big kiss on the cheek.

"Get off, you clown!" Dylan laughed at him. "How about one last beer from the magic fridge?"

"We're just about to leave and you finally have a great idea," Matt teased.

"It's nine o'clock in the morning," I called after them.

"Don't worry, we'll get one for you too," Matt shouted back.

"It's far too early," I complained but took a swig from the beer bottle Dylan had given me anyway. They'd passed them out to everyone, cameramen included. Only Carl and Adam had accepted. The other cameramen hadn't even reacted to the offer.

"Someone should propose a toast," Kelly suggested.

"Okay!" Matt volunteered, raising his bottle. "Here's to magic beer fridges, free holidays and …" He paused and took a dramatic deep breath before continuing. "To the most awesome people you could ever hope to find in the street on a Friday afternoon, with nothing better to do than jet off to Spain with a bunch of strangers!"

I returned Adam's smile when he raised his beer with the rest of us, and took a long drink. It was all getting far too emotional for me, and I slipped inside the house in search of Maria. I wanted to say goodbye to her. I found myself alone while I wandered through the house, and shouted for Maria when I reached the top of her staircase.

When there was no reply, I ran down the stairs and into the dimly lit hallway below. This time no one blocked my path and I pushed open the door nearest to me.

It was Chrissie I saw first. There she was, walking beside the pool, head thrown back in laughter – except she was *here*, in this room, on a computer screen. There were so many screens! Another showed Matt, the camera zooming in while he tipped his beer bottle to his lips, smiling at something Kelly was saying.

Every room in the house was covered: the kitchen, our bedrooms, the bathrooms, everything!

My stomach lurched and I felt shaky as the reality of it all set in. It was one thing to *think* the house might be rigged with cameras, but another thing to see it like this.

"You're not really a catering assistant, are you?" I asked quietly. The two guys sitting in the room, focusing on the screens, swivelled round in their chairs. The larger of them was the one who'd stopped me when I'd tried to come in here before.

"I already told you – you're not allowed down here," he told me gruffly. They turned back to continue what they were doing and my eyes roamed the room, trying to take everything in. This must be what Ryan had found!

"You should leave now," the smaller guy told me impatiently.

Shocked and dazed, I managed to get my legs moving and made my way back upstairs. Adam was in the kitchen. He sounded concerned when he asked if I was okay, but I couldn't bring myself to look at him. I walked past him and through the house.

My head spun and I struggled to process it all. I couldn't believe Ryan had seen all this and not told us! Actually, maybe I wasn't so surprised by Ryan; he was childish and mostly just interested in having a good time. Adam, on the other hand, should have warned me. I swung around in the dining room to find him behind me, looking sheepish.

"I think you can get rid of that now, can't you?" I snapped, swiping at the camera. He lowered it and took a step away from me, tilting his head to one side as words formed on his lips.

"You should have told me!" I shouted before he could say anything. "You knew and you didn't say anything."

He moved towards me, sighing. "I couldn't. I wasn't allowed t—"

"Yes, you could! You had plenty of opportunity to tell me. I presume there aren't any cameras in that cupboard downstairs! You could have told me then. Or last night!"

Adam's gaze drifted over my shoulder and I turned to see everyone watching my outburst.

Matt stepped forward. "What's going on?"

"There are cameras everywhere!"

"Yeah," he said slowly, glancing at Carl and Adam, then looking back at me like I was crazy.

"Not them! There's more. They're everywhere!" I glanced around, wondering where they were. Hidden among all the random ornaments and decorations, no doubt.

Chrissie moved towards me. "Are you okay?"

"There's some sort of control room downstairs," I explained. "You can see the whole house on computer screens: they zoom in and change the camera angles. They've filmed everything … bathrooms, bedrooms, everywhere! They were watching us all the time."

"Oh my God!" Chrissie gasped. "Are you serious?"

"Ryan saw it too," I told them. He was hanging around at the back of the group and avoided my gaze when I glared at him. "You saw it, didn't you?"

"Maybe …" His eyes narrowed. "I didn't want to tell you and spoil all the fun!" His weak smile made him look pathetic as he tried to explain himself. "Plus they took me off for that so-called interview and swore me to secrecy. I didn't want to ruin the TV show." His voice went all squeaky as he looked at us nervously. "It's not such a big deal, is it?"

"So we might actually get on TV, then?" Kelly said, sounding excited. "We might be famous?"

Nobody answered her. We were lost in our own thoughts, trying to comprehend what it all meant. We'd been tricked. Chelsea's heels clicked on the stone floor when she walked in to stand among us. Her voice cut through the tense atmosphere.

"Sorry to break up the party, kids, but it's time to go home!"

Part 2

Hannah Ellis

Chapter 23

The mood was sombre when we made our way through Manchester Airport. We'd spent much of the journey home discussing the hidden cameras. We talked in circles until we finally concluded there was nothing we could do; it had already been done. We just had to wait and see what would happen next. Jessica had avoided commenting, saying there'd be time to ask questions once we were back in the UK.

Despite the hidden cameras, I still felt sad the week was over. A week ago, I was worried about what I was getting myself into – and now I was panicking about going back to my life. I glanced at Matt and Chrissie beside me and felt my eyes fill with tears. I didn't want to go home. It was like we were in a little bubble while we were away, and I didn't want to leave it.

We were ushered straight outside the airport, having been informed that our bags would be collected for us and delivered to our homes. Checking where the cameras were – where Adam was – had become an unconscious action. When I glanced around, I felt panic rise when I realised there were no longer any cameras on us. The cameramen had all vanished. I tried to think of where I last saw Adam, as though that might help. I'd caught his eye when we exited the plane but had looked away, irritated. I'd not seen him since. As I lingered on the kerb, my eyes darted in all directions, but there was no sign of Adam – or any cameras.

I was still looking around for him when I climbed into the waiting minibus. Jessica embarked with us, informing us that we had one stop to make before we went home. I had no idea where we were going – and I didn't care. I was happy to drag things out for as long as possible. I wasn't looking forward to the goodbyes.

Adam played on my mind. He'd said he wanted to see me again, but then I'd been angry with him. The anger was receding quickly now that I didn't know if I'd see him again. He'd just been doing his job, after all. We hadn't said even goodbye. The tightening in my chest was a sign that I couldn't let myself dwell on it for too long. What would be, would be.

We pulled up outside an office block, then followed Jessica through the deserted corridors and into a large conference room. She instructed us to take a seat at an oval table, and paced the room as she addressed us.

"As I think you already know, the house in Spain was rigged with hidden cameras to capture your every move at all times of day and night. What you don't know is that the footage we captured over the last week has already been aired." She paused, letting her words sink in, a hint of a smile on her lips. "You were broadcast to the nation every evening on RDT1 – a prime-time slot – and the response has been overwhelming. You caused quite a stir and viewing figures have been tremendous."

When she paused again, Dylan jumped in. "You can't do that! You can't put us on TV without permission."

She shook her head – in sympathy or amusement? Perhaps a bit of both. A nod at her assistant sent him hurrying around, handing us each a printed document. I recognised it as the contract we'd signed before we flew out to Spain.

"We had your permission," Jessica told us. "The document you signed before you left was drawn up by a team of top lawyers. We definitely had your permission."

"But you said we probably wouldn't even be on TV," Chrissie chimed in. "And if we were, it would be on some weird channel in the middle of the night."

"I said probably, possibly, maybe ..." Jessica looked bored, sighing as though she were losing patience. "It was all written down in front of you – if you'd read the contract before you signed it."

I flicked through the pages as I attempted to take everything in. I'd definitely been led to believe that they were filming to see if this was a viable concept, and told that the footage *may* be shown at some point in the future. I'd had no idea that it would be aired immediately.

"I would advise you to familiarise yourself with the document in hand," Jessica said. "You'll notice that the contract forbids you from making any public comment about your experience for the next three weeks, at which time you are required to attend a live show."

She paused and my heart sank as I began to digest what she'd told us – though I should really have been expecting it. I knew the house was filled with cameras. I'd seen it for myself down in that basement room filled with screens. If they'd gone to that much trouble, it made sense that they would actually air the footage: that it would be a big deal.

I'd not believed that, though, until Jessica had announced it. My mind whirred and I attempted to make sense of my memories from the last week. I thought back to the conversations we'd overheard: Jessica shouting that we were boring and that the TV show would never be aired. Had all that been staged?

I wondered which bits had been shown on TV. Snippets of conversations ran through my head. I'd definitely been scathing about both of my parents, but I couldn't remember exactly what I'd said. At least Dylan had stopped me from saying too much.

I suddenly remembered to breathe. My head felt like it might explode.

"I realise this is a lot to take in," Jessica continued, while her assistant handed us back our phones. "And I'm sure you're all looking forward to getting back to your own homes. There are cars waiting outside to take you home."

She continued talking about our luggage, the cars we'd been promised, and various other things, but I had switched off. Her words washed over me until she moved and held the door open for us.

"I look forward to seeing you all at the live show in three weeks." She smiled at us as we filed out of the room.

"Can you believe that?" Chrissie asked when we walked back along the corridor.

There was a spring in Ryan's step. "We're gonna be famous!" he said joyfully, from the front of our group. "It's gonna be amazing!"

I wasn't sure what to say about it all, but just moved, dumbfounded, with the rest of them. In the lobby I heard a noise – shouting and cheering – and turned to look at the commotion through the big windows. There was a crowd outside: people with cameras, people holding banners. My eyes landed on a group of girls screaming for Ryan and holding a banner with his name and hearts on it. I felt a hand pull roughly at my elbow, and turned to see Jessica.

"Come with me," she said urgently, pulling me back into the corridor.

"What's going on?" I asked.

"I forgot to mention, you caused a bit of a media storm! Apparently someone found out you're here – it's all over social media. Follow me. We've taken your car around the back."

I trailed behind her, glancing back over my shoulder. "What about the rest of them?"

"They'll be fine. I'm sorry, Lucy, you weren't portrayed very well, and I'm afraid the public might not like you very much."

I was confused, partly because she didn't sound sorry and partly because I couldn't really understand what she was saying. What did I do to make people dislike me?

She opened a back door and pointed at a shiny black car. "There's your ride home. If the media attention is too much, or you have any problems, feel free to get in touch and we'll see if we can help."

"Okay," I said, but the door closed as soon as I stepped outside, and Jessica was gone.

On the half-hour journey home, my mind whirred. I'd not said goodbye to anyone, and I didn't even have their phone numbers. We'd laughed at Margaret when we were getting ready to leave the finca and she suggested we write down our contact details for each other. Matt had jokingly asked her if it was 1995. He'd said, "Let's save the paper and ink and wait until we've got our phones back!" *Bloody Matt and his great ideas!*

Jessica's mention of a media storm had left me feeling overwhelmed and confused. We'd been on TV and the show had been popular! What had happened? What had people seen? Why had I come across so badly that I was ushered out of a back door?

I tried to rationalise everything. I had known at the start what I was letting myself in for. I couldn't quite figure out how I'd been fooled into thinking that the TV show might not be aired. The rational part of me insisted it wasn't so bad; I'd still had a great week and made brilliant friends. Okay, some things, which I didn't think were being filmed, had been filmed, but I hadn't done anything terrible or irredeemable. Everything would be fine.

Chapter 24

"Lucy Mitchell?"

I smiled at the man who was standing at my front door when I arrived home. I'd been battling my suitcase and had a head full of jumbled thoughts, so I hadn't seen him until the last minute.

"I wonder if I could talk to you for a few minutes? I'm with *Now* magazine and we'd love to do an article on you ..."

Slightly stunned, I noticed for the first time the other people hanging around my front door. This seemed to be an invitation for them to all speak at once.

"Sorry." I squeezed through them with my suitcase, putting my head down when someone raised a camera. "Excuse me. I just need to get inside." My hand shook as I fought to get the key in the lock, finally bursting through the door and pushing it firmly shut behind me.

I shouted a quick hello to Melissa, but the place was quiet and I stood in the living room, trying to digest all that had just happened. It was exhausting attempting to make sense of everything. There were reporters at my door. It felt like I was trapped in some weird dream; this couldn't actually be real. This couldn't really be my life.

I thought of Adam and my new friends, who had all disappeared as abruptly as they'd appeared in my life. After spending the last week surrounded by people, the silence was unsettling and I paced the living room, not quite sure what to do with myself.

I picked up the home phone and punched in my dad's home number, suddenly desperate to speak to my stepmum, Kerry.

"It's me," I said when I heard her voice.

"Oh, hon! You're home." She sounded relieved. "Are you okay?"

"Yeah, I think so. I just got back and my head is spinning."

"How was it?"

"It was good." Then I got choked up and couldn't stop the tears. "It was really good."

"Everything will be okay," she soothed. "Don't worry."

"I had a great time," I told her, laughter mixing with my tears. "I'm so glad you told me to go. I didn't know it was actually going to be on TV, but it doesn't matter; it was the best week of my life."

"That's great," she said, sounding as though she was humouring me. "And don't worry about Matt. You'll soon forget about him."

"What?" I said. "*Matt?*"

"Yeah," she said slowly. "I was worried that the whole situation would have upset you …"

"What situation?" I felt like my memory was playing a trick on me. I tried to think of what she might have seen that she could be talking about. She must mean Adam. I'd see him again though, somehow. It would all be okay.

"You're home!" Melissa's voice interrupted us, and I turned to find her standing behind me.

"I'll call you back," I told Kerry and hung up.

"Hi!" I flung my arms around Melissa. I was relieved to have company. It felt as though I hadn't seen her for months, not just a week.

"Hi," she said flatly, pulling away. "How are you?"

"Fine. Yeah, I'm good."

"I saw you on TV," she informed me. "And you're all over the papers. I've had reporters at the door for days …"

"Sorry," I replied automatically, slightly taken aback by her coldness.

"I bet you wished you'd listened to me now, don't you?" she asked. "Didn't I say it was a stupid thing to do?"

"I'm glad I went," I told her. "I had an amazing time."

She gave me a condescending look. "They made you look stupid. Don't you care that it's all been shown on TV for everyone to see? You made a fool of yourself over a man with the whole country watching. I don't think you'll ever be able to show your face in public again. Aren't you embarrassed?"

My heart started to race as visions of Adam flicked into my mind. What had I done that was so embarrassing? Surely there hadn't been cameras in that little cupboard. That was why Jessica had been trying to get Adam on the walkie-talkie; she knew we were out of shot. And even if it had been filmed, it wasn't really that bad.

The phone rang and I answered it to hear my mum's voice.

"I hope you're not going to blame me for all this," she asked. "I had no idea what would happen. Sometimes things don't turn out quite how we'd like them to but, honestly, this will all blow over before you know it. You've got nothing to be ashamed of. Matt was leading you on – and eventually everyone will see that. Don't you worry."

"Okay," I replied. "I'll have to call you back." I hung up the phone. Immediately the doorbell went and I moved like a zombie to answer it.

"Delivery of a Peugeot to a Miss Lucy Mitchell?"

"That's me," I told him, as reporters shouted at me over his shoulder.

"I'll need to see some ID – and there's some paperwork."

I invited him in, closing the door on the wolves. When the paperwork was taken care of, I thanked him, and he handed me a key. Following him out of the door, I hurried past the reporters and climbed into my brand-new car.

Chapter 25

"Did you record it?" I asked Kerry when she opened the door to me.

"Yes, but …"

"I need to see it," I told her, wiping tears from my cheeks.

"Okay. We can watch it together. It's not so bad." She wrapped her arms around me and squeezed me tightly before I pulled away and moved into the living room to park myself in front of the TV.

I braced myself for the seven hours of viewing ahead of me.

The first hour was painless; it showed Chelsea and the cameras running around the streets, desperately trying to convince people to do the show, and ended with the seven of us arriving at the finca with wide eyes. But in the second episode, things started to get confusing.

My stomach turned all fluttery while I watched myself chatting easily to Adam. I smiled at the memory, waiting impatiently for Adam to appear on the screen. But when the cameras panned round, it was Matt looking back at me.

"That didn't happen!" I told Kerry, shaking my head in confusion. "Matt wasn't there!" The scene changed from me apparently looking lovingly into Matt's eyes to me lying in bed, giggling, as I confided in Chrissie how lovely I thought Matt was and how much I liked him. "It's all been edited!" I said in disbelief. "I didn't say that about Matt!"

Kerry looked at me sympathetically and I felt the anger rising in me.

"Is Adam in this at all?"

She shook her head. "Who's Adam?"

The whole show had been edited and cut until it was unrecognisable to me. None of the cameramen made an appearance; it was as though they weren't there at all. Entire conversations had been fabricated, and I struggled to understand what I was seeing. One scene showed Chrissie and me from behind as we chatted about Matt. None of that conversation had happened. Part of me was impressed at the editing team; they must have cut our individual words from other conversations to make us say whatever they wanted. It soon became clear that I was supposed to be head over heels for Matt. My emotions were all over the place: anger rolled through me and my confusion was overwhelming.

I watched, bewildered, as the tree-climbing afternoon came on screen. In this version it was Matt who swooped in and pulled me up when I fell. My hero, Matt, his fear of heights magically eradicated. There was no sign of Adam.

I was a few hours in when my dad arrived home with my little brothers. I hugged Max and Jacob and played with them for a while, as they demanded. At five, at least they were oblivious to my humiliation. They jumped on me and wrestled me before I untangled myself from them and joined Dad and Kerry in the kitchen. Dad gave me a perfunctory hug and asked how I was. Even at the weekend, when he wasn't in a suit and tie, he still had a stuffy air about him, and his rapidly greying hair made him look every one of his fifty-two years.

"They've cut and edited the show so much," I told him. "It's not what happened at all. They've made me into a laughing stock, haven't they? I should've known it would end badly."

"Well, if you put yourself in these situations, you leave yourself open to this sort of thing," he told me. "Just learn your lesson and move on."

"Stuart," Kerry hissed at him.

"What?" He genuinely didn't know what he'd said wrong.

"Can't you be a little bit sympathetic?" Kerry shook her head at him.

"I am sympathetic!" he said, his face softening slightly. "Why don't you show me the contract you signed, and we'll see if there's anything we can do? Maybe you could sue them and you can tell the *real* story."

"I looked through it. They can show any footage in any way they choose. There's about twelve pages of small print in the contract. They knew what they were doing and they covered themselves well."

"Well, it just goes to show that you should never sign anything without first reading every word …"

"Stuart!" Kerry slapped his arm.

"Well, I'm right, aren't I?"

I couldn't help but smile at him. Everything was always black and white with my dad.

"Is it okay if I finish watching in the spare room?" The boys had taken over the living room.

"Of course you can," Kerry told me. "And it's your room." She'd always insisted that I had my own room in their house. I appreciated the gesture, but I'd never stayed with them more than the odd night and it was definitely just a spare room.

"I'm sorry if you think I'm insensitive," Dad told me under Kerry's cold stare. "And I'm sorry that things didn't work out how you wanted, but this will all blow over quickly. It will all be forgotten about before you know it."

"I hope so," I replied.

"I'm going to make us a cuppa and come and join you," Kerry told me. "Stuart, you'll have to get the boys some dinner."

"Okay," he agreed, giving her a quick kiss.

I was so glad we had Kerry; she made my dad so much more bearable and had always been a good friend to me. She was naturally pretty with bouncy blonde curls, which seemed to match her light and happy personality. At forty-four, she was eight years younger than Dad, and had always seemed so much cooler than him. I'd been delighted when she got pregnant with the boys through IVF, after a long time of trying. The boys were non-identical: Max had Kerry's blond curls, while Jacob's blond hair was dead straight.

The house was always full of fun with the boys in it, and Kerry had given up her career in physiotherapy to be a full-time mum until the boys started school. She worked part-time now and always cooked a hearty meal for the four of them to eat together in the evening. I tried not to compare the twins' childhood to mine too much, but sitting down for a family meal every evening seemed fairly idyllic.

I settled down on the bed in the spare room and

prepared to torture myself some more. It was tempting to walk away and not put myself through the heartache of watching it, but I needed to see for myself what everyone else had seen. Kerry followed me in with tea and a box of tissues.

"That bad?" I asked her.

"Just in case." She smiled at me.

As the show went on, a love triangle appeared to develop between Matt, Chrissie and me. It was full of me grinning at Matt with big puppy-dog eyes and then him and Chrissie clearly getting cosy behind my back. It made me look like a lovesick teenager, oblivious to everything going on around me. They'd even cut a scene where Dylan was gently telling me to be careful. It looked like he was worried about Matt hurting me. In reality, he'd been warning me about the cameras and telling me to watch what I said about my family.

"I'd actually been saying what terrible parents I have!" I told Kerry. "So at least they didn't show that." She laughed sympathetically and patted my leg.

I was made to look more and more like a creepy stalker, and it was increasingly uncomfortable to watch. The night I fell asleep on Adam morphed into a shot of Matt fast asleep, with me creeping up to get cosy and snuggling into him while he was blissfully unaware.

I started to laugh hysterically at that point. It was all so ridiculous. I wasn't sure how they had managed to cut it so it really did look like I was with Matt. I rewound it and watched it again. Adam's camera must have been somewhere nearby, but it was nowhere to be seen and his belt with his walkie-talkie had mysteriously vanished. *I* even wondered if it was Matt, not Adam.

"Wait!" I moved closer to the TV and pressed rewind, then pause. There was a brief close-up of me asleep on Adam/Matt's shoulder before the camera cut to me moving into him and resting my head on his chest. The camera zoomed in so that the shot was mostly of me – but just for a moment, at the edge of the screen, I caught Adam's arm moving around my shoulder and his hand stroking my hair.

"He stroked my hair," I told Kerry.

She stared at me as though I had lost the plot.

"Not Matt," I explained. "Adam. That's Adam stroking my hair!" I smiled as I thought of him, and for a split second I forgot all about the TV show and just remembered Adam. When I'd found out about the hidden cameras I'd felt like he'd betrayed me and was so angry with him. Suddenly, I didn't care at all; I just wanted to see him again.

"I think you should stop watching this," Kerry suggested kindly. "You're going to drive yourself crazy."

"That might be enough for one day," I accepted. "How does it end? Give me the highlights …"

"You catch Chrissie and Matt kissing and go a bit crazy; you cut up her T-shirt and push her in the pool, then pour a bottle of Coke over Matt."

"It's all very clever. I'll give them that." I hid my head in my hands and Kerry patted me affectionately on the back.

"Your dad's right. You could tell your side of the story. Get on one of those morning TV shows …"

"They've made me look crazy, though, so anything

I say will be disregarded as ramblings. People believe what they want to believe, don't they? Besides, I'm not allowed to discuss it publicly for three weeks. It's in the contract."

"Why three weeks?"

"Presumably because by then the interest will have died down and no one will care what any of us have to say." I shrugged. "I don't know. We have to do a live show in three weeks. I don't know what will happen then."

Chapter 26

More reporters blocked the doorway when I arrived home. Squeezing my way through, I politely said I couldn't speak to them and went inside, with the intention of hibernating for a long time.

I started to unpack my bag and laughed when I found the T-shirt that Chrissie had cut away at. A wave of sadness washed over me and I made a conscious effort not to let myself spiral into a pit of despair. I threw everything in the wash and then wandered the apartment aimlessly. Kerry had warned me not to watch the TV. Apparently we were getting a fair amount of coverage. She told me it was big news that we had arrived home, and there was a lot of media speculation about our public silence.

Melissa shouted hello as she came in, then disappeared to her room. I sat on the couch with a book in my hands, though I couldn't focus on it and read the same page several times. I got ready for bed and paced the apartment in my pyjamas, sure I wouldn't be able to sleep.

"Hi," I said to Melissa, hovering in the doorway to her bedroom.

"Hi," she said without looking up from her computer.

"How are you?" I asked awkwardly.

"Fine. Busy. You okay?"

"Yeah. I can't stop thinking about all this TV stuff. Nothing really happened the way they showed it."

"It's just a stupid TV show." She finally looked up at me. "It amazes me that anyone watches that sort of thing."

"You watched it, though?"

"Just because you were on it. I bet you wish you'd listened to me and stayed at home."

I wasn't sure why she enjoyed being right on this occasion.

"I'm glad I went," I told her. "I had fun. Plus, I got a nice watch and a new car." I held my arm out to show her, but she went back to tapping away on her computer.

"Doesn't really seem worth it if you ask me. Anyway, did you want something? I'm kind of busy."

"No," I smiled at her. "Just thought we could chat – but it doesn't matter. Goodnight."

***

I slept well but woke feeling groggy and with no desire to get out of bed. Waking up to a morning chat with Chrissie had been much more fun. I wanted to be back in Spain. I'd get up to find Adam waiting outside my door and go down for breakfast and my daily exchange with Maria. My thoughts settled on Adam and my heart ached. I'd just stay in bed forever, I decided.

I dragged myself up briefly to answer the door, returning to hide under the bed covers when it turned out to be a reporter from a women's magazine asking for my story. I ignored the doorbell the next few times it rang, but forced myself to answer the home phone when it rang late in the morning.

"I'm at the door," Mum told me. "Let me in, will you?"

"Hi," I said drearily when she'd come in and closed the door behind her.

"Hello!" She gave me a big hug. "My daughter – the celebrity! It's so exciting!"

"Not really, Mum," I argued. "I don't think I really came out looking very good, did I?"

"Who cares? You're famous!" She grinned. "Let's have a cuppa and you can tell me all about it. Kerry's really worried about you. She said I need to make sure you're eating properly. And she thinks you should go and stay with them for a while."

"You don't need to talk to Kerry about me," I told her. When Kerry married my dad, Mum had decided that they should be friends since they were co-parenting. So Mum rings Kerry now and then to talk about me, and Kerry is ridiculously patient about the whole situation.

"Well, we worry about you," she told me firmly. "I knew you'd have been straight over to talk to her, and I wanted to know how she thought you were doing."

"Are you upset that I went to her, and not you?" I asked. I'd always been close to Kerry, and Mum had never commented on it or seemed to care.

"No. I'm glad you've got Kerry. Considering you're not blood relations, you're quite alike. I wasn't having a dig at you. It's just the way things are. Anyway, *are* you eating?"

"I haven't eaten today," I confessed. "I could

probably manage some toast."

"Okay, go and sit down and I'll make you something."

She joined me in the living room five minutes later and placed a plate of scrambled egg on toast in front of me before returning to bring in two cups of tea.

"Tell me all about the week, then …" she prompted after I'd eaten. "What really happened?"

I took a deep breath and launched into my account of the week and the friends I'd made. It was fun telling her all about everyone and everything that had happened, comparing it to the snippets of information she'd got from the media. Apparently the clip of Dylan playing his guitar had been shown, and it had been suggested that he was dark and brooding due to so many knock-backs from the music industry, not because he'd fallen out with his dad. I felt a little better after talking to Mum, and she stayed with me for most of the day.

I spent Sunday with Dad, Kerry and the boys, which was a welcome distraction, but then I retreated back to the safety of my apartment and wondered what life as a recluse would be like.

***

By Tuesday morning, I was in a fairly dark place. I lay on the couch and ignored the doorbell yet again, preferring to stare at the ceiling and wonder what to do with the rest of my life.

"Lucy!" a voice called impatiently. Then there was a banging on the door and the bell went again – and again. The press were getting pretty obnoxious. I contemplated calling the police.

"Lucy! It's Adam!" The voice came again. My stomach lurched as I jumped up and ran to the door.

"Hi," I said cautiously, resisting an almost overwhelming urge to throw myself at him. "Come in, quick," I told him as reporters snapped away. At least they'd taken up camp at a slightly more respectful distance now. My heart was racing when I closed the front door, leaving us alone in the hallway.

"You're a hard one to track down," he told me as I motioned for him to follow me into the living room. Sitting beside him on the couch, all I could think about was kissing him again. His cool and calm demeanour was at odds with the nervous breakdown which I was trying desperately to keep bottled up inside. "I've been trying to call you."

"I've not switched my mobile on since we got back," I told him. "How did you get my number, anyway?"

"Chrissie called me. Matt got in touch with Jessica and bullied her into giving up our phone numbers. The whole gang went over to Dylan's pub on Sunday and had a little get-together in the back room. I called in and had a quick drink with them. Everyone missed you."

"Really? Everyone was together?" Jealousy hit me like a truck. "I couldn't have come anyway. I'm so embarrassed."

"Why?"

"What do you mean, *why*?" I asked, turning to face him. "Haven't you watched it? They made me look like a crazy person."

"Yeah." He looked at me, humour in his eyes. "But

it was great TV!"

"Hey!" I gave him a shove. It felt good to laugh again.

"I'm joking, I can't believe they edited everything like that but you can't sit around here, hiding from the world forever."

"Not forever," I said. "Just for a little while."

"You should go to Dylan's pub tonight," he said, shifting to the edge of the couch as though getting ready to leave. "I can give you the address. Chrissie gave me strict instructions to find you and get you to come …"

"Are you going?"

"Yeah, I think so. I just have to head home first to pick up a few things, I'm on my way now."

"Do you live nearby?" I realised that I didn't know much about him.

"No. I've got a place out in Havendon."

I looked blankly at him.

"It's a little village, about an hour's drive. I stay with Carl when I'm in town. I told you in Majorca, remember? Their garage is converted into a flat, and they let me use it in return for babysitting."

"Carl's got kids?"

"A little boy, Josh. He's a cutie."

"That's nice." I stood up with Adam, and wished he didn't have to leave so soon.

"I'd better get off if I want to make it back into town this evening … Here's the address for the pub and everyone's numbers." He handed me a slip of paper and moved towards the door.

"I'll see you later, then?" There was a definite hint of desperation in my voice when he reached to open the front door.

"Yeah." He hesitated, his hand on the door. "Unless … do you want to come with me? If you don't have any plans for the day?" He looked vulnerable while he waited for me to reply.

"Yeah … okay."

"It's not the most exciting of trips, but …"

"I'd like to come," I interrupted him.

"Great."

"I just need to jump in the shower quickly."

"That's fine," he told me, following me back into the apartment.

"I'll be quick," I promised while I backed into the bathroom.

"Is it okay if I grab a coffee?"

"Kitchen's there," I pointed. "Help yourself."

Panic set in as I rinsed the shampoo from my hair. I'd eagerly agreed to spend the day with Adam, but now I was overcome with nerves about spending time alone with him. It was so easy in Spain when he was just always there in the background. It had been such a surreal situation. There was a chance that in the real world we wouldn't get on at all.

I also started to panic about what to wear. I considered turning my phone on, to call Chrissie for advice, but I didn't know how I could pull that off without Adam noticing, since the piece of paper with Chrissie's number was in the living room. With deep breaths, I attempted to pull myself together. It was just a drive out to the country with Adam. No big deal.

I realised I'd have to go from the bathroom to my bedroom with just my towel wrapped around me, and hoped that Adam was still in the kitchen so I could make a dash without him seeing me. Of course, he'd seen me in a bikini, but it felt different being alone in my apartment with him.

I'd almost reached the bedroom when he called my name, walking out of the kitchen with his mobile in his hand. "It's for you," he told me. "It's Chrissie."

"Great!" I gripped my towel tighter. "Chrissie! Hi!" I tried to keep my voice casual. "How are you?" I flashed Adam a smile and then moved into my bedroom, closing the door behind me.

"Where've you been?" Chrissie asked. "I tried to call you."

"Sorry," I told her, perching on the edge of my bed. "My phone's off. Isn't it crazy what they did with the show? They made me look terrible."

"I know; I can't believe it."

I heard a noise in the living room and remembered Adam was waiting for me. "You have perfect timing, by the way. I need your help! Adam's here …"

"I know, I just called him!" She laughed at me. "What's going on?"

"I'm going to his place with him," I told her, getting up and opening my wardrobe. "It's out of town somewhere. I don't know what to wear!"

"Oh, wow! Do you think he's secretly rich and has a massive house in the country?"

"No! I don't know! What should I wear?"

"Hmm. Just go with jeans and a T-shirt or vest top … something tight and preferably low-cut. Go casual."

"Okay, I think I can manage that."

"Just wear something comfortable but not too

geeky."

"Got it." I laughed and started searching for something appropriate. "I'm really nervous. I've never been alone with him."

"Apart from that one time in the cupboard," she teased.

"Apart from that!"

"You'll be fine; just relax and have fun. Adam's a nice guy. And you just spent a week on holiday with him. Don't freak out about a day out."

"You're right," I agreed. "I'm being silly."

"You're coming to the pub tonight, aren't you?" she asked.

"Yes, I can't wait to see everyone again. It's been weird being alone."

"I know. I felt completely lost when I got home on Friday."

"How're things with Matt?" I asked.

"Good. I'll fill you in tonight. You'd better get on and not keep your date waiting."

"It's not a date," I protested.

"Yes, it is." She laughed. "Have fun!"

Chapter 27

I kept my head down as we left, ignoring the shouts from the reporters and ducking quickly into the safety of Adam's car.

"Bloody cameras!" Adam quipped as he pulled away, making me smile.

"How long before they leave me alone?" I asked.

"Not long, I imagine. They'll get bored and move on to the next thing pretty quickly. Especially if you don't speak to them."

"No fear of that. Even if I was allowed to talk."

"I heard about that," Adam said. "It's all a bit weird."

"How much did you know about everything?" I asked.

"Not much," he told me as he slowed for traffic lights. "I knew that they wanted you to think it was only our cameras, no hidden ones. We were supposed to hang back wherever possible so they could cut us out easily. I didn't know they planned to edit it to obscurity, though." He glanced over at me, trying to gauge my reaction. "I had no idea about that."

I nodded, believing him.

"I wasn't sure you'd even speak to me today," he went on. "You looked so mad at me on the last day in Spain."

"I was," I said. "I went to look for Maria to say goodbye, and found that room downstairs full of TV monitors, and the two guys zooming in and changing camera angles. It freaked me out."

"And that was all my fault?"

"No. But you were there to trick us and I took it personally for a while."

"I was just doing my job. I wanted to tell you but I couldn't. And honestly, when I heard about the show, I thought I'd be filming a bunch of idiots. I never expected to *like* any of you."

The urge to kiss him came out of nowhere and I looked out of the window to distract myself. "I keep wondering, do you think they'd always planned to edit it like that, or was it because we were a bit boring?"

"I think they planned it all along." He smiled at me. "You weren't that boring."

"What about the food poisoning thing? Was that a lie too?"

"Yeah. They wanted fewer cameramen around, but didn't want you to get suspicious so they made up a story about them being sick."

I paused, trying to get my head around everything. "I still can't believe I actually agreed to go in the first place. It all feels a bit surreal."

"Until you were on the plane, I was convinced you were going to change your mind and refuse to go."

"Me too!" We settled into a comfortable silence as we drove away from the city and into the winding roads that meandered through pretty little villages.

"How did you end up living so far out of town?" I asked as we drove along a narrow road bordered by fields and rolling hills.

"I grew up in a village, and I never really took to city life. I had a place in the city for a while, but it never really felt like home. My dad had a mild heart attack a few years ago and I moved back for a while, to be around while he recovered. I settled back into village life and didn't really have any desire to move again. I sold my place in Manchester, and Carl said I could stay with them when I had jobs in town. It worked out quite well."

"Erm …" I hesitated, not quite sure how to ask the question. "Do you live with your parents?"

He paused, a smile playing on his lips. "No! God, no! I'm thirty. Did you really think I lived with my parents in the country?"

"No," I ventured, embarrassed. "I don't know! I don't know anything about you."

"Okay," he said. "We can fix that."

"Here we are," he announced ten minutes later, pulling up in front of a semi-detached house in the middle of a quaint little village. "My house. Where I live alone … without my parents!"

"Don't tease me," I told him, mock seriously. "Are you going to give me the tour?"

"Yep." We stepped out of the car and I followed him up the path to the front door.

"It's nice," I told him as we wandered through the living room and into the little kitchen. There was a neat rectangular lawn visible through the back window, surrounded by a wooden fence. It was very cute.

"It's nothing special," he told me. "But I like it."

"Chrissie thought you might be rich and have a big house in the country," I confided.

"Sadly not," he said with raised eyebrows. "You want to see the upstairs?"

"No." I laughed at his boyish smile.

"Oh, now you go all coy! Shame I don't have a little cupboard for you to drag me into!"

A blush coloured my cheeks and I shifted my weight, feeling awkward as I shook my head, not sure what to say.

"Sorry. I didn't mean to embarrass you," he said as I avoided meeting his gaze.

"You didn't," I lied, and looked around the kitchen. "It's very clean," I commented to change the subject. "I didn't have you down as a neat freak."

"Well, I like to keep the place nice," he told me.

"Hmm, okay."

"What?" he asked with raised eyebrows.

"I feel like you just lied to me …"

He made an attempt to look offended, before he sighed and let me in to his secret. "My mum might have a key," he mumbled.

"Really?" I failed to hide my amusement. "Your mum comes round and cleans for you?"

Now he was the one looking embarrassed. "Maybe."

"Does she do your washing too?" I glanced at the duffle bag that he'd dumped in front of the washing machine in the corner of the kitchen.

"Not always."

"So it was hilarious that I thought you might live with your parents, but your mum actually does your washing and cleaning for you?"

"Don't judge me!" He looked suddenly bashful and it was endearing.

"I bet you just let her do it because it makes her happy, right?"

"She likes to look after me!"

I eyed him suspiciously and he glared back at me. "I can look after myself!"

"Sure you can, Mummy's boy!" I gave him a nudge and moved back to the living room.

"Hungry?" he asked.

"A bit. Are you going to cook?"

"I thought I'd take you to the pub for lunch. I can give you a tour of the village."

We walked down the street in glorious sunshine, Adam pointing out the sights as we went. Havendon boasted a post office, a little shop, a community centre, a playground and a pub.

"That's pretty much it," Adam told me as we got to the pub.

"It's nice."

"I know it's not that impressive, but I like it."

"Adam!" the barman greeted him cheerfully.

"Hi, Mike. How's things? Did I miss any excitement while I was away?"

"You wouldn't believe what's been going on here," he said, his voice full of mirth. "It's been crazy!"

"I always miss the fun," Adam told me before looking back to Mike.

"Little Lily Stevens lost her pet rabbit again!" he told us excitedly.

"No? You're having me on!" Adam laughed.

"Don't worry; it turned up after ten minutes in Mrs Johnson's garden."

"Phew!" Adam sighed and I smiled at their little joke.

"And …" Mike took a breath. "You won't believe this, but John had a nasty cold …"

"No way!"

"And there was no post for a day! Things really start to fall apart when the postman gets sick. It was chaos. No post! For a whole day!"

"Shocking!" Adam declared. "I might need a beer to calm my nerves now."

"Coming right up. And the lady friend?" He leaned on the bar and gave me a once-over.

"This is Lucy." Adam introduced me.

"I'll have a beer too," I told him, surprising myself. I think I'd developed a drinking problem over the last week.

"I'll bring them over," he told us with a smile.

We sat at a table in the corner and I relaxed in Adam's company. It was nice to spend time with him in a normal environment, and I enjoyed listening to him chat about his childhood in the village and his work in TV production. We switched to soft drinks since Adam was driving, and the time passed quickly. We ate lunch and I was disappointed when Adam suggested we start the drive back to the city. "I'll be in trouble if you don't put in an appearance at Dylan's place tonight."

"It'll be nice to see everyone." I would've liked to keep Adam to myself for a little longer, I thought.

We were getting up to leave when a plump, dark-haired woman approached us. I was expecting her to have recognised me and be intent on telling me what a terrible person I was, so I was surprised when Adam greeted her.

"Hi, Mum."

"I saw your car and came looking for you," she told him, giving him a warm hug. "What happened to your hand?"

"I cut it. It's fine. This is my friend, Lucy."

"I'm Ruth." She hugged me before turning to Adam. "Were you going to bring Lucy up to the house?"

"It's a bit of a flying visit, actually," he told her. "We were just about to head back to the city."

"Stay and have a coffee with me before you disappear, will you? I've not seen you properly for ages."

Adam glanced awkwardly at me.

"Coffee sounds good," I said.

"Great." She turned to look over her shoulder. "Bring us three coffees, will you, Mike?"

Adam mouthed an apology at me and I smiled in reply as I sat back down.

"What do you think of Havendon then, Lucy?"

"I like it. It's pretty."

"These are all local …" She pointed to a framed photo hanging on the wall close to us. There were a few similar ones dotted around the pub, with differing landscapes.

"They're great." I gazed at the one nearest us, a peaceful sunset over farmland.

"They're Adam's," Ruth told me proudly.

"Really?" I stood to get a better look. "You took these?"

"They're old," he told me while I peered at the picture. "They're not my best ones."

"They're really good," I told him, moving back to my seat. He shrugged, and his silence reminded me of Spain and all the times he couldn't talk to me.

"He's an amazing photographer," Ruth told me.

"But he's very modest."

"The one of the churchyard is my favourite," Mike said when he appeared with our coffees. He pointed to the door, and I walked over to look. It was stunning. Delicate bluebells sat in the foreground, creating an eerie contrast with the lonely church and heavy headstones beyond.

I sat back down to my coffee. "It's amazing."

"I don't know why he insists on wasting his life working in TV studios," Ruth commented while she stirred her coffee.

"The TV work is okay," Adam said. "I get to meet some interesting people."

I caught his eye and he gave me a sly smile.

"It's your life, I suppose!" Ruth said.

We chatted over our coffees and were interrupted twice as customers entered the pub and came to say hello to Ruth. It seemed that she knew everyone. A hazard of village life, I guess. Ruth told us about the church fete she was helping to organise, and talked a bit about Adam's dad, who had apparently driven an elderly neighbour into the next town for her hair appointment.

She didn't ask about me. I wasn't sure if she knew about the TV show, but if she did she was politely avoiding the subject.

"You'll have to come up and have dinner with us sometime," she told me while I drank the last of my coffee and Adam went to the bar to pay.

"That would be nice," I told her.

"All set," Adam said. "You heading home, Mum?"

"No, I'm going to go and see how Stan is." She glanced at the old gentleman who'd waved at us when he came in a few minutes earlier. "His wife died recently, and I like to keep an eye on him." She hugged me goodbye and I thanked Mike as we left.

"Sorry about that," Adam said as we fell into step and headed back to his place. "I can't believe my mum just gate-crashed our first date."

"This was a date?"

"I thought so," he said, slipping his hand into mine.

Chapter 28

We'd just found a parking spot around the corner from the pub when Adam's phone rang. It was Carl, he told me as he answered it. I listened while he told Carl where we were, and had a brief conversation.

"I think I'll take the car home so I can have a few drinks," Adam told me when he ended the call. "Carl wants to come for a drink so I'll get a taxi back over with him."

"Okay," I told him. "Probably a good idea to get rid of the car."

"Especially if Matt's around. He's got a thing about shots."

"I'll see you later, then." I said, opening the car door.

"I won't be long."

I walked straight into Dylan in the pub and was overjoyed to see him.

"Hey, stranger!" He left the empty glasses he'd been collecting and gave me a big hug.

"Isn't that Lucy?" I heard someone on the next table say. I turned at my name and smiled vaguely, but the looks I received weren't particularly friendly. I'd almost forgotten about everything that was going on while I'd been out with Adam. It was all coming back to me now.

"Come on." Dylan put a hand on my back and ushered me towards the bar, where I found Chrissie sitting alone.

"I thought you'd fallen off the planet!" she exclaimed, embracing me tightly. Dylan moved around the bar to serve a customer and I noticed an older version of him pulling pints.

"Hello!" he said, beaming at me. "I think I recognise you from the telly!"

"I'm Lucy," I told him.

"Jack," he replied. "I'm Dylan's dad. I'm busy, but come around and give me a quick hug."

I glanced at Chrissie.

"He's harmless," she told me. "He likes his hugs. And we get free drinks so we go along with it!" She smiled over at him while she spoke; they seemed to be familiar with each other. Jack gave me a big squeeze, then asked me what I wanted to drink. I ordered a beer and wondered again at my increasing alcohol consumption.

"Why on earth didn't you have your phone on?" Chrissie demanded when I took a seat next to her at the bar. "You had us worried."

"Sorry. I didn't know you'd be trying to get in touch."

"Why not?" she asked. "It's all completely crazy. We need to stick together!"

"Yeah, I know. I just wanted to hide when I saw what they'd shown on TV." I smiled at Jack, who put a beer on the bar in front of me.

"Don't hide from us, though. Didn't you miss everyone? I felt so lost on Friday night. I didn't know what to do without you guys."

"Yes, I really missed everyone," I told her, picking up my drink. "It was so weird; I just wanted to be back in Spain with you all. And I missed our bedtime chats."

"Me too!"

"I heard you've all been hanging out without me?" I pouted.

"Only because we couldn't get hold of you."

"What did I miss? I presume you've been having fun with Matt without me around to sabotage you?" She laughed at my comment, and then couldn't stop.

"It's not that funny!" I insisted, but laughed with her anyway.

"Sorry." She coughed as she calmed down again. "It was pretty funny, though."

"I just don't think I'm ready to laugh about it yet," I told her sadly.

"I know," she said. "They really set you up, didn't they? Anyway, let's not talk about it now. I want to know about your date with Adam …"

I opened my mouth to fill her in, but a tall, butch-looking woman suddenly loomed over us, interrupting our conversation. "Everything okay?" she asked, her eyes on Chrissie.

"Fine, thanks," Chrissie told her, politely.

"Is she bothering you?" she asked, glancing at me.

"No," Chrissie answered slowly.

"Because I can give her a slap for you if you want. She deserves it."

I was taken aback by her tone and my heart raced. She was very intimidating.

"Oh, it's that Lucy!" A man appeared next to the woman and glared at me. "I can't believe you're talking to her," he told Chrissie. "Crazy bitch!"

"She's not crazy," Chrissie snapped at them. "And she didn't do anything wrong."

"It's that weirdo from the TV," someone else commented as they walked past, drawing the attention of the whole pub.

"I just offered to give her a slap," the big, scary woman announced.

"Nobody's slapping anyone," Jack shouted from across the bar. "Sit down and drink quietly or get out!"

"I think it's Lucy the lunatic you ought to be throwing out," someone else called.

"Leave her alone." Dylan elbowed his way to us and took my hand as I slipped off the stool. "Come on." He led me around the bar and through a back door. "Take her upstairs," he told Chrissie. "I'll sort the rabble out."

My heart was still racing when I took a seat on the couch in the living room of the apartment above the pub.

"That was crazy." Chrissie seemed as shocked as I was. "Are you okay?"

"I think so," I replied, on the brink of tears.

"I really hate Jessica and the stupid TV people," Chrissie commented. "I don't know how they can mess with our lives like that."

"Jessica's career certainly isn't over, is it?" I said. "Those conversations we overheard were all set up, weren't they?"

"I guess so. I'm a bit confused by everything, to be honest."

Margaret and Kelly appeared in the doorway.

"Hi!" I jumped up to hug them both.

"Are you okay?" Kelly asked. "Dylan said there was a bit of trouble in the bar."

"I'm okay, I think. I'm not sure," I told her honestly. "I'll survive, though."

"Yes, you will," Margaret agreed, giving me a big hug. "We missed you!"

"I can't believe everything that's going on," Kelly commented.

"I take it you didn't lose your job?" I asked her.

"No!" She laughed. "Business is booming. Apparently celebrity waitresses are even better than pretty ones! I got a pay rise!"

"That's great," I told her with as much enthusiasm as I could muster.

"Sorry. Am I being really insensitive? They really screwed you over, didn't they?"

"It's fine. It's not your fault. I'm glad it worked out well for you."

"Not that well," she said. "Didn't you see how they made me out to be a blonde bimbo?"

"Yeah," I said slowly, biting my lip in an attempt to keep a straight face. Kelly looked from me to Chrissie, who was concentrating on her feet.

"I'm not a bimbo!" she screeched, breaking into a laugh.

"No, you're not!" I said.

"I don't think they needed too much editing to make you look that way, though," Margaret told her.

"What about me?" Chrissie said, chuckling with the rest of us. "They made me look like some pathetic lovesick little girl."

"Well …" I looked around. Everyone looked

thoroughly amused.

"That's not how I am!" Chrissie was adamant. "Nobody came out looking that great really, did they?"

"Ryan did all right," Kelly argued. "He's getting a lot of female attention now and he's loving his new celebrity status. Dylan came out looking fine too."

"That's true," I agreed. "What's happening with you, Margaret? Are you going to stay in the UK longer now you're a big celebrity?"

"Well, I have to stay a bit longer to do the final filming. Kelly got me a job at the restaurant with her for now, just to keep me out of trouble!"

"That's nice," I told her. "I bet it's fun working together."

"It is," she told me. "And we can get away with anything, what with us being such big celebs!"

"I don't know what I'm going to do about a job," I told them glumly. "I don't have the energy for job-hunting. I might have to sell the Rolex and the car to tide me over. I'm nervous about going out in public at the moment anyway, what with reporters and the general public after me."

"Just keep a low profile for a couple of weeks," Chrissie told me. "As soon as the three-week gagging order is over, we can all sell our stories and set the record straight."

"So just three weeks of this hell, then?" I said, and felt bad as they looked at me so sympathetically. "Sorry. I'm not a lot of fun, am I?"

"It's understandable," Margaret told me. "You definitely got a bad deal."

"Yeah, well, just wait," I told Margaret. "As soon

as the three weeks are up, I'll be telling everyone about you and your cradle-snatching ways! That should take the attention away from me!" There was a pause before Margaret grinned at me and we all erupted with laughter. "How is Ryan?" I asked. "Have you seen him?"

"Yes. He's fine," Chrissie replied. "He'll probably turn up later. I put out an alert to everyone that you were off the missing persons list."

"I'm glad Adam came to find me. I was going crazy at home."

"Shall we go down and get a drink?" Kelly suggested. "We demanded a night off work to celebrate your return. Let's have some fun!" She smiled at me mischievously.

"I can't go down there," I told her. "People were mean to me!"

"Jack said we can use the back room. It's all great publicity for him and the pub, so he wants to keep us sweet!"

"Go on, then," I agreed. "I think a drink might be just what I need."

The back room of the pub boasted a small bar and a pool table. A long wooden bench stretched along one wall of the room, and small round tables and stools were scattered around the place. Dylan came in, told us to help ourselves to drinks and took a food order to the kitchen for us. It was a nice set-up.

I had a beer and chatted with the girls. It almost felt like we were back on holiday when Margaret insisted we play pool. She and Chrissie were pretty good, but Kelly and I were hopeless, and it led to a fair amount of laughter.

I was still reeling from the incident in the bar, but it was good to laugh with the girls. I felt better being surrounded by my holiday gang. It was as if I was in a bubble again.

"Ladies!" Ryan beamed at us when he arrived.

"Hi!" I grinned and gave him a big hug. "I missed you," I told him, surprised by the strength of my feelings.

"It's good to have you back!" he told me. "It wasn't the same without you."

"I love how we all sound like you've been gone for years, when it was actually only three days," Chrissie laughed.

"It felt like a lifetime to me," Ryan commented as he released me from the hug and moved to the bar. "How amazing is this place?"

"It's pretty cool," I agreed.

"I love being a celebrity." Ryan laughed as he got himself a beer, and passed more around when he saw we were almost empty. I could already feel myself getting emotional with the alcohol, but I didn't care. "It's brilliant," Ryan went on and clinked his beer bottle against mine. "The girls are all over me! All the time. It's amazing." He gave me a goofy smile and I couldn't help but laugh.

"We're not supposed to talk about the fame stuff," Chrissie chastised him. "Lucy's only had abuse."

"Oh yeah, shit. Sorry. They made you look a right tool, didn't they?"

We all stared at him, speechless at his tactless comment. I ruffled his hair and laughed at him before taking a swig of my beer.

"It's actually very weird being a celebrity," Kelly

told us. "I was working last night and a guy asked me to sign his bum so he could get it tattooed!"

"No way!" I laughed at her. "That's ridiculous."

"I was there!" Margaret said. "He was fairly inebriated but he did ask."

"What did you say?" I asked.

"I took his pen and signed his forehead. Told him he could go and get that made permanent if he wanted!"

"Seriously?" I asked.

"I swear, I'm telling the truth. We couldn't stop laughing. It's so much fun working there now. Especially since it seems to be optional. There's no way I'm getting fired anytime soon. The place is packed. It's the same here."

Dylan brought our food through and sat and chatted to us for a while. The bar was busy, he told us, so he had to keep going to check everything was going okay, but he'd keep nipping back to hang out with us whenever he could.

"You all right?" he asked, pulling up a stool next to me.

"Yes, I'm much better now," I told him while the others chatted among themselves. "Did you know about the cameras the whole time?"

"No." His forehead wrinkled as he frowned. "I was suspicious but I only really figured it out that night in the restaurant when I spoke to you about it."

"I can't believe Ryan didn't tell us," I said, loud enough for him to hear.

"I already explained," Ryan said with a sigh. "Jessica made me promise not to say anything, and she can be quite persuasive when she wants to be.

And, actually, I thought it was fun that you didn't know."

"Thanks, Ryan!" I said sarcastically.

"Dylan!" Jack put his head around the door. "I need you out here. They're asking for a song!"

"They can dream on." he said, standing to leave. "Make sure you eat everything," he instructed, indicating my plate of fish and chips, which I'd only picked at. "I don't want you fading away on me!"

"Yes, boss!" I replied, smiling.

I picked at a few more chips and then pushed the plate to one side.

"You'll end up drunk," Ryan warned me. "You're a lightweight at the best of times, and drinking on an empty stomach is asking for trouble!"

"Too late!" I told him and raised my drink to his.

"Just don't expect me to carry you home," he said. "There are a lot of women after my body out there!"

I took a long drink of beer. "They only love you because you were on TV."

"Fine by me!" he said.

"Shall we play pool again?" Chrissie asked. "You might be better now you're a bit tipsy, Lucy!"

"Go on then." I stood and turned to see Matt, framed by the back door. It was probably the beer, but the sight of him made me really emotional.

"Well, this is awkward," he said. "It's my crazy stalker!"

Tears sprang to my eyes and he strode across the room to give me one of his big bear hugs. "Where've you been hiding?" he asked as he lifted me off my feet. I couldn't find my voice, and I buried my head in his neck as sobs shook my body. "It's all fine," he reassured me. "You'll be okay."

"I know," I sniffed into his shoulder. "Sorry!"

"It's fine. I've had a few tears on your behalf too! Don't let it get to you. Let's get drunk and pretend we're in Spain with you trying to seduce me again!"

"In your dreams." I laughed and wiped the tears from my face.

Then there was another voice from the back door. I glanced over to see Adam and Carl watching me.

"Hi." I attempted a smile and turned away to wipe my face with my sleeve.

"Are you okay?" Adam asked, appearing by my side.

"Yeah." I looked around to see everyone staring at me. "I'm fine!"

"Some people had a go at her in the bar," Chrissie explained. "One woman threatened to hit her."

"Seriously?" Adam asked, wrapping me in a hug. "People are idiots. Don't let it get to you."

"What's going on?" Dylan asked when he came back in. "Look at the state of you." He walked over and wiped the tears from my cheeks. "Only one thing for it … let's all get drunk!" He moved behind the bar and lined up a row of shot glasses before pouring some golden liquid into each of them for us.

"Don't ask if I'm okay!" I warned Carl when he came and put an arm around my shoulder, giving me a squeeze. "I'm a bit drunk and an emotional wreck. You'll set me off again!"

"I wasn't going to!" he told me as we took our shots. "You're a tough 'un. You'll be fine."

"I will." I told him. "It's weird seeing you without a camera."

"Don't worry," he said, beaming. "I'm rigged with a hidden one!"

Chapter 29

"You haven't told me about your date today," Chrissie whispered when Adam headed for the bathroom.

"It was good," I told her. "We went to his house. And no, he's not rich. It was nice. We had lunch … Actually, it was a bit weird, but we ended up having coffee with his mum."

"What?" Matt leaned in to join the conversation. He was sitting next to Chrissie and had been pretending not to listen. Kelly and Margaret had gone through to the bar to do a bit of mingling, and Carl and Ryan were experimenting with mixing cocktails behind our private bar. "You met his parents?" Matt asked. "On your first date?"

"Yeah. His mum, anyway."

"He took you to meet his mum on your first date?" he asked again.

"He didn't take me to meet her. We just bumped into her."

"Hmm." Matt looked dubious. "But he lives in a little village, right? So it wasn't a big surprise that you saw his mum?"

"What's your point?" I sighed.

"Well, I just don't understand why anyone would do that … unless …" He smiled to himself.

"What?" Chrissie demanded.

"I'm just wondering if Adam might be a genius," Matt mused.

"What are you talking about?" Chrissie asked.

"Nothing. Never mind. Carry on talking. Pretend I'm not here!" He moved away slightly and picked up his pint so I turned back to Chrissie and ignored him.

"What's his mum like?" Chrissie asked.

"Really nice," I told her. "She invited me to go up and have dinner at their place sometime."

"Yep," Matt slipped back into the conversation. "The guy's a genius!"

"Seriously?" Chrissie snapped at him. "What are you talking about?"

"He knew you'd end up meeting his mum," Matt told me with the tone of a detective uncovering the truth. "He had it all planned!"

"No, he didn't," I protested.

"That's the most elaborate seduction plan I've ever heard of," Matt said through a grin. "It was risky, but it seems like it might just pay off. I love that guy!"

"Will you shut up?" Chrissie laughed at him. "You're such an idiot."

"I'll have to high-five him," Matt announced. "He's my hero. He's coming. I'm high-fiving him!"

"Don't you dare!" I hissed. "Don't say anything."

"What's so funny?" Adam asked when he came back to sit with us.

"Nothing." I took his hand as he sat on the stool next to me.

"Oh, I forgot to tell you," Matt began. "My mum wants to meet you all. She's invited everyone over for a barbecue on Friday."

"Did I miss the joke?" Adam asked when Chrissie and I burst out laughing.

"Not really." I squeezed his hand.

"What's so funny?" Matt said.

"Your mum has really invited us all over?" Chrissie asked.

"Yep. She wants to meet everyone. She's been obsessed with the show and is excited about having a houseful of celebrities."

"It sounds fun, actually," I told him.

"Just one problem, Lucy. You might have to sit in the car and I'll bring you a hot dog … Mum's not your biggest fan. She specifically said not to invite the crazy girl who threw poor Chrissie in the pool. Sorry!"

"Shut up! That's mean. Did she really say that?"

"Nah," he grinned. "Maybe!"

I covered my face with my hands in embarrassment.

"I'm joking!" he said. "Get over it already!"

"Shall I hit him for you?" Chrissie asked.

"Yes, please!"

"I'm just having a bit of fun." Matt laughed. "Let's change the subject then and go back to Adam and his elaborate seduction technique. I cannot believe you took Lucy to meet your mum!"

I hid my face in my hands again. "Your boyfriend's annoying," I told Chrissie out of the corner of my mouth.

"You told them that was an elaborate seduction technique?" Adam asked. "Why would you say that? Surely there's a man code about that sort of stuff?"

"So he's right?" I asked. "It was all part of an evil

plan?"

"Yes!" he replied. "No. I'm kidding. It definitely wasn't a plan. Not an evil plan, anyway!"

I gave him a friendly shove and he glanced at Matt. "I can't believe you said that! I think we need to have a chat over a game of pool." He gave me a quick kiss as he stood up, and my stomach fluttered.

"Anyway," Matt said, grinning as he got up. "I'd still like to high-five you if that's okay?"

Adam shook his head and bumped shoulders with Matt when he headed for the pool table. He passed Matt a cue and then winked at me.

I turned to Chrissie with a sigh. "I like him so much."

Chapter 30

"The room is spinning," I told Chrissie as I looked up at my bedroom ceiling.

"It was a fun night, though," she remarked, getting into bed beside me. "Looks like you and Adam are getting on well. I saw you kissing him."

"I saw you kissing Matt," I retorted.

"Yeah …" She laughed.

"And he didn't look too happy when you said you were going to stay here with me." We'd been standing outside the pub when Chrissie announced that she missed our night-time chats and was coming home with me.

"No, I don't think he was too impressed." She hesitated. "I slept at his place the last two nights."

"Really?" I said. "You kept that quiet."

"I know. I don't know if we're rushing things a bit."

"It's not that fast," I told her. "You've known him a week and a half now, haven't you?"

"When you say it like that, it sounds terrible!"

"But?" I asked, turning on my side and pulling the bedding up to my chin.

"But it feels like I've known him for years. It doesn't feel too fast; it feels … right."

"It does seem like we've all known each other for a

long time. I can't believe that ten days ago none of us had met."

"And he's such a nice guy. He's so sweet." She had a lovesick grin on her face, and it made me smile.

"Aww, you love him!" I teased.

"Shut up!"

"He is lovely, though, if slightly annoying!" I said. "I think you've got yourself a keeper."

"I hope so," she said, shifting to get comfy. "I still can't believe you met Adam's mum."

"I know; he swore it wasn't planned."

He'd seemed quite embarrassed about it in the pub.

"Anyway, you'll be meeting Matt's parents on Friday," I told her.

"That's true."

***

Although I tried to lead Chrissie astray, I couldn't convince her to skip work in favour of keeping me company for the day. We ate a breakfast of tea and toast together and, as she left, she told me to turn my phone on.

I did as I was told and plugged my phone in next to my bed, making myself comfortable while I settled down to listen to voicemails and read through texts. I was amused by a few messages from Matt. In one message he asked if we were playing hide and seek again, and told me I was winning. He'd sent another one immediately after that, saying they'd been checking all the cupboards and couldn't find me, then had sent one to say that Adam had turned up and I was nowhere in sight so they were out of ideas.

I laughed out loud when I listened to a voicemail of the gang, in the pub, telling me how much they missed me. Then my heart started to race at the sound of Adam's voice on the next message. It was short and sweet, saying he hoped I was okay and to call him when I got his message. I was tempted to do just that, until I remembered the message was days old. I pressed a button to listen to it again, enjoying the sound of his voice.

I'd just put the phone down and was staring at it when it rang, making me jump.

"You finally switched it on," Adam said. "So you're having a productive day so far?"

"It was top of my list of things to do today."

"What's next?"

"That was the whole list. It's been a successful day!"

"Good. Can I tempt you away from your apartment, then?"

"I don't think I can be seen in public," I told him.

"What if I promise we won't see anyone?"

"I could probably be persuaded." I smiled into the phone.

"Great. I'll pick you up in an hour."

***

"You were lucky I chose sensible footwear." I took Adam's outstretched hand as I moved cautiously over the boulder-ridden stretch of path beside the stream. Thankfully the path evened out ahead.

"Erm …" He paused, his mouth twitching into a smile.

"You think I don't own anything other than sensible shoes?"

"I really wouldn't like to comment." The path opened out, leaving room for us to walk comfortably side by side.

"Just so you know, I have some really wild shoes in my wardrobe." I'm not sure why I felt the need to lie about this, especially since the look on his face made it clear that Adam neither believed me, nor cared about my shoe collection. "Honestly, I have some heels you wouldn't believe … They're like this …" I stretched out my index finger and thumb as wide as possible, shrinking the distance slightly to try to make it more believable. He smiled, pressing my finger and thumb closer together. "Okay." I stopped him when the gap was about half an inch. "I have some really hot flats though! And really strong, healthy feet … I might stop talking now …"

"That would make a change."

"I don't talk much," I protested.

"Yeah, I think you've told me that a few times."

"I'll be quiet then." I pouted. He smirked, and we walked in silence for a while. It took a concerted effort not to speak, which was strange because I'd genuinely never considered myself much of a talker. With Adam, I relaxed and felt like I could talk to him all day, about anything that sprang to mind. "Where are we going?" I asked.

"Wow, that was almost a full two minutes," he joked, glancing at his watch. "Just for a walk," he told me. "It's hard to know where to go on a date if we're limited to places where no one else will be."

"So this is a date, is it?"

"Yes," he said, a look of amusement on his face. "Or have I misread things?"

"No," I told him, stopping to take a seat on a boulder at the edge of the stream. "I don't think you misread anything." Just then, the sun came through the clouds, making kaleidoscopic patterns as it streamed through the tree branches.

Adam pulled off his shoes and socks and walked into the middle of the stream, moving carefully over the rocks underfoot. "Can I hazard a guess and say you don't date much?"

I smiled and suddenly felt that I could tell Adam anything. "I had a rebellious phase when I was fifteen and dated Paul Green." 'No' would probably have sufficed, but I really did seem to be developing a problem with talking too much. "He was two years older than me, and a goth! He wore way more make-up than me and rarely spoke, which I always found to be a good thing. Occasionally, he'd take me to McDonald's or to the cinema, but mostly we just hung out in the park or in bus shelters. Thankfully none of my family paid any attention to my little rebellion, so I gave him up pretty quickly."

"I'll be honest." Adam eyed me from the middle of the stream. "I was expecting you to get all embarrassed and clam up."

"You're the one who said I talk a lot," I reminded him. "I'm just trying to live up to your expectations. You'll have to listen to the entire dating history of Lucy Mitchell now, and you've got no one but yourself to blame."

"Go on, then." He kicked water up at me, making me laugh. I removed my footwear to submerge my feet in the soothing, cold water.

"Let's see, there was Ben Finchley. I was at university and I met him one evening in the laundry on campus. He used to take me for dinner in the cafeteria, which was pretty cheap of him because we had meal vouchers for living on campus. His room was in the building next to mine and our windows faced each other, so he used to play his music full blast and yell at me to name that tune. It was always U2 or Queen and he'd only manage two songs before everyone else in the building would shout at him to shut up."

"What happened?"

"I moved off campus in the second year. I rented a house with some girls on my course and we just drifted apart. After uni, I dated Dale Davies for six months until he left to go backpacking around Vietnam and Cambodia. We decided to call it a day and I never saw him again."

"And after him?"

"Some guy called Adam," I replied, smiling as I watched him standing in the broken sunlight, his thumbs hooked loosely into his back pockets. "I don't know his last name …"

"Lewis?" he suggested.

"Adam Lewis," I pondered. "That could be it. Anyway, he was handsome in his own way but had this nasty habit of following me around with a camera. Very annoying!"

"But you dated him anyway?"

"Yep."

"What happened to him?"

"He judged me on my choice of shoes and my short

dating history, and left me in the woods one day."

"Interesting," he mused, looking down and shifting his weight from one foot to the other.

"And your dating history?" I quizzed.

"It's slightly longer," he said with a grin. "But almost as boring as yours!"

"Hey!" I kicked out a foot to splash him.

"I dated a girl not long ago who always wore these really high heels," he told me. "The stupid stiletto ones? They looked great, but she always looked so unstable that I kept imagining how easily I'd be able to push her over …" His eyes flashed with mirth and I let out a short laugh. "You can't really date someone if you're always thinking about pushing them over."

"It does seem like a doomed relationship," I agreed, as he moved through the water towards me.

"It was." He reached out a hand and I joined him in the water, enjoying the feel of his arms around my waist. "Sturdiness is underrated."

"Are you calling me sturdy?" I asked, my arms hanging loosely around his neck.

"No," he told me. "Because that sounds bad!"

"It certainly doesn't sound like a compliment."

"I think the best thing for me to do now would be to kiss you and pretend that word never came up."

"Good plan," I told him as his lips came down to meet mine, our bodies moving together. My stomach lurched and my body reacted to him. Never in my very limited dating history had I felt like this about anyone.

I really needed a pause button. Some moments are so amazing that you want them to last forever. This was one of them. It was an amazing, tender moment –

right up until something bit my foot and I leapt out of the water as though it was shark-infested.

"If I'm moving too fast, you can just say." Adam grinned and followed me out of the water.

"There was something on my foot," I said, struggling to catch my breath.

"Fish," Adam announced, peering into the water. "There are loads of them."

"Sorry," I told him, a hand on his back, looking down at the tiny fish darting around. "I think I killed the moment!"

"Some women pay good money to have fish nibble their feet, you know?"

"Crazy women!" I told him and he kissed me briefly before sitting to put his shoes back on.

"Just so we're clear," he said when we set out along the path again, "I like your footwear and your short dating history."

"And I'm glad you don't spend your time thinking about pushing me over."

"Well, it's not like it *never* crosses my mind …" He grinned and gave me a gentle shove.

"I'm sturdy," I told him proudly, holding my ground.

Chapter 31

"He's keen," Chrissie commented when I told her about my hiking trip with Adam and the movie night I'd had with him the previous evening.

"I didn't see him today." He'd gone with Carl to a photography exhibition, so I'd spent the day cleaning my apartment and lazing around.

"Apart from now," Chrissie pointed out.

"Yeah." I smiled as I looked over at Adam, who was standing over the barbecue with Matt.

"So things are going well?" she asked.

"Yeah, really well. He's amazing."

"I have a question." Ryan plonked himself down on the plastic garden chair next to me. "Do you think Margaret's got a thing for me?"

"No!" Both Chrissie and I laughed at the genuine concern on Ryan's face.

"I feel like she's after me," he told us quietly. "She gives me these looks. It's starting to get creepy."

"The fame might be going to your head," Chrissie told him. "You think all women are after you."

"All women *are* after me," he told us seriously before looking thoughtfully up to the sky. "Maybe you're right. I might have a problem!"

"I think so," I said.

"That's good, then. I don't have to look out for

Margaret. She's just being friendly?"

"Yes," Chrissie replied. "She definitely isn't interested in you."

"Thanks, girls. Anyone need a drink?" We shook our heads and he left us alone again.

I got a stern look from Matt's mum as she walked outside with a plate of burger buns and a bowl of salad. "I hope you're behaving?"

"All calm so far, Wendy." I smiled at her but her 'jokes' were beginning to wear thin.

"I have to say, it's lovely having all these young men in the house." She winked at us as she set the food on the table next to the barbecue before squeezing Adam's bicep. I didn't dare catch Chrissie's eye, certain I'd get the giggles. The look on Adam's face was funny enough. "That Pierre's a bit of all right too, isn't he?"

Pierre was Kelly's date, and so far he'd confused me by telling me that he was French, in a heavy Welsh accent. He was making himself useful, helping Wendy in the kitchen.

"He seems nice," Chrissie commented, falling silent when Kelly wandered out through the back door.

"You won't believe this," she told us in hushed tones as she sat beside me. "I think Margaret's trying to steal Pierre. She's all over him! She's laughing at his jokes – which aren't even funny – and she keeps touching his arm. Honestly, it's quite disturbing. Can't she find someone her own age? I've seen her giving Ryan the eye as well."

"She's had a glass of wine," Chrissie pointed out. "I think she's just one of those people who flirts with anyone after a drink."

"Yeah, you might be right. She needs to leave Pierre alone, though, or I'll have to have a word."

"So you met him at the restaurant?" I asked.

"Yeah, he's the new wine waiter. They're trying to be fancy now the place is so popular. To be honest, I don't think I'm that keen on him, I was just intrigued. I've never met anyone who's half French and half Welsh. It's a bit weird, actually!"

"Burgers are ready," Matt shouted.

"I'm starving," Kelly said, walking away from us.

"It's like a revolving door of entertainment," Chrissie said as Margaret fell into the empty chair, laughing. "You have to tell us something funny if you sit there!"

"You Brits are so easy to wind up." Margaret said as the laughter subsided. "I've got Ryan thinking I'm in love with him and Kelly thinking I'm after her boy-toy!"

"Poor Ryan," I said, smiling. "We told him he was imagining it."

"I'd watch out for Kelly," Chrissie said. "She has an air of someone I wouldn't want to get on the wrong side of – if you know what I mean."

"Yeah," Margaret said. "She can be quite scary in the restaurant. I'd say she has a violent streak. Maybe I should stay away from Pierre."

"I need food," I told them, getting up and moving over to the barbecue. "Everything under control, boys?"

"There's a burger with your name on it," Matt told me, reaching for a plate and flipping the meat on it for me.

"Put the chicken legs on now," Wendy instructed

Matt. "I know how Ryan loves his chicken!" She howled with laughter and Matt rolled his eyes.

"I can see where you get your sense of humour from, Matt."

He glared at me and swatted me away with a spatula.

"How was your day?" Adam asked while I built up my burger and loaded salad on my plate.

"Fine," I told him. "Pretty boring. How was yours? Did you enjoy the exhibition?"

"It was fine." He paused and switched to a whisper. "I missed you."

"I missed you too." I beamed as my stomach flipped and my appetite disappeared.

"I need a group photo," Wendy announced after the food. "Everyone go and stand against the hedge over there." We did as we were told, while Wendy barked orders at us. "Sorry, not you," she told Pierre. "Just the famous people. You get out of the way too," she told Adam. "Actually, you're the camera guy, aren't you? Could you take the photo? You'll know what you're doing. Matt, where's your dad?" We all winced as she screamed for Matt's poor dad, Graham, to come outside.

"I've just seen you all on the telly," Graham said when he joined us, standing at the edge of our group for the photo.

"You know how to use that, don't you?" Wendy asked Adam, who held up her battered-looking phone.

"I think I can manage." He smiled politely back at her. "Say cheese!"

"You would think they'd have run out of things to

say about us by now," Chrissie replied to Graham.

"It was an advert for next week's show," he told us. "It was all very mysterious."

"The live show's in two weeks," Matt told him.

"It didn't look like a live show. It just said there would be an extra show with shocking new footage. Can you all stop staring at me?" he said. "That's all I know."

Much to Wendy's dismay, we abandoned the photo and headed for the kitchen, where we huddled around Matt while he did a quick internet search on Graham's laptop. "Found it," he told us, and the screen flashed with our smiling faces before it changed to a shot of Chelsea, who invited viewers to tune in next Friday for an unforgettable hour of entertainment. "You won't believe your eyes," she promised, before the advert ended.

"I'm sure people *will* believe their eyes." I sighed. "They believe anything that's fed to them."

Hannah Ellis

Chapter 32

The restaurant where Kelly worked felt like a fast-food place. The décor was minimal and tacky, with dusty plastic flowers on every table. I listened to the easy conversation at the table, but didn't feel very sociable.

"Lower the weapon, please." Adam reached out for the knife that Matt was waving around while he told us another teaching anecdote.

"Sorry, mate!" Matt laughed. "I think maybe I should just let *you* stab *me*, and then we can shut up about it. You're milking it a bit now."

"You've literally scarred me for life. I think I'm allowed to milk that!" Adam said.

"I've done you a favour," Matt told him. "Women love scars."

"So I should be thanking you for almost severing my hand?"

"You're so dramatic," Matt said. "If you want me to kiss it better, just say so!"

Adam rolled his eyes and turned to me. "You okay?"

I was quietly staring at the menu, using it as a shield. Chrissie had convinced me to join them for a meal, but it already felt like a bad idea. In the two days since Matt's barbecue, I hadn't ventured out much. I'd received a load of nasty looks and someone had shouted at me when I went to the local shop for groceries, and I decided I was better off hiding away indoors.

When Chrissie argued that I couldn't hide forever, I decided there was safety in numbers and agreed to come out. We were subject to stares and murmurs as soon as we walked in and, even though Kelly had attempted to conceal us in a corner, I was still aware of the looks we were getting.

"I'm fine," I replied.

"People are just curious," Chrissie said. "Ignore them."

I smiled weakly, keeping my thoughts to myself. She had no idea; all she'd had was positive attention. It was hard to describe how it felt to have strangers in the street giving you abuse. It wasn't so easy for me to brush off, but I didn't want to ruin the evening by dwelling on it. I'd just eat and make an excuse to leave, I decided.

"This place is full of celebrities tonight," Kelly whispered after taking our order. "Try and be cool, won't you?"

"We're always cool," Matt said.

"It's very weird that we're celebrities," Chrissie said. "I can't quite get my head around it. Are you coming to Dylan's after work?" she asked Kelly.

"Maybe. I'll see what time I finish. It might be a late one. Once word gets out about all the famous people hanging around tonight, we'll probably get busy."

"It's already pretty busy," I said.

"This is nothing. They'll be queuing up later. I'd

better get on. Food won't be long."

She was right: the food arrived slightly too fast for my liking and wasn't particularly good. I slipped my hand into Adam's and decided I'd finish my drink and get him to take me home.

The toilets were at the opposite side of the room, beyond the bar. I walked quickly, in time with my heartbeat, trying to ignore the looks I was getting.

"You're that crazy one off the TV, aren't you?" a girl asked when I walked out of the toilet cubicle. She only looked about eighteen, and I had the feeling she'd followed me into the toilets on purpose.

"Yep. That's me," I told her, rinsing my hands quickly and heading for the door.

"Can I get a selfie with you?"

"No," I told her. "I'd rather not."

"Suit yourself!" she called after me as I made a quick exit.

I was trying to bypass a group of guys by the bar when one of them stepped directly into my path. "Excuse me," I said politely, trying to keep my head down and be invisible.

"Hey! What's up, Lucy?" he asked as though he knew me, loudly enough for his friends – and anyone else in the vicinity – to hear. His companions sniggered, and I went to move around the other side of him but he blocked my path.

"Can I just get past, please?" I looked up at him. His crooked smile was making me nervous.

"Come on, Lucy, stay and chat to me. Just because Matt's not keen doesn't mean no one else is interested." I got a whiff of his alcohol-fuelled breath and glanced over his shoulder, searching for Adam. "I don't mind them a bit crazy either," he leered loudly, to the amusement of his pals.

"Excuse me," I said again, but when I went to walk past him, he put a hand on my hip and pulled me back. I pushed his hand away and stepped aside just in time to see a fist whizz past me and land squarely in the middle of his face.

"Has anyone else got anything to say to my friend?" Kelly asked, inspecting her knuckle while her victim stared at her in shock, catching drops of blood as they fell from his nose. "Good! Then I'm going to ask you all politely to leave now. Or do I need to call the police?" They glanced at each other before placing their drinks on the bar and shuffling off through the restaurant.

"Come with me." Margaret appeared and led me behind the bar and into the corridor beyond.

"Are you okay?" Kelly patted my arm and I remembered to breathe.

"I need some air," I told them. Margaret announced she was going to get Adam, and Kelly led me out of a back door and into an alleyway.

"Thanks for rescuing me," I said to Kelly, who smiled and flexed her fingers. "Is your hand okay?"

"I'll survive," she told me. "What a creep."

"What's going on?" Adam appeared, looking worried. Chrissie and Matt were following close behind.

"I just want to go home," I told him and he put an arm around me. I really didn't want to fall apart behind the bins; I needed to get home quickly so I could collapse into a blubbering mess in private.

"Margaret said some guys were hassling you?"

Chrissie said.

"She's fine," Kelly told them. "Just take her home, Adam."

"Shall we come with you?" Chrissie offered.

"It's fine. I want to be on my own. I'll talk to you later." I made a poor attempt at a smile and walked quickly towards the road, with Adam hurrying to keep up.

"What happened?" he asked in the car, but I could only shake my head. I put all my energy into keeping tears at bay until I got home. He rested a hand on my knee and I turned away from him, leaning my head on the cool window.

"I'll call you tomorrow," I told him when he pulled up in front of my place. He put a hand on my arm but I jerked away, practically falling out of the car in my haste to escape. I made for the shelter of my apartment, ignoring Adam, who was calling my name. I shut the door behind me and blocked out the noise of the doorbell and Adam knocking at the door. Pacing the living room, I tried to control my breathing. The room spun and I gripped the back of the couch as a sob escaped me.

I wished Adam would leave. I heard him call my name again. Then I wished he would stay. Panic set in as soon as it went quiet, and I ran to open the door. He looked so solemn standing in the doorway. He looked at me for a moment before we moved at the same time, crashing into each other. I clung to him. Once I started to cry, I couldn't stop.

He moved me into the living room and onto the couch, cradling me until my hysterics subsided. I was reluctant to move my face from his shoulder – partly because I was sure I wasn't looking my best, but also because I didn't want to see the pity in his eyes. I was also quite comfy.

"I'll get you some water." He kissed the top of my head as I wiped away my tears. Finally deciding that making myself look decent was an impossible task, I gave up, lying on the couch and closing my eyes until Adam reappeared and placed a glass of water on the table before perching on the couch beside me.

"How did all this happen?" I asked vaguely. "I should never have gone to Majorca. Why didn't I just carry on home instead of stopping to talk to Chelsea?"

He looked hurt. "Don't say that."

"I can't even leave the house any more," I said.

"That's okay. We can just stay inside. It's not so bad." His mouth twitched into a half smile. As I sat up to kiss him, something primal kicked in and I suddenly just wanted to forget everything that was going on in my life. I pulled him roughly towards me and kissed him hard, moving back moments later to pull his T-shirt over his head. I could feel his apprehension, and knew he was probably worried about my current mental state, and whether or not I was fully in control of my actions.

I ran my fingers through his hair as I kissed him urgently, and when I eased back to lie on the couch I gave him no choice but to follow me, covering my body with his. I hushed him when he tried to speak, swallowing his words until he finally gave in and relaxed into me. My skin tingled with a million tiny electric shocks as I caressed his back and he kissed my neck.

"Hi!" Melissa's voice caught me by surprise,

leaving me confused and gasping for breath. "Don't mind me," she said loudly, with more than a hint of eye-rolling, then we heard her bedroom door slam shut. Adam collapsed onto me, letting out a low guttural sigh before pulling himself up and reaching for his T-shirt.

"Sorry," I told him sheepishly.

"No problem." He smiled. "Can I get a beer?"

I nodded and tried to compose myself when he went to the kitchen. I sat up to steal a swig of his beer and then lay back down, resting my feet in his lap as I finally told him what had happened in the restaurant, and how Kelly had come to my rescue.

"I wish I was the sort of person who could just punch someone in the face when they hassled me," I told him. "Although I'd probably have been arrested several times in the past week!"

"It's better to have friends who will beat people up for you," he mused, massaging my feet.

My eyelids slowly became heavier while we chatted, and at some point I drifted into a deep, dreamless sleep.

Waking to a combination of sunlight and birdsong, I pulled my duvet around me – before realising that I was still on the couch and Adam had gone. I was making coffee when I heard a shrill beeping coming from my bedroom. I stood in the doorway for a moment, looking at Adam, who was sprawled peacefully face down on my bed.

Silencing the incompetent alarm, I sat down to nudge him awake.

"How come I got the couch and you got my bed?" I asked when he forced his eyes open.

"You looked comfy." He stretched. "I didn't want to wake you and I couldn't be bothered to drive home."

He propped himself up on one elbow and I moved to kiss him. Then he reached for his phone to check the time. "I'm late for work," he groaned.

Chapter 33

"I'm so sorry, I honestly wanted to cook." Carl's wife, Lizzie, apologised to me for the third time.

"I'm more than happy with pizza," I said, watching Adam bounce nine-month-old Josh on his knee and pull faces at him.

"There's a guy coming to fix the oven tomorrow," Carl said.

"I'm fairly sure we need a new one," Lizzie told him. "Adam had a look at it and he couldn't fix it."

"Since when is Adam an expert on fixing ovens?" Carl sank on to the couch beside me.

"He's just handy with stuff like that." Lizzie looked at me. "He's an angel. Nothing would ever get done around here if it weren't for Adam."

"Hang on a minute," Carl said. "I'm perfectly capable of doing odd jobs!"

"We had a door that creaked for two years," Lizzie told me. "Adam was here two days and he fixed it."

"So he's handy with a can of WD-40!" Carl said.

"Well, you couldn't manage it!" she told him.

"It was on my list of things to do."

Adam grinned through their exchange. "There was that window that wouldn't open too."

"It took Adam all of about three minutes to fix that!" Lizzie smiled at me. "He's not a bad cook either."

"Are we trying to sell him, or what?" Carl said.

"No! He's not for sale. I couldn't cope without him. We're going to keep him with us forever. He's the glue that holds our marriage together!" She passed a bottle of milk to Adam. "See if you can get him to sleep before the pizzas get here, so we can eat in peace."

Adam sat back in his chair, cradling Josh in the crook of his arm before popping the bottle in his mouth.

"He's great with the baby too," Lizzie told me.

"Okay," Carl said. "Adam is wonderful. I think we've all got the message. We've not even mentioned the photos yet!"

"Aren't they gorgeous?" Lizzie looked up at the mantelpiece, which was adorned with framed family photos. "Adam takes the most fantastic photos."

"I had a look earlier. They're amazing." I glanced at Adam, whose eyes were on Josh. He was gently rocking him and hushing him as he gave him his bottle.

"Adam said the media attention has been pretty tough," Lizzie said, changing the subject.

"Yeah. I'm starting to feel a bit claustrophobic at home."

It was Wednesday, and this was the first time I'd left the apartment since the incident at Kelly's restaurant on Sunday. "I had to get my mum to go shopping for me yesterday. I couldn't bring myself to go to the shop."

Lizzie looked sympathetic. "People are awful, aren't they?"

"I can't believe how crazy it's all been. It feels like a bad dream."

"I wonder what they'll show on Friday," she mused.

"He's asleep," Adam announced, looking at Josh.

"I'd better take him up," Carl said. "Prove I'm not completely useless."

"If you wake him, I'm divorcing you and marrying Adam," Lizzie told him with a warning glance.

"Do I get any say in that?" Adam asked as he handed Josh to Carl and joined me on the couch.

"No," Lizzie said with a grin. "Are you working tomorrow?"

"Yeah, I'm in the studio tomorrow and then I have a week away from the place. I've got some private photo shoots lined up."

"That's good," she said.

The doorbell rang, and Adam went to answer it.

"Thanks for inviting me over," I said to Lizzie. "It's nice to get out of my apartment."

"You're welcome. Any friend of Adam's is a friend of ours," she told me. "We quite like him, in case you haven't noticed!"

"Me too," I replied automatically and felt myself blush as Lizzie smiled at me.

It was a lovely relaxed evening. Carl was such an easy-going character and I loved the affectionate bickering between him and Lizzie. They were warm and welcoming and the evening flew by.

"Come again, won't you?" Lizzie said, embracing me when we finally went to leave.

"I'd love to," I told her, hugging Carl before stepping outside with Adam and turning to wave at them.

"Want to see my room?" Adam asked as the security light came on and illuminated the driveway. I nodded and followed him to the garage at the side of the house.

"It's nice," I told him when we were inside.

"It's all Lizzie's decorating," he said as I took in the flowery wallpaper on one wall.

"Hmm, yes, it is quite feminine," I commented.

"They said I could redecorate but I'd feel bad about it. They'd only just done it up when my dad had his heart attack and I got rid of my place in the city." He went to sit on the edge of the bed, and I joined him. "It was supposed to be a guest room for when Lizzie's parents come to stay, since they don't live nearby. I was killing myself commuting to the city until they insisted I stay here."

"That was nice of them."

"They're amazing."

I nodded. "I had a great evening."

He leaned closer to me as the conversation fizzled out, and I relaxed into him. He brought his hands up to frame my face, then caressed my hair while he kissed me.

"Do you want to stay here?" he asked as he kissed my neck. I'm not sure why I tensed, but he obviously registered it. "Or I could drive you home?" he said.

I hesitated and my mind whirred while I tried to figure out what to do. I had no idea why I was reluctant to stay. The other night, at my place, I'd thrown myself at him and now, all of a sudden, I was unsure. I felt as though I couldn't trust myself to make decisions any more. In the past few weeks my life been had turned on its head several times, and my emotions were all over the place.

"I'm not sure," I said.

He planted a kiss on my nose. "I'll drive you home."

"Sorry," I said as we stood.

"It's fine."

"I just don't want you to think …" I trailed off, not sure what I was going to say.

"I don't think anything." He kissed me again before taking my hand and leading me out to the car. He chatted away in the car and I was glad that it wasn't awkward. I was laughing at his stories of him and Carl getting drunk and getting into trouble with Lizzie as we pulled up at my flat. I smiled lazily at his profile and regretted my decision not to stay with him.

"What?" he asked me.

"I feel like I'm going mad," I told him. "My head is such a mess with everything that's been going on. Is it completely crazy that I want to invite you in?"

"I'm going to go with fickle rather than crazy."

"Sorry," I said again and he leaned over to kiss me.

"It's really not a big deal. Get some sleep and sort your head out. I'll call you tomorrow."

"You're working tomorrow, aren't you?"

"Yeah, and it'll be a long day. I'll see you on Friday, though?"

"Great." I kissed him goodbye and got out of the car, kicking myself all the way inside and into my cold lonely bed.

Chapter 34

The gang assembled in the back room of the pub on Friday night and had a couple of drinks before moving upstairs to Dylan's apartment to watch the show. It was cramped with all of us in the cosy living room, and there was the usual banter, along with some speculation about what they were going to broadcast, while we waited for the show to begin.

Margaret suggested that after the success of the first show they would move straight to another and film the first show live this time. I didn't think they were finished with us yet, and grew increasingly nervous as the adverts came on before the show. I was sitting on a shabby beige couch, sandwiched between Chrissie and Adam. I leaned into Adam and he squeezed my hand reassuringly.

"Maybe they've engineered more footage and it's an hour of the girls in their bikinis fighting over Matt!" Ryan's voice reached me from somewhere behind me.

"Someone hit him, please," I called over my shoulder.

"Hey!" he shouted and I turned to see him cowering from Kelly who swatted at him playfully. "Maybe even mud wrestling," he added bravely and darted across the room to avoid Kelly. I turned and rolled my eyes at him before Dylan shushed us and turned up the volume on the TV.

We muttered our disdain when Jessica appeared on the screen. She was sitting on a blue couch, wearing a white suit and looking, in my opinion, like a complete bitch. There was a large screen to her left and she smiled into the camera which zoomed in on her.

I didn't trust Jessica and her production team one bit, and I was terrified of what lies she would tell next. I just wanted all the media attention to die down, but I had the feeling she wanted the exact opposite and would do anything to get her way.

She introduced herself as the show's producer, and then made some generic comments about the success of the show and remarked on the viewing figures before her tone changed.

"As I expected, the show caused quite a media storm, and we've all read and heard stories about our seven participants. What I can now reveal is that the majority of those stories were fabricated by my team and leaked to the press."

I was confused by her words. Had she really just admitted that they had made things up? I held my breath, waiting to see what would come next.

"I can also tell you that what you believed to be a reality TV show was far from reality." She paused. Her words hung in the air. "In the next hour we will begin to reveal the truth behind *A Trip to Remember,* and show you how the media can twist the truth until it is entirely unrecognisable. We used multiple camera angles and voice technology in order to create an entirely fake show. We'll reveal how we went from this …" She indicated the screen beside her and footage of us came on. This time it showed exactly what had happened, and I watched myself fall from the rope in the trees and dangle there, shouting at Matt, who looked down at me helplessly, leaving Adam to come to my rescue.

"My hero!" I grinned up at him, only to see a look of panic appear on his face.

"Well, there goes my street cred," Matt complained.

"To this," Jessica introduced the next clip, showing the edited version of us in the trees. This time, Matt came to my rescue. Or so it appeared.

"To be honest, I think their version is better," Matt said and received a slap on the leg from Chrissie.

"In case you're wondering who the real hero was," Jessica continued, "it was one of our cameramen, Adam Lewis. Which brings us to the next twist in the tale. Not only were our participants' words and actions distorted, but they were also led to believe that we were merely trialling a concept for a show. As far as they were concerned, the show would probably never be aired. They didn't know that the house was rigged with hidden cameras. We used camera operators in order to create a situation where the participants believed they weren't always being filmed.

"This evening we will show you the truth behind some of the pivotal moments in the show." She looked at the screen again and footage appeared of Chrissie and me laughing by the pool, right before I pushed her in. They then showed how they had made it look completely different by never showing our faces and editing what we said. It was amazing how easy it looked.

We were glued to the screen for the next hour while we watched ourselves on screen, both edited and unedited clips. It was fun to watch, and we laughed as we relived our holiday. At the end of the show, Jessica looked directly into the camera to address the audience again.

"Reality TV shows are always engineered to provide maximum entertainment. The contestants are chosen specifically for their entertainment value, and only the most TV-worthy moments will make it to your screen, displayed in the most dramatic way possible." She paused, re-crossing her legs and leaning towards the camera. "With *A Trip to Remember* we wanted to show you just how easy it is to manipulate footage." We waited in complete silence when she paused again. "But we won't do it again. RealTV24 will give you the chance to watch genuine, unedited footage of real everyday people. You'll be able to watch as we find people at random and follow them from packing for their holiday until they return home. To kick this off, over the course of the next week, we will broadcast the entire footage from *A Trip to Remember*, unedited, on RealTV24. You can switch over now to begin watching Lucy and the rest of our contestants twenty-four hours a day, or tune in every evening here on RDT1 to see the highlights. I'm confident you'll find the unedited version just as entertaining as the show we engineered! Good evening!" She sounded like a newsreader when she ended the show. Dylan immediately grabbed the remote to change to RealTV24.

"That's not good," Adam complained.

"What?" I looked at him to see if he was serious. "It's amazing! I don't have to convince people I'm not crazy. They'll see it for themselves."

"I hate to break it to you," Matt said, "but you probably come off as slightly crazy anyway!"

"I can live with *slightly* crazy," I told him.

I looked behind me and noticed that Ryan had gone as white as a sheet. "I need to go and find a rock to live under," he told me as he caught me looking at him. "No offence," he said to Margaret, making us all laugh.

"Oh no!" Chrissie suddenly looked horrified. "They're going to show everything!"

"And?" Kelly asked. "It's not so bad, is it? Unless you're Margaret or Ryan!"

"It's just that everything will be shown," Chrissie said. "Every conversation we had. Even when we thought there were no cameras around."

I began to think of all my late-night chats with Chrissie and realised that Adam would know everything I said about him. That would be embarrassing.

"What are you so worried about?" Matt asked Chrissie.

"It's just going to be embarrassing, that's all. I said some things when I thought we weren't being filmed."

"Were you talking about me?" Matt asked her in a silly voice as he squeezed her cheek.

"Get off!" She swatted his hand away as a smile crept over her face.

"Oh, wait!" Dylan said, his eyes twinkling. "I don't think you should be teasing anyone, Matt! You might have said something about the girls, if I remember correctly." He gave Matt a knowing look, and I watched in amusement as Matt's face fell.

"Oh crap," he said slowly as his eyes went wide. He raised his hands to cover his face briefly and then gently squeezed Chrissie's arm. "Well, this has been fun, babe. Maybe we should just end things on a positive note and go our separate ways …"

"What did you say?" she growled at him, and he winced as he glanced at me.

"Don't tell me it involves me too?" I asked.

"Oh, God." He sighed as he glanced at Kelly and then Margaret. "Right. I'm sure we all said things behind closed doors which we'd rather people didn't see, so I think we should make a pact that none of us watch it … and maybe go and live in a cave somewhere?"

"Oh!" I gasped as a thought hit me. I looked at Kelly and cringed. "Matt and I were mean about you."

"What did you say?" she glared at us.

"What?" Matt jumped in. "When?"

"On the plane," I reminded him.

"That wasn't really mean." He grinned. "I think we judged you by your blondness. But you didn't prove us wrong!"

"And, in Matt's defence," Dylan jumped in, "he later rated you ten out of ten for looks …"

"Shut up!" Matt shouted. "No spoilers! If people want to know their ratings, they need to watch the show. Now let's go downstairs and I'll buy everyone a drink."

"That would be nice!" Dylan said. "I've been thinking it might be time people started paying for drinks."

"But we only hang out here for the free drinks," Kelly told him with a cheeky grin.

"Are you okay?" I asked Adam, who'd gone suspiciously quiet.

"Hey! You're going to be a TV star now too," Matt said.

"I think I'm going to go home," Adam said.

"Why?" Matt asked. "We're going down for drinks now."

Adam shrugged and we started to make our way downstairs. "I'm going to head off," he told me while the rest of the gang helped themselves to drinks in the back room of the pub.

"What's wrong?" I asked.

"Nothing," he said when I followed him out of the backdoor. "I'll call you tomorrow. Will you be okay getting home?"

"I'm fine." I tried to smile, but my confusion must have been evident.

"Sorry – it's just that I'm going to be splashed across the media now too. That's why they didn't care that I interacted with you. They knew it would make great TV."

"It won't be so bad. Most of the time you weren't doing anything. Besides, it can't be worse than what I've had to deal with."

"But you *chose* it!" he snapped. "They asked you to be on a TV show and you agreed, even if you didn't really know what you were getting into. I was just doing my job."

"Okay." I stepped back, stunned by his tone. "I didn't really choose for everything I said and did to be twisted."

"I know." His eyes softened and he took a step towards me. "I'm sorry. I didn't mean it like that."

"It's fine. Just go home."

"I'm sorry," he said again, pulling me to him. "I want to talk to Carl and check over our contracts. I hope they can't air all the footage of us legally, but due to the nature of the show, they updated our contracts. I didn't think anything of it at the time, but I guess they've covered all their bases. You go back inside and have a good night. I'll talk to you tomorrow."

I gave him a quick kiss and went back inside.

"What do you want to drink?" Ryan shouted over the bar. He was mixing cocktails again.

"Nothing, thanks. I'm going to go too."

"Is everything okay?" Chrissie asked. "What's going on with Adam?"

"It's fine," I told her. "He's just stressed."

"Do you want me to come with you?" she offered.

"No, stay and have fun. I'll be fine. I just don't really feel very sociable."

"I'll come and make sure you find a taxi," Matt said.

"You don't need to; I'm quite capable."

"Shut up and let me be a gentleman!" He nudged me towards the door and I shouted goodbye to the rest of the gang.

Chapter 35

Max and Jacob jumped all over me the minute I walked through the door the following evening.

"How are you?" Kerry asked, shooing the boys out of the way to hug me.

"Okay, I suppose."

"So I get to watch what really happened now?" she said. "This is going to be fun."

"Don't watch it," I pleaded with her. "I'm embarrassed. And actually, I wanted to talk to Dad. I said some things … and I just thought I'd better talk to him in case he sees it."

"Okay." She looked at me sympathetically. "We were just going to eat, though."

"Great, I'm starving. I'll talk to him later. I presume there's enough food for me?"

"Always," she told me cheerfully.

Over dinner, the boys flicked from one bizarre conversation to the next, and we covered topics from where dinosaurs go to buy shoes to why some eggs are for hatching and some are for eating. They never stopped talking, and they never failed to make me laugh.

"You two clear up," Kerry instructed Dad and me. "I promised the boys I'd play a game with them before bed."

I smiled at her, knowing that was my cue to chat to Dad.

"Have you started job-hunting yet?" Dad asked when I followed him into the kitchen with plates in both hands.

"Not yet."

"Sorry, Kerry told me not to ask. I just wondered, that's all."

"It's fine. I can live off my savings for a couple of months. With all this TV stuff, I haven't had time to think about getting another job. I'd like to find something I really want to do, rather than just take what I can find."

He nodded vaguely as he started loading the dishwasher. I scraped and washed the dishes and handed them to him. "Are you okay with all the stuff on the TV now? Kerry was worried it'd upset you." He was clearly uncomfortable with the subject.

"Yeah, it'll all be fine," I told him. "But I did want to talk to you about it … They're going to show everything now. An uncut, unedited version …"

"Yeah, I watched the show with Kerry last night."

"Okay." I hesitated, not quite sure how to go on. "I just wanted to warn you. I think I said some things about you and Mum … not really bad, but just …"

"I don't care," he said, straightening up from the dishwasher to look me in the eye.

"I can't remember exactly what I said, but it definitely wasn't complimentary." I bit my lip, feeling terrible.

"Look …" He flicked the kettle on and passed me the biscuit tin. "I'm well aware that you didn't have the easiest of childhoods, and I'm sorry about that …"

He put his hand up to silence me as I tried to butt in. "I know how it was with your mum, and I definitely didn't win any Father of the Year awards. Nothing you say on that TV show is going to make me think or feel any differently about you."

"Okay," I said as tears filled my eyes.

"You'll be okay," he told me. "Kerry says that when all this media stuff blows over, all you'll remember is that you had a great time. And she's usually right! But don't tell her I said that." He smiled at me, heading for the living room with a cup of tea for Kerry.

"How's things with Adam?" Kerry asked cautiously as Dad took the kids to read them their bedtime story.

"Great," I told her.

"You've been seeing a lot of him?"

"Most days since we got back. It's all a bit of a whirlwind, really, but everything's great." I felt my face light up as I spoke about him. I'd felt pretty deflated the previous evening, but he'd called in the morning and we'd had a good chat. I'd laughed with him on the phone and hated hanging up when he had to go to work. Whenever I wasn't with him I was thinking about when I'd see him next.

"Just be careful," Kerry warned. My face fell slightly at her negative tone.

"I am. I know it all seems pretty fast …"

"It *is* fast," she corrected. "How long have you known him?"

"Not long …"

"Just a couple of weeks. I'm worried about you."

"Why? I'm happy – happier than I can ever remember being."

"I just don't want you to get hurt. Let's be honest: when it comes to men you don't have much experience."

I took a breath, not liking where this conversation was going. "Why does that matter?"

"Go slowly, that's all I'm saying. You don't need to rush things. I don't want you to get your heart broken."

"It's not a fling," I told her defensively. "I love him." It was the first time I'd said it aloud but it was true. I had fallen for him completely.

She didn't react, but I felt as though she was making a determined effort not to roll her eyes. "Does he love you?" she asked.

"I don't know. I think so. Maybe." I hoped so. I really thought he felt the same way but I didn't know. Kerry's words sparked my insecurity. What if I was being naïve and rushing into things? What if, for him, this was just a fling?

"I'm sorry." Kerry's features softened as she looked at me. "I love that you're so happy. I'm just worried about you, that's all."

"Thanks. You don't need to worry, though. Everything is going to be fine."

Chapter 36

I picked up the phone to call Adam late on Sunday morning and hesitated before I pressed dial, suddenly worried that I'd seem too keen, which was ridiculous. He called me all the time.

I relaxed and sank back into the couch as soon as I heard his cheerful voice.

"What are you doing today?" I asked, deciding that I could be the one to ask him on a date for a change.

"I have to work," he told me, sounding distracted.

"Oh, okay." I didn't quite manage to hide my disappointment.

"What have you got planned for the day?" he asked.

"Apart from my busy schedule of hiding from the world?" I joked. "Not much. I might go and see Dylan later; some of the others will probably be there too."

"You could come with me if you want," he said.

"To work? At the TV studio?"

"No, I'm doing a family photo shoot. You could be my assistant. The pay's not great, but it might be fun."

"What does your assistant have to do?"

"Hold my camera bag, keep an eye on the lighting …"

"I could probably carry the bag," I told him. "I'm not sure about the lighting."

"Well, we'll be outside, so it's basically watching

out for clouds."

"Maybe I could manage that."

"Great. It's a bit of a drive – out near my place."

"I don't know." I wavered. "Won't I be in the way?"

"No. It'll be fun. I'll take you out for dinner after."

"Okay, then. If you're sure?"

"It's fine. I'll pick you up in an hour."

I hung up and smiled to myself. Only an hour until I saw him.

It was a beautiful summer's day and I opted to wear a cute green sundress and a pair of ballet pumps. I didn't even have to call Chrissie for wardrobe advice. Adam kissed me when I opened the door to him, and I wrapped my arms around him. He held my hand when we walked to the car, and we settled into an easy silence as we headed out of town.

"What are you grinning at?" he asked me.

"Nothing," I told him. "I'm just happy."

"Good," he told me, reaching for my hand.

"How's the hand?" I asked, inspecting the bandage, which looked smaller than the original.

"Much better, but don't tell Matt. I'll keep making him feel guilty for as long as possible!"

Without thinking, I pulled his hand to my face and kissed his knuckle, just beside the bandage. I blushed as he turned to look at me, retrieving his hand to change gear when he slowed for the traffic lights. "Sorry," I whispered.

"You're quite distracting," he told me when he stopped at the lights, drawing me to him for a kiss.

"Sorry!" I said as he returned his attention to the road, pulling away when the light turned green. I went back to smiling to myself as I took in the scenery out of the window. It felt good to get out of the city. There was something peaceful about the narrow country roads that weaved through the fields and villages. I felt like I might burst with happiness. Just being in Adam's presence made me feel drunk.

I thought about Kerry's advice about being careful and not getting hurt, but I dismissed it. I just wanted to enjoy every moment. I didn't want to miss out on something because I was too scared to take a chance. Even though I'd not known him long, I felt so comfortable with Adam.

"So what are we doing today?" I asked.

"Family photos for Ben and Angela, with their two kids Harry and Zac. We're meeting them in a park near their house. We'll just follow them around and take photos. Easy!"

"How old are the kids?" I asked, thinking that if they were five-year-olds like my brothers it definitely wouldn't be easy.

"I think they're about four and seven. Something like that. Nice kids."

"You know them?"

"Angela went to school with my sister, Becky. I bumped into her a while back at my parents' place. She was helping Mum prepare for some bake sale or something. Anyway, I ended up keeping the kids entertained while she was helping Mum, and when she found out I still did photography, she asked me if I'd take some photos for them."

"That's nice."

"Yeah, they're a lovely family, so it should be fun."

***

They were ready and waiting for us when we pulled up. "Can we play now?" I heard the younger boy whining as we approached them.

"Hi." The young mother greeted Adam with a kiss on the cheek. "I told the kids they couldn't go to the playground. I didn't want them getting all dirty before the photos."

"Your mum's right." He looked down at the boys. "Let's take some photos and then we can play." He reached to shake the dad's hand before turning to me. "This is Lucy, who has volunteered to help me out today," he told them. "'Volunteer' might not be quite the right word," he admitted as Angela and Ben introduced themselves with a handshake.

"Can we play football?" the older boy asked, eyeing the ball Adam had tucked under his arm.

"Later," he replied. "First let's have a race up to that tree over there …" He pointed to a huge oak tree at the other side of the field. "First one to touch the tree gets to take the first photo." He handed me the football and pulled his Nikon out of its case. The boys looked thoroughly impressed. "I knew you'd come in useful," he told me, smiling, as he passed me his backpack and camera case, keeping hold of the camera.

"On your marks, get set, go!" he shouted. The boys took off at a run and Adam paused before jogging after them. "See you up there," he called back to us.

"He's got far too much energy," Ben commented.

"It's because he's not got kids," Angela told him. "People who don't have kids are always full of energy."

"How old are they?" I asked.

"Zac's the eldest," Angela said. "He's seven. Harry's just turned five."

"They look like fun."

"Yeah," Ben sighed. "I'm getting too old for fun, though!"

I watched Adam racing up the hill with the boys. When Harry started to lag, Adam scooped him up, carrying him to keep up with Zac, who was getting ahead. He deposited the delighted little boy back on the ground in time for him to reach the tree at the same time as his brother.

"He might just have averted World War Three there," Angela commented.

"So what do you do, Lucy?" Ben asked. "When you're not volunteering to help Adam?"

"Oh, I … hmm. I'm sort of between jobs at the moment."

"Sorry." Ben grinned at me. "Did I ask the wrong question?"

"No, it's fine. I was working in an office but I was made redundant recently. I'm supposed to be job-hunting, but I've no idea what I want to do."

"So you're kind of on holiday?" Angela suggested.

"I guess that would be one way to look at it!"

We approached Adam, who was crouching with the boys on either side of him, fascinated by his camera. He looped the strap over Zac's head and passed him the camera. Zac aimed it in our direction. Next he gave it to Harry, who looked very proud of himself while he snapped some photos of us.

"What took you so long?" Adam asked us when we

joined them.

"Some of us are old and weary!" Ben said.

"You want this?" Angela asked, producing a green tartan blanket from her shoulder bag.

"Yes." Adam took it from her and laid it out under the tree. "It's better if it's your own stuff in the pictures."

"I'll move the bags out of the way," I said, picking up Angela's bag to add to the collection draped over my shoulder.

"Thank you," Adam told me, a twinkle in his eye.

"There's a cloud just there, by the way." I smiled, pointing to the lone cloud in the perfectly blue sky.

"I don't know how I ever managed without you," he teased as I wandered away. There was a bench further up the hill and I parked myself on it, scattering the bags on the ground around me and tilting my face to the sun. It was an amazing location. The huge oak tree was stunning in the vast green field. At the edge of the field was a stream, then the start of a forest. I was sure the photos would be amazing.

I watched while the family positioned themselves on the blanket and Adam snapped away. He'd stop and chat to them, making everyone laugh, before taking more photos.

They moved over to the edge of the forest, Adam hopping over stepping stones to get to the other side of the stream to photograph them from there. The kids took off their shoes and socks to paddle in the shallow water, and I watched Adam do the same. I couldn't see what happened next, but I heard some sudden shrieks of joy and watched Adam move to Zac and place something in his hands.

"We caught a frog!" he shouted up to me, and I smiled when Ben took it from Zac to chase Angela with it. This caused much hilarity, and Adam snapped away while Ben and Angela played with their kids. I loved watching Adam work. He was completely different than he'd been in Majorca. That had seemed like a job, whereas today he was concentrated and focused but also full of life and passion. He obviously loved what he was doing, and it was fascinating to watch him.

"You okay?" Adam jogged over to me and reached into his backpack for a bottle of water.

"Yeah, it's beautiful here."

"You're not bored?"

"Not at all. I'm quite happy."

"Good." He gave me a quick kiss. "I have to go and play football now," he told me, grinning as he retrieved the ball from under the bench and headed back to the boys, who were running around the tree.

"You got a good spot." Angela joined me on the bench, leaving the boys kicking the ball around with their dad.

"It's gorgeous," I told her.

"That's our house over there." She pointed back down to the road where we'd parked the car. "The yellow one."

"So you have all this on your doorstep? It's amazing."

"Yeah – village life can get claustrophobic sometimes but I can't complain about this." We watched Adam and Ben chase the kids around the field for a while before Angela broke the silence. "I saw you on TV, by the way."

"Oh no! Really?"

"I told Ben not to say anything, but I think it's killing him."

"I thought maybe it hadn't reached you out here…"

"You think we don't have TV?" she asked me with a laugh.

"No!" I said. "I just thought that maybe you had better things to do or something."

"No! We live in a village; nothing ever happens here. TV addicts, the lot of us! It was fun seeing Adam on TV yesterday," she told me. "Then when you stepped out of the car with him today, I thought Ben's eyes would burst out of his head! We don't get many celebrities round these parts."

"I'm really embarrassed now," I told her. "I've hardly been out in public since we got back. I thought I'd be safe here."

"I feel awful for you," she told me sympathetically. "It's amazing how easily they twisted everything, isn't it?"

"Yeah. When I watched the edited version, it even confused me. I almost believed it was real. I thought I was going mad."

"So what really happened? Can I get some spoilers?"

"I've lost track of what's been shown on TV," I told her, trying to think of something to tell her. "Margaret and Ryan had a drunken snog …"

"No!" Her eyes went wide. "Really?"

"Yeah. He was mortified." I reached into Adam's backpack for the bottle of water. "It was hilarious. He's going to be so embarrassed when they air that."

"That's brilliant! How was it really? Did you enjoy

it?"

"I had a fantastic time," I told her, replacing the cap on the water and stretching out my legs in the sunshine.

"What was everyone like?" she asked eagerly. "Do you mind me asking? I'm fascinated by it all."

"I don't mind," I told her. It was actually really nice chatting to her. "Everyone was lovely. I got on with everyone. We've been meeting up since we've been home as well. They're like family to me now."

"What about Matt?" she asked. "I really believed you were in love with him, but that was obviously not true … Oh, but that moment when you were watching Adam sleep and he woke up – that was the cutest thing ever!"

My shoulders shook as I started laughing and couldn't stop.

"Sorry!" Angela told me. "I'm being weird, aren't I? Don't tell Ben. Not after I told him not to say anything to you!"

"Matt's lovely," I told her when I got my laughter under control. "But we're just friends."

"So what about you and Adam?"

"We ended up kissing in a cupboard during a game of hide and seek," I confessed with a smile.

"Brilliant!" She sighed. "And I guess things are still going well if you're having dinner with his parents. I had to call and drop some papers off with Ruth earlier and she was panicking about whether or not you were a vegetarian. I told her I'd seen you eat chicken on TV so I thought she was safe! Sorry," she said quickly as my eyes went wide. "I'm being really weird, aren't I? Knowing what you eat …"

"It's not that," I told her. "It's knowing where I'm having dinner that's surprised me. Because I didn't know that."

"Oh my God!" She put a hand to her mouth. "Are you serious?"

"Adam said he'd take me out for dinner … but he never mentioned where."

"I've put my foot in it, haven't I?"

I nodded but found it amusing. "It seems like it."

"He must like you, though, if he's taking you for dinner at his parents' place. And Ruth obviously took a shine to you, so you're doing well. You know, I had the biggest crush on Adam when we were teenagers, but I was terrified of his mum and his sister." She stopped talking suddenly and looked at me, her eyes big. "What is wrong with me today? I keep saying stupid things! I'm sorry. I should have just left you in peace."

"Don't worry," I reassured her. "It's usually me talking too much, so this is a nice change. Anyway I thought you were friends with his sister?"

"Becky was my best friend … but she was still terrifying! Come on, let's go and join them."

We walked in silence back to the blanket, where Adam and Ben were chatting. The boys were still happily kicking the football to each other.

"Guess what?" Angela said to Ben when she sat down beside him on the blanket. "Ryan kissed Margaret!"

"No way!" Ben replied. "That's not true." He looked at Adam, who nodded. "Wow!" Ben laughed. "What else? Tell me more!"

"You need to get a life!" Adam laughed at him as I

took a seat next to him on the grass and he moved his hand to my knee.

"These two kissed in a cupboard!" Angela told him excitedly, making me burst out laughing.

"The cupboard didn't have any cameras in it," Adam informed them, a smile spreading across his face. "So it's basically Lucy's word against mine. And we all know she's a bit crazy!"

"Hey!" I shoved him until he lost his balance and ended up lying on the grass.

"Why are you telling them the one thing that happened away from the cameras?" he said through his laughter.

"I forgot there weren't any cameras," I told him. "It just slipped out!"

"We got an exclusive," Ben turned to high-five Angela. "We can dine out on this for weeks!"

"Speaking of dining out … where are we going for dinner tonight?" I asked Adam with raised eyebrows.

"Well, it was going to be a surprise," he replied cautiously. "But I'm guessing village gossip has ruined that."

"Sorry," Angela shrugged, looking fairly sheepish.

"Didn't you promise the kids ice creams?" Ben looked at Angela with wide eyes. "Now would be a good time for ice creams, wouldn't it?"

"Perfect!" she agreed, telling us they'd be right back and mouthing another apology at Adam.

"How did Angela know?" Adam turned on his side to look at me. I shrugged and he took my hand. "I'd already arranged to have dinner with my parents before I spoke to you. I don't know why I didn't tell you that. I guess I thought you might not come."

"You were probably right there," I told him plainly.

"Sorry. We don't have to go …"

"She's already cooked!"

"True." He raised an eyebrow. "Do you mind?"

"I guess not," I told him. "But if this is some elaborate seduction plan, then I have to say it's a bit weird. And Matt's going to have a field day when he finds out!"

"How about we don't mention it to Matt …" he suggested, pulling me down to lie on the grass beside him.

"Okay," I agreed. "But maybe next time you could warn me about stuff like dinner with your parents."

"Deal!" He moved up on one elbow and leaned over to kiss me. I stroked his hair as he lingered over me, our noses touching. He kissed my forehead before sitting up to look down the hill and wave at the boys, returning with ice creams in their hands.

Adam reached for his camera and took some more photos of the boys, happily licking their ice creams and getting messier by the second.

"Here, give me that." Angela reached for Adam's camera. Adam put an arm around my shoulders as Angela aimed the camera at us. I rested my head on Adam's shoulder, letting Angela capture a moment of pure happiness.

Chapter 37

"I've seen you on the TV," Adam's dad, Tom, told me bluntly when we were introduced. "But apparently I've got to pretend you're not a lunatic!" He winked at me and we took a seat in the living room. It was a cosy room, neat and orderly but homely, with an array of ornaments and framed photos along the mantelpiece.

"I said to pretend you've not seen her on the telly!" Ruth clucked as she moved out of the living room.

I asked if I could help with anything, but she told me to stay put.

"I knew there was something I wasn't supposed to mention," Tom chuckled. "How was the photo shoot this afternoon?"

"Don't talk about that yet!" Ruth shouted from the kitchen. "Or come in the kitchen if you want to talk …"

Tom's eyes sparkled and he flashed me a grin. "She doesn't like to miss out! She worries she'll miss some gossip to share at her committee meetings. She's on about seven different committees; I think they mostly meet to swap gossip."

"What are you saying?" Ruth's voice drifted through to us.

"Come on." Adam nudged my leg and stood up.

"It'll be killing her, thinking she's missing out."

"I'd better get drinks too before I get shouted at," Tom told me. He radiated warmth and I liked him immediately.

"Tom!" Ruth shouted as we walked into the kitchen. "Get drinks for everyone, will you?"

Tom rolled his eyes and pulled a bottle of wine from the rack in the corner of the kitchen. "Everyone all right with red?" he asked.

"We've got white if you'd prefer, Lucy?" Ruth turned to me. "Or beer …"

"Red's fine. Are you sure I can't help?"

"Yes, everything's ready. Let's go and sit down." We followed her out of the kitchen and into the back room of the house.

"We're eating in the dining room?" Adam commented. "It's not Christmas, is it?"

"We often eat in here." Ruth tutted, moving around the table. "Take a seat, Lucy."

I pulled out the chair nearest to me, setting my wine down while Ruth reached for my plate and served me a square of lasagne.

"By often, she means once every year," Tom told me quietly.

"Oh shush, you two!" Ruth reprimanded them, handing Adam a plate of lasagne. "It's nice to eat in here sometimes."

I saw Tom eyeing the lasagne, looking slightly puzzled as he handed his plate to Ruth. "This looks great," he told her.

"Oh, it's not for you," she told him, jumping up and rushing out of the room.

"I thought it was too good to be true," Tom

commented. "Don't ever have a heart attack! I've not been allowed anything tasty to eat in a long time."

Ruth came back with a piece of grilled chicken for Tom. "Sorry, I forgot all about it. There's salad too."

"I think you just like torturing me," he told her, looking longingly at the lasagne.

"Sorry, but Adam's here and lasagne's his favourite," she told him, returning to her seat. "Tuck in," she instructed, waving her fork at me.

I did as I was told and felt sorry for Tom; the lasagne was delicious. Silence settled over us while we ate. I hadn't realised how hungry I was until I had started eating.

"Tell me about this afternoon, then," Ruth prompted as she reached for her wine glass. "Did you have a nice time with Angela and Ben?"

"I had a great time," I told her.

"Did you get some good photos, Adam?"

"I hope so. I'll start going through them tomorrow."

"They're a lovely family, aren't they?" Ruth remarked.

"They're really nice. Angela was good fun," I told her. "You've known her a long time?"

"Since she was a little girl. She had a bit of a wild streak as a teenager, but she turned out well."

I couldn't help but smile at Ruth's assessment.

"I wouldn't say she was wild," Tom commented. "But she did have her eye on Adam, and Ruth thought she wasn't good enough for our little prince so we had to make her feel as unwelcome as possible!"

"What?" Adam asked with his mouth full. "Angela never had a thing for me."

"Oh, she did!" Ruth argued. "And she was two

293

years older than you."

"He was such a geek," Tom told me, a glint in his eyes. "He's been obsessed with cameras since he was big enough to pick one up. When he was sixteen, Angela would come around wearing Wonderbras and skirts no bigger than my belt ... Adam didn't even notice. He was too busy taking photos of daffodils!"

"That's not true!" Adam laughed. "Why are you making up stories? Angela only ever came over to hang out with Becky."

"No, she had a crush on you," I grinned at him while I loaded up my fork. "She told me today!"

"See!" Tom said.

"Why did she tell you that?" Adam smirked. "What's wrong with the woman that she can't even keep her own secrets?"

"I thought she was funny."

"If she had a crush on me, I never knew it," Adam said.

"You were the only one who didn't notice," Tom shook his head. "I don't think Becky was impressed that her best friend had a crush on her little brother. Poor Angela never stood a chance."

"Does Becky live nearby?" I asked.

"No," Tom said. "She lives in France."

"We hardly see her," Ruth complained. "And she's got two beautiful girls. I never get to see my grandkids."

"That's not really true," Tom said. "They visit quite often."

Adam looked at me. "Mum can't understand why anyone would leave the village."

"Well, I would've understood if she wanted to

move into the city," Ruth said. "But France?"

"Awful place," Adam said in a mocking tone.

"Full of baguettes and croissants!" Tom laughed. "And people talk funny, you know?"

"Don't tease," Ruth told them. "Is it really so terrible to want to have your family around you?"

She tutted and returned her attention to her plate as Adam and Tom exchanged a look.

"That was great, thanks," Adam said, pushing his plate away and leaning back in his chair. I nodded my agreement as I finished. "We might have to go soon," Adam announced.

"You can't go," Tom said. "We've not shown Lucy your baby photos yet!"

"Well, that would be fun!" Adam rolled his eyes. "But we have to drive back to Manchester tonight so we can't stay long. I'll help tidy up." He stood and started to stack plates, but Ruth moved round the table and took them out of his hands.

"Your dad and I will clean up. Why don't you show Lucy the garage?" she said over her shoulder as she walked out of the room.

"Come on." Adam took my hand, standing up and leading me through the house. He turned to me when we stepped out of the front door. "I should definitely not have brought you over for dinner."

"Why?" I asked. "It was lovely."

"I always thought I had quite cool parents," he told me. "I never realised how embarrassing they are."

"They're not that bad!" I said and reached up to kiss him.

"I can't believe my dad called me a geek!"

"Your dad's so sweet."

"Yeah, he's pretty cool, actually – when he's not calling me a geek!" He pulled me around the side of the house towards the garage.

"I think you're still a bit geeky," I teased, bumping shoulders with him.

"Well, these days I do at least notice hot women flaunting themselves around me!"

"What's that's supposed to mean?"

"You, in your tiny little bikinis," he said, grinning. "It was like torture!"

"They were Chrissie's bikinis," I corrected him, embarrassed. "What's in the garage, then?"

"My photos," he told me. He unlocked the side door and stepped inside, feeling around for the light switch.

"Wow," I gasped when the lights flickered on and I stepped inside. Framed photos of every size lined every wall. "This is amazing. Is this your niece?" I moved to admire a photo of a little girl blowing a dandelion clock, sending the tiny white umbrellas flying out against the bright blue sky. She had eyes the same colour as the sky – and the look of wonder in them was amazing.

"Yes, that's Emily. That's from their last visit, a couple of months ago. That's her sister, Hailey," he added as I moved to look at another picture. Hailey was walking through a field, looking over her shoulder to smile straight into the camera. It was simple but stunning.

"They're beautiful girls," I told him, unable to take my eyes from the pictures.

"Nah, I'm just good with a camera … They're ugly little things in real life."

I smiled at the humour in his voice and turned to see him perching on a wooden table in the middle of the room. My eyes were drawn back to the picture of Emily. It was incredible. I picked it up to take a closer look.

"It looks as though she might just step out of the picture," I said. "It's amazing." I felt Adam's eyes on me while I wandered around trying to take everything in. "Is this where we were today?" I asked, looking at a picture of a stream flowing next to a forest.

"Yeah."

"You were right about the photos in the pub. I thought they were great, but these are something else. They're stunning. How do you take photos like that?" I couldn't quite get my head around it. "I feel like I'd get my hand wet if I touched it. The water looks as though it's flowing."

"It *was* flowing!" he told me with a cheeky grin.

"You know what I mean." I looked up at him, but he just shrugged. "They're brilliant," I told him, overwhelmed by his talent. "Where do you sell them?" I asked while I browsed some more.

"I don't, yet."

"Not at all? Why not?" I hopped up beside him on the table and my eyes wandered around the room, drawn to the beauty of the photographs.

"I'm not sure. The TV work pays well, and it's a pretty steady income. I love taking these," he indicated the photos, "but I only really think of it as a hobby. It's taken me years to build up a collection. I find a place that I want to capture and then keep revisiting the same spot until the light is exactly right. I worry that if I was dependent on photography for an income, the pressure would take all the fun out of it."

"It just seems a shame. You looked so happy today when you were taking photos of Angela and Ben and the kids."

"I love doing the photo shoots too, but it's hard to make a living from it. A lot of the work can only be done at the weekends and evenings. That's the stuff I really enjoy: when I get to be part of people's lives. Weddings, baby photos, family photos, graduations … I like the thought of taking photos that people will treasure, and kids growing up with my photos on the walls of their home. Plus, it's just nice work. But it's sporadic. The TV work isn't that reliable either, but in the past few years I've managed to line up contracts steadily. The money's good but the contracts are only ever short. A six-month contract is considered a lottery win."

"But if you sold these as well as doing the photo shoots, can't you make a living that way?"

"That's the plan," he told me. "I guess the TV work is just less of a risk. Once the mortgage is paid off I'll give it a go. That's what I keep telling myself: pay the bills and then chase the dream."

"It's such a shame that you keep all this hidden away, though."

"Now you sound like my mum!"

"Well, she's right. Why can't you sell them now?"

"I need to set up a website and stuff …"

"Are you worried that they won't sell? Because they would." I moved from the table to take a closer look at the rainbow he'd captured arcing over hills, while oblivious ducks swam on a pond in the foreground. "They would definitely sell. You wouldn't even need a website to start with – just ask a few cafés to display them for you. Anyone would want these hanging on their walls."

"You and my mother might be biased," he told me. "Come on, I'd better get you home."

"I might be biased," I conceded when he turned off the garage light. "But I'm also right. You're really talented and they would sell themselves. I would buy one. More, if I could afford it! How much are they?"

"You couldn't even afford *one*." He pulled me to him.

His lips had just brushed mine when a knock interrupted us. I looked towards the house and saw Ruth standing in the kitchen window, peering out at us and holding up a cup. "Tea?" she mouthed.

Adam sighed and led me back to the front door. "Time to say goodbye. Stop laughing," he ordered. "It's not funny!"

"It's a bit funny," I told him.

We said our goodbyes and headed back down to Adam's house to pick up the car. I enjoyed the weight of his arm around my shoulder when we walked in silence into the village.

Darkness was falling over the village and a quarter-moon hung over the pub, beckoning me to it. "Do you want to get a drink?" I asked.

"I shouldn't drink any more," he told me. "And I'll probably fall asleep at the wheel if we don't get going soon."

"Okay." I hesitated when we reached his house. "Or we could just stay here tonight and drive back tomorrow …"

"We could do that," he agreed.

"Okay." I tried my best to sound confident. "Good." I walked up the path to the house.

"Thought you wanted to go for a drink?" he said, following me.

"I changed my mind. Do *you* want to go for a drink?"

"Not really," he said with a boyish grin. "I'm just hoping that my mum's been and tidied my bedroom recently!"

I smiled, shaking my head as I followed him over the threshold and inside.

Chapter 38

I woke blissfully happy: my head on Adam's chest, an arm draped over his torso, and my legs tangled with his. I had to fight the urge to tell him I loved him when he kissed the top of my head and whispered, "Good morning".

"Can we stay here forever?" I murmured into his chest.

"Yeah," he said and I lifted my head to look at him, then lowered my lips to his.

Forever didn't last long. Adam got up to answer the door mid-morning, and was greeted by a gaggle of reporters wanting interviews and obnoxiously snapping photos before he closed the door on them.

"Maybe you should've put a T-shirt on," I told him from the stairs as he pulled the curtains in the living room, dressed only in a pair of jeans.

"It looks better on you," he said, glancing up at me.

I tugged at his T-shirt which I'd thrown on, and smiled before heading to the shower. Afterwards, I went downstairs, feeling refreshed and back in my own clothes. A mug of coffee waited for me on the table and I picked it up and moved to where Adam was sitting at his corner desk.

"They look great," I said, when I caught sight of yesterday's photos on his laptop.

"Yeah, they came out well. I just need to cut eight hundred photos down to thirty or forty now and then make sure they're perfect."

"Does it take long?"

"Yeah. Do you mind hanging around here today?" He looked up from the laptop. "I've got a job nearby this morning. I could drive you home after that?"

"Fine by me. I might go in search of breakfast."

"I can run across to the shop," he told me. "There's quite a crowd outside."

"It's okay." I peeked out of the curtain and saw that he was right: the street was full of cars and I heard someone shout my name before I hastily replaced the curtain.

"I can't send you out to the wolves." Adam stood behind me, circling his arms around my waist as he kissed my neck.

"You've got work to do." I turned to kiss him. "I think I can survive a trip to the shop."

And I did. I was back five minutes later with a packet of bacon, a loaf of bread and a stack of business cards from reporters, offering to pay for my story.

"How was it?" Adam asked, glancing up at me.

"Mission accomplished," I told him, holding up my wares. "I love that photo." I peered over his shoulder to get a better look at little Harry, proudly holding up the frog to show his dad. "I'll make bacon sandwiches," I suggested, sensing I was in the way.

"Thanks." He went back to work and seemed lost in it when I handed him a plate with a sandwich on it five minutes later. I went out into the back garden to eat my breakfast and then lie on a towel in the sun.

"I'm really sorry," Adam told me, kneeling down beside me an hour later. "I've got to go. I'll just be a couple of hours and then I'm all yours."

"I really should've got you to drive me home last night," I said. His face fell before he caught the teasing in my eyes and tickled my ribs.

"I'm glad you didn't."

"Me too." I sat up and shielded my eyes from the sun. "Go to work. I'm fine – quite happy here, actually. Apart from the fact that you're reminding me that people work and I should probably get a job too."

"You'll find something."

"I might if I looked for something!"

"I won't be long," he promised, kissing me briefly before heading out.

I found my phone as soon as he left, and called Chrissie. "Where've you been?" she asked after a quick greeting. "I tried calling you last night but got no reply."

"I stayed at Adam's," I told her, a foolish grin on my face.

"Ooh! Love is in the air, is it?"

"I tagged along to a photo shoot he was doing yesterday and then we had dinner with his parents, since we were nearby."

"So Matt was right?" She laughed. "The crazy seduction technique actually works!"

I couldn't help but laugh along with her.

"Did you see the papers today?" she asked. "Adam's really stealing the limelight now. Everybody loves him."

"I know – there were a lot of press on his doorstep this morning."

"It's annoying, isn't it? Kind of kills the romance."

"Yeah, I'm trapped inside again. I thought I was safe in the village."

"It'll calm down soon, I'm sure. Anyway, I'm just going to work, but we're all going to Dylan's on Wednesday night. Can you and Adam come?"

"I'm sure I can find time in my hectic schedule for you!"

"Brill! I'll see you then. Have fun with Adam!"

"I will." I laughed as I hung up.

I got bored pretty quickly. Peeking outside, I saw that most of the reporters must have left with Adam, but there were still a few hanging around so I didn't feel like venturing out. I was lying in the garden, ignoring my rumbling stomach, when I saw movement in the house and sat up to shout to Adam.

"I'm out here," I told him and was surprised to see Tom's face appear at the back door.

"Hi!" He greeted me with a huge grin.

"Hi. I thought you were Adam getting back."

"Sorry to barge in. I tried ringing the bell. I was in the pub for a late lunch and overheard a reporter saying that Adam had gone out and left you home alone. Thought I'd see if you wanted to keep me company for lunch ..."

"I'd love to. I'm starving!"

"Adam working?" he asked while I shook out the towel I'd been lying on and folded it.

"Yeah. I'm not sure how long he'll be. Where's Ruth?"

"She's over at a friend's. They're knitting hats for premature babies. She never stops – there's always some project. It gives me a bit of peace at least." His

304

face lit up when he smiled.

"Are there many reporters in the pub?" I asked once we'd made it past the few outside the house. I'd ignored them, keeping my head down.

"Just a couple. You needn't worry. I'll protect you!"

I looked up at him, trusting him completely.

"Now, you can't tell Ruth about this," he told me when we settled ourselves at the table in the corner. "Not about the food, anyway. I'm supposed to eat the salad she made for me. I'll just tell her I kept you company while you ate."

"Do you think she'll believe it?"

"No. I can't get away with anything. She's got spies everywhere. It's worth the lecture, though."

"When did you have the heart attack?" I asked.

"A couple of years ago now." He paused and shook his head. "It was scary. I thought I was a goner."

"You must have scared Ruth too."

"I'd say I scared everyone. Ruth went on a mission to never let me eat anything I liked ever again; Becky was flying back with the kids every weekend; Adam bought the house out here." He smiled at me. "It was pretty nice, actually. I had all my family around me again. I stopped working and life slowed down."

I took a sip of lemonade and looked around the pub: there was an elderly couple eating at a table near the door and a couple of reporters sitting at the bar. Tom had firmly told them not to bother me and they seemed to take him seriously. "Sorry, I'm chatting away and you're starving, aren't you? Do you know what you want?"

"What are you having? I'll go and order," I told

him, standing up.

"You can order, but I'm paying, okay?"

"Deal."

"Fish and chips for me, then," he requested. I chuckled to myself as I headed over to Mike at the bar.

"What did you do before you retired?" I asked when I re-joined Tom at the table.

"For ten years before I retired I was the caretaker for all the schools in the area."

"I can imagine you doing that," I told him.

"I loved it. I knew all the kids in a ten-mile radius. It was nice work."

"What about before that?"

"I was the warehouse manager for an agricultural supplier. I worked for them for thirty years and then they made me redundant. Replaced me with some kid."

"I just got made redundant," I mused.

"If it's any consolation, it turned out well for me. Sometimes things happen for a reason."

"I think you're probably right," I said to him, thinking of how my life had changed since my last day at work.

"That's not what I ordered," Tom told Mike when he set down two bowls of broccoli soup on the table.

"I didn't think so," Mike laughed. "But it's what Lucy ordered for you!"

"Not you as well," Tom groaned as he toyed with the soup.

"I don't want to get into trouble with Ruth," I explained, picking up my spoon.

"You know, for a while there, I thought you and I

were friends." He shook his head and I couldn't keep the smile from my face. He grinned back at me as he slurped his soup.

"I don't know what to do about work," I confided. "I should be looking for a job, but I've no idea what I want to do."

"How old are you?" he asked.

"Twenty-six."

"Pff." He waved a hand in front of his face. "You've got your whole life to figure out what you want to do. Not everyone is like Adam and knows what they want to do at four years old!"

"Why doesn't he sell his photos?" I asked. "There is so much amazing stuff hidden away in your garage."

"Who knows? He's putting it off. There's always some reason. I've stopped asking."

I broke up my bread roll and dipped it in the soup. "He's so talented."

"I know. I have brilliant children, though I'm not sure how that happened."

"What does Becky do?"

"She's an English teacher. She only intended to be away for a year, but she fell in love with France, and then Will. It'd be nice if she were closer, but she visits regularly and we go over to them occasionally. She's happy – that's what matters."

"I thought about teaching. I'm not sure I'd be any good at it, though."

"You won't know unless you try." He winked at me.

"There you are," Adam arrived, looking tired and stressed.

"What's wrong?" I asked.

"I didn't know where you were. Why don't you have your phone on?"

"It's on," I said, drawing it from my handbag and registering the missed calls. "Oh, I think it's on silent. Sorry."

"Do you want a drink, kid?" Tom asked.

"No, we need to get going. I should take Lucy home, then I've got more work to do. Are you finished?" he prompted.

"Yes," I said, standing and thanking Tom for lunch. "No dessert!" I said sternly as I hugged him.

He grinned at me. "You're a killjoy, you are!"

I slipped my hand into Adam's as we walked through the pub. Reporters circled us when we walked the short way back to his house. "I just need to run inside and get my laptop," he told me, as though there weren't people shouting questions at us, and cameras flashing too close to my face. My heart raced and I was glad when we finally made it to the front door and ducked inside.

"Did you see the newspapers when you were in the shop this morning?" Adam broke the silence without looking at me while he packed up his things.

"Yes." His face had been splashed across the front pages of the tabloids. I'd skimmed through some of the articles, and found them to be complimentary, mostly just uncovering who the mysterious man was.

"You could have warned me," he said without emotion.

"Sorry, I just thought I'd go for the 'ignorance is bliss' approach."

He sat down beside me on the couch, looking

deflated as he rubbed his eyes.

"It's not so bad," I said. "Everyone likes you."

"I just went to a job and all they wanted to do was talk to me about the show, and I had reporters annoying me the whole way there and back. Someone got hold of our contracts. There's nothing to stop *me* talking to them, so they're persistent."

"It will all blow over soon."

"Come on, I'll take you home," he said after a fleeting kiss.

Hannah Ellis

Chapter 39

My dad's timing was pretty good. It was Tuesday morning and I'd just checked my bank account, working out how long I could survive without a job, when he popped round with a cheque that covered about three months' rent. I had savings so I was fine for a while anyway, but I hated the thought of burning through the money that I'd spent so long putting away.

I'd wondered if he'd seen the show and heard me telling Kelly how he had never helped me out financially. He'd laughed when I asked, swearing he'd not been watching and knew nothing about it.

Ironically, now that he was helping me, I'd snapped at him.

"Why now? I could've used some help before when I was studying and working part-time as well."

He'd looked at me seriously across the living room, and I felt bad for barking at him.

"You don't have a job, and I thought it would help – give you some breathing room while you look for a job. You were always so capable and determined, I didn't think you needed money before …"

"I didn't," I replied. "I made sure I was fine because I didn't feel that I had any choice."

"I'll always help you out when you need it."

I smiled sadly; maybe he should have made that clearer before.

"Thanks for this." I waved the cheque in my hand. "I need to chase up my redundancy money and start job-hunting."

"I'll leave you to it," he said, giving me a quick hug and heading for the door. "Take care."

I got to work, updating my CV and trawling the internet for jobs. Adam was working all day. I'd had a text from him in the morning apologising for his bad mood yesterday and promising to come over when he'd finished work.

He arrived early that evening. I'd made pasta for us. He was quiet and distracted as he lay on the couch, his head in my lap.

"Are you okay?" I asked, running a hand through his hair.

"Yeah, I just hate all the media stuff." I'd thought the media attention was bad before, but that was nothing compared to the days since they'd been airing the unedited footage. Adam and Carl had been thrust into the spotlight too. While Carl seemed to enjoy it, Adam wanted to hide from it. Public opinion of me seemed to be slightly better. I'd ventured to the shop in the afternoon without getting any abuse, so that was positive. People didn't seem to hate me any more, but I don't think I was very popular either. I tried not to watch any of the show, but in moments of weakness I flicked on and saw myself as quite geeky.

"It will blow over," I told him: that was what he'd said to me when I'd been panicking about the media coverage.

"Maybe."

"It will. As soon as the show is over, people will find something else to obsess over."

"It's not the general public that worries me," he said, sitting up. "It's the fact that I need to make a living and I'm being shown as the most unprofessional cameraman ever. Stuff like that doesn't just blow over. Employers will remember that."

"I don't think it's that bad; everyone loves you."

"I'm not interested in winning popularity contests," he said angrily. "I'm worried about how I'm going to pay my mortgage when no one will employ me."

"Okay." I turned away from him.

"Sorry." He reached for my hand. "I didn't mean to take it out on you. Hopefully, I'm overreacting. I just hate the reporters and the press coverage. I can't stand people recognising me. I want life to get back to normal."

"It will," I said, gently. "We'll look back and laugh at all this one day."

"Hi," Melissa shouted as she came into the apartment. We shouted greetings but she disappeared into her room and slammed the door.

"I need to find somewhere else to live." I sighed. "I don't know how long I can put up with Melissa and her moods."

"Yeah," Adam mumbled. I wasn't convinced he'd heard me.

"Do you want to watch a movie?"

"I think I might just head home." He turned to kiss me and I moved closer to him.

"You could stay here," I suggested.

"I've got a meeting first thing in the morning at the

TV studios and it's easier if I go from my place."

"Okay." I smiled, trying to hide my disappointment.

"Sorry. I hardly slept last night and I'm in a crappy mood. I just need to go home and get some sleep."

"That's fine." I kissed him again and moved away to let him up.

"I'll talk to you tomorrow," he said at the door.

"What's the meeting about?" I asked.

"I've no idea; they just asked me to come in. It was all a bit mysterious. I'll find out tomorrow."

I closed the door on him and felt as though the perfect little world we'd created was falling down around me. Of course things wouldn't stay happy and shiny forever but I hated seeing Adam so down. Hopefully things would get better after this week. We'd do the live show and then the media attention would gradually die down until we were completely forgotten about. Things could only get better.

***

"Hi!" Melissa sounded strangely cheerful as she walked into the living room the next morning. "I was just on my way to work," she told me, "but I saw this outside the corner shop and thought you'd want to see it." She dropped a tabloid newspaper in front of me. My heart sank when I glanced at the headline: *How I found out my boyfriend was cheating on me on a reality TV show.* There was a picture of Adam with a woman who looked like a model. Maybe not. I guess she could be a supermodel. She was gorgeous.

Melissa turned to leave and I looked up at her. "What's your problem?" I asked angrily.

"I don't have a problem," she said innocently.

"Then why are you being so nasty? You've not had anything nice to say to me since I got back from Spain."

She hovered in the doorway, looking uncomfortable. "I just think it's so pathetic, all this media stuff. I feel sorry for you. You've made such a mess of your life."

"You feel sorry for me?" I asked. "Why have you been so horrible if you feel sorry for me?"

She looked at me, rubbing her forehead as though searching for an answer.

"It seems more like you're jealous," I suggested.

"You've got no job," she snapped. "And you're splashed all over the tabloids. What's to be jealous of?"

"I've got a boyfriend," I said and caught the look on her face. I was right; she was jealous. "And friends, and a life!"

"Pff!" She raised her eyebrows and glanced at the paper on the table. "Are you sure you've still got a boyfriend?" Abruptly, she turned and left.

I kept my cool while I read the article. It seemed that Adam's girlfriend, Felicity Carter, was just a regular old model – nothing super about her. So that was a relief. She talked about how she'd been dating Adam right before the show started and how he'd been acting strangely ever since he'd left for Spain. She'd suspected something was going on, but didn't know what until the unedited show started on Friday and it gradually became clear that he'd been having some sort of romance with one of the contestants. "Some sort of romance?" I laughed as I repeated the

315

words aloud.

I took a deep breath and struggled to straighten things out in my head. I tried to convince myself that she was just a bimbo trying to make some money by making up a story, but there were pictures of her with Adam and they looked genuine. To make matters worse, they looked great together.

The next minute, I threw the paper down onto the coffee table, realising it was all lies as I glanced at the picture again. At least, I hoped it was lies.

Chapter 40

I opened the door to a nervous-looking Adam later that day. "I was just going to make a cup of tea," I told him. "Do you want one?"

"I'd love one." He hovered in the kitchen doorway. I decided I'd let him sweat rather than come out and ask about Felicity Carter. I was hoping he might bring it up, but I'd purposely left the newspaper out on the coffee table as a little conversation starter, presuming he wouldn't mention it if I didn't.

"How was your day?" I asked, handing him his tea.

"Fine. I got a lot done. I finished working on the photos from Sunday and sent them over to Angela, so I'm just waiting to hear what she thinks."

"She'll love them, I'm sure."

"I hope so. I always get a bit nervous waiting for people's reactions. Oh ... you saw that, then?" he asked, looking at the newspaper lying on the table.

"Yeah. I can't believe you never mentioned your girlfriend to me. She's very pretty."

"I'm glad you think it's funny. I was expecting you to slam the door in my face. Now I'm a bit concerned that you're not bothered." He sat beside me on the couch. "So do you just not care that I have another girlfriend, or is it really so unbelievable that she could be my girlfriend?"

"It was the shoes," I told him, flicking to the remainder of the story on page five, which included a full-length picture of Felicity. "I know how you feel about ridiculously high heels." The shoes she was wearing would be considered extreme by most people's standards – not just flat-heeled me.

He sighed and leaned back. "I'm also not that interested in the sort of person who would make up stories just to make a few quid."

"Did you date her?" I asked calmly.

"I went on one date with her," he told me, reaching for my hand. "And that was one too many. I promise you there's nothing going on."

"I didn't think there was." I moved closer to him and ignored the niggling doubts in my mind. I did believe him, but there was a tiny part of me that wondered if I shouldn't be so trusting. After all, I'd only known him a short time. I felt as though I knew him so well – but I was also aware that my feelings for him made me vulnerable.

"Thanks for not freaking out," he said softly, wrapping his arms around me and resting his head against mine. "I was worried that you'd believe it. I can cope with all this media stuff, just so long as it doesn't come between us."

"It won't." I stroked his bandaged hand. "Where did the photos come from?" I asked, wondering how on earth anyone goes on one date with someone and ends up with photos like the ones in the newspaper.

"I didn't even know her then." He picked up the paper to look at the pictures. "I was working and she was in the studio for a photo shoot. She just dragged me on set. I think she was drunk, to be honest."

I took the paper from him and folded it up, not wanting to look at it any more. "What was the meeting about this morning?"

"Well, they had a few lawyers present while they asked me some questions about my hand, so I guess they're worried I'm going to sue them or something."

"That's all they wanted?"

"Some boring work stuff. Discussing upcoming contracts ..."

"So they will employ you again?"

"Seems like it."

"That's good, isn't it?"

"Yeah." He didn't sound too sure. "They also want Carl and me on the live show with you guys on Friday."

"Really?" I was immediately excited at the thought of Adam being there too. "I'm dreading it. It'll be much better if you're there."

"I'm not doing it." He shook his head slightly. "I told them to take a running jump. There's no way I'm doing that. Would you do it, if you had a choice?"

"I don't know." I was dreading doing a live show, but it was also nice to think that we could finally have our say. It seemed like a fitting end to things somehow. "I guess not," I told him, wanting to be agreeable but also upset that he wouldn't be there.

"I think Carl will do it," he commented. "He loves all the media attention."

Hannah Ellis

Chapter 41

Ryan and Matt looked up from their game of pool when we walked into the back room of the pub early in the evening. It had been less than a week since I had seen them, and less than a month since we met, but we embraced like family reuniting following a long separation. We sat around drinking, chatting and laughing while the rest of our gang arrived over the next hour or so.

Margaret and Kelly both looked tired; they complained they'd been working and partying too much and were in desperate need of sleep. They announced they couldn't stay long and sat down with a glass of wine each.

Chrissie squeezed me tightly when she arrived. I felt great with the whole gang around me.

"You should've invited Carl," I told Adam, realising we were one person short.

"I asked him earlier in the week," Adam said. "But his in-laws are visiting or something."

"I spoke to him earlier," Matt chimed in. "He said he'd call in."

"Really?" Adam asked. "I might give him a call and see what he's up to …" He moved away from us, his phone to his ear, and came back when there was no answer.

"You okay?" I asked.

"Yeah, fine." He draped his arm around my shoulder while I waited for my turn on the pool table. Matt had us all playing some game, but I wasn't entirely certain what was going on, so I just took a shot when I was told to. I was fairly sure I was losing.

"Sorry I'm late," Carl told us merrily when he finally arrived. "Matt promised you wouldn't start the fun without me, but I think he lied!" He grabbed a beer and came and joined Adam and me at the bar. "Congratulations on the job!" he said, beaming at Adam. "Some people have all the luck. I'm starting to regret the whole wife and kid thing."

"What job?" Chrissie asked, hovering between the pool table and us with a cue in her hand.

"They offered us permanent contracts. Unfortunately for me, it's six months of the year in Spain for as long as this holiday reality show lasts. Lizzie vetoed it, so I'm out. I'm so jealous." He slapped Adam on the arm. "Easy work, too: since everyone knows the house is rigged, it's only the bits outside the house. It's basically a load of money for sitting in the sun half the year. The usual studio work the rest of the year, but a permanent contract is like gold dust."

"Congratulations!" Chrissie said, glancing at me. I avoided eye contact with her and smiled benignly, trying my best not to react.

"It sounds great," I said, forcing cheer into my voice. I felt Carl's eyes on me and saw the panic on his face when he realised that Adam hadn't told me the news.

"I'm just going to say hello to Margaret and Kelly,"

he muttered, slapping Adam lightly on the back and moving away from us.

"I was going to tell you," Adam leaned in towards me. "I haven't even accepted it yet. I said I needed to think about it."

My heart pounded in my chest. "Was that what the meeting was about today?"

"Yeah. I was still trying to get my head around it all."

"It's brilliant, though, isn't it? I mean, you were worried about getting work. And you said the contracts are usually short, so a permanent one must be a big deal." I was talking too fast. I didn't want anyone to see how I really felt. "Working in Spain will be amazing. When do you start?"

"They want me to fly out on Sunday. They're going to do another show straight away."

"Can you tell Maria I said hello?" Matt jumped in to the conversation. "I can't believe you'll be there without us. I bet the next lot will be boring. The show will be a disaster and you'll be back in a week."

I lifted my beer bottle to my lips and felt my hand tremble. I really wanted to get out of there and away from Adam's awkward looks. I wasn't sure how long I could keep the fake smile on my face. Finishing my drink, I announced that I needed my beauty sleep.

"Can I come with you?" Adam asked quietly once I'd said my goodbyes.

"I'm staying at my dad's," I lied. "I said I'd take the boys out in the morning. Trying to be helpful, while I have the time."

"Can we talk?" he asked, escorting me out of the back door of the pub. "About Spain and the job."

"Look." I turned to him, taking a deep breath and hoping I could keep calm. "It's okay. It sounds like an amazing opportunity, and it will probably be nice for you to get away from all the media hassle."

"What about us?" he asked.

"We can see each other whenever you're back," I told him, feeling suddenly sick. "Lots of people have long-distance relationships."

I didn't mention that I wasn't one of those people. It wouldn't work for me: I'd hate every second of being apart and I couldn't put myself through it. The thought of it was bad enough. "I don't think you should pass up such an amazing opportunity," I said, with as much conviction as I could muster.

"Really?" He frowned. "So you're okay with me going?"

I couldn't formulate words, so I did some combination of a shrug and a nod. I could hardly tell him not to go. We'd only known each other a matter of weeks, and I didn't want him to end up resenting me because he missed out. That's if he would even turn it down for me.

"I'll talk to you tomorrow?" he asked as we reached the main road. Thankfully there were plenty of taxis around, and I managed to flag one down immediately.

"Yeah. I'll give you a call."

"Maybe we can have dinner together?"

"That sounds nice." I kissed him and climbed into the taxi, turning to wave when the car pulled away. When the driver asked where I was going, I gave him my dad's address. I couldn't face going back to the apartment. Dad and Kerry's house was more homely and I really needed to be somewhere comforting. I leaned back against the headrest and let the tears fall down my face.

I was silently congratulating myself on making it all the way through the house and up the stairs to the guest room without waking anyone when the hall light came on and bathed me in light.

"Sorry," I whispered to Kerry. "I was trying to be quiet. Is it okay if I stay here?"

"Of course," she murmured, squinting into the light. "Is everything okay?"

I really thought I was just going to say yes, but I surprised myself by calmly telling her that Adam was moving to Spain and I was going to die alone. She shuffled past me into the spare room and closed the door behind us before taking a seat on the bed, patting the space next to her.

"What happened?" she asked, stifling a yawn.

I fell backwards to lie on the bed. "He got offered more work in Spain. They want him to leave on Sunday."

"How long for?" she asked, patting my knee.

"I'm not sure – maybe six months. He wants to keep in touch, have a long-distance relationship or whatever."

"And you don't?" she asked.

"No," I told her, sitting up on the bed to look at her. "I don't want him to go."

"Did you tell him that?"

"No. I can't tell him that. We've not known each other long. Please don't say I told you so."

"Do you really think I would?" Kerry sighed. "It seems bad now, but things tend to work out how they should. If it's meant to be, it will be. And if you really love him, you can figure out the distance."

"I feel really stupid," I sobbed, leaning into her as she wrapped an arm around my shoulder. "I thought this was something serious. I already planned out my life with him" – I laughed bitterly – "and it didn't involve him spending half the year in Spain."

I straightened up and wiped my tears, insisting I was fine and telling Kerry to go back to bed. I couldn't fall asleep, though. Apparently I was going to be awake all night enduring the torture of my own thoughts. I'd let myself get carried away and jumped ahead to my happy-ever-after way too soon. I couldn't believe he'd be leaving on Sunday. I didn't even have the chance to get my head around it: he'd be gone before I knew it and I'd spend the rest of my life being miserable.

The good thing about not being able to sleep at night was that I could effectively kill a good portion of the following day lying in bed, dozing. I drifted in and out of sleep as the rest of the house woke up and filled the place with noise and bustle. When it went quiet again I dozed for a few hours. Chrissie rang at lunchtime, and I told her that, no, I had no idea that Adam was going to Spain until the exact moment everyone else found out yesterday. She did her best to console me, but I felt no better after I'd hung up. If anything, her sympathy made me feel slightly worse.

I dragged myself out of bed at Kerry's insistence and sat and ate a late lunch with her.

"Why don't you call and talk to him?" she asked.

"I don't know." I rested my head on the table pathetically. "I can't decide whether I should make the most of the time before he leaves or cut my losses and avoid him."

"Seems like you're going for the avoiding him approach."

"I don't know if I can bear to see him. I might just end up begging him not to leave me and clinging to his leg!"

I laughed at the smirk on Kerry's face and banged my head lightly against the table. Needing something to occupy me, I offered to pick the boys up from their holiday club in the local community centre, and only checked my phone after I'd walked them the ten minutes home. There were four missed calls from Adam and I was contemplating calling him back when Max burst into the spare room, demanding that I help him build a train track.

When we finished, the track took up every inch of floor space in the boys' bedroom and I was quite proud when I slotted the final piece into place and watched Max and Jacob couple up their trains. My brothers came in useful sometimes: they were a great distraction. I decided I'd call Adam back later, when it was too late to meet him, but I'd at least get to hear his voice. We'd had vague plans to go out for dinner, but I couldn't face him. Tomorrow was the live show and the TV network was sending a car for me early in the afternoon so they could prep us for the show.

I left my phone in the spare room and gave Max and Jacob my attention. My mind kept wandering to Adam, but I pushed the thoughts from my head and focused on playing cars and trains and trying not to wince too much when the boys decided they wanted to pretend to be hairdressers, with me as their model.

Dad called to say he was running late, so we ate

without him, and I was engrossed in a giant floor puzzle with the boys when the doorbell rang. Kerry went to answer it. My heart started to pound when Kerry came back into the living room with Adam behind her.

"Who's he?" Jacob asked.

"This is Lucy's friend, Adam," Kerry told him when I lost the power of speech.

"Hi." Adam waved and I managed to smile up at him.

"Finish the puzzle quickly, boys, and then it's time for bed," Kerry told Max and Jacob.

"Can he help?" Max pointed at Adam.

"I'm not very good at puzzles," Adam told him, coming down to kneel beside Max and survey the pieces.

"It goes there." Max pointed to the middle of the puzzle when Adam picked up a piece.

"So it does!" Adam grinned at him. They went on like that, the kids directing Adam when he picked up a piece, until it was finished.

"Come on, then," Kerry cajoled. "Let's go up and read some stories before bed."

"Can Adam read to us?" Jacob asked.

"No, he can't," Kerry said, chuckling. "Say goodnight and get upstairs."

They shouted goodnight and scampered away. "Help yourselves to anything," Kerry told us as she followed the boys. "There's leftovers in the kitchen if you're hungry, Adam …"

He thanked her before turning to me. I busied myself tidying the puzzle away and tried to get my emotions under control.

"I thought we were going to have dinner together," he said while he helped me pick up the puzzle pieces.

"How did you know where I was?"

"I asked a reporter," he told me. "If you give them twenty quid they can find out most things. I did try calling you …"

"My phone's upstairs."

"So you don't want to see me, or what?"

"I do." I finally met his gaze. "I was just thinking about your job in Spain …"

"And you thought you'd distance yourself before I'd even left?"

"Maybe," I said. "Why didn't you tell me about it? I don't understand why I heard about it from Carl …"

"I wanted to talk to you about it. I wasn't going to leave without discussing it with you. I just didn't want to freak you out; we've not known each other long, and it felt weird to start having serious conversations about our future."

"You didn't have to ask my permission," I told him, putting the last puzzle pieces away and turning to look at him. "But it would've been nice if you'd told me … Anyway, it sounds too good an opportunity to pass up."

"Okay." He sighed. "It might work out. I wouldn't be working round the clock like when we were in Spain. I'd be able to fly back regularly, and you could visit me. And the work in Spain isn't going to be forever. It will probably be short-lived. I don't want things to end between us because of my job …"

"Me neither." I told him. "But maybe we can make it work." I'd have to give it a try, I realised, because even though the thought of being away from him was hard, the thought of not having him in my life at all was incomprehensible.

"You don't sound too sure?"

"Sorry." I felt a smile flicker at the corners of my mouth. "I'll just miss you, that's all."

"I'll be back before you know it," he promised. "I won't be able to stay away for long."

"Good." I rested a hand on the back of his neck as he leaned over to kiss me.

***

We ended up drinking red wine back at my place, and once I'd had a couple of glasses I decided it might be fun to watch ourselves on TV. So far I'd done a great job of avoiding it, but I was feeling merry and decided it would probably be entertaining. Adam groaned when I voiced the idea, but I ignored him and reached for the remote.

It was actually really good fun to relive the holiday. It felt like so long ago already. Now that there was so much more footage to show, the screen was split, with the main action shown in the middle and other boxes in the corners of the screen showing what was happening elsewhere in the house. Adam and I chatted through the boring footage of us all getting ready for dinner, then focused on the screen again to watch me getting out of the minibus and enter the restaurant where we spent our final evening.

It was fun to watch, and I wasn't even too embarrassed when I saw myself stealing glances at Adam on screen. I remember being annoyed that night because he wouldn't look at me, but suddenly there was a shot of him staring at me while I chatted to Matt and Chrissie.

"Can we turn this off now?" he asked.

"No, I want to watch!"

"They're messing around with the editing again," he complained when we saw another shot of him gazing at me, this time while I danced with Dylan and then Matt. The screen version of me walked over to the table to sit alone. I remember being in a bad mood, angry that Adam wouldn't meet my eyes.

"Turn it off," Adam demanded, reaching for the remote. I grabbed the remote and held it away from him, watching as the TV showed Adam looking at me so intensely that it gave me goose bumps. Real-life Adam reached around me to snatch the remote and press the power button. He didn't say anything and I stared at the blank screen.

"I love you," I blurted out quietly. The silence enveloped me before the fear hit me. Fear that I'd just ruined everything. That he'd turn and run a mile. The sound of my blood pumping around my body was suddenly deafening.

When I finally turned to look at him, he had that look in his eyes again. The intense look I'd just witnessed on TV.

"I love you, too."

Hannah Ellis

Chapter 42

I woke tangled up with Adam and, for a moment, felt that everything was right with the world. Then my brain kicked into gear and I remembered that he'd be in Spain in a couple of days and I had to appear on live TV that evening. My feelings of contentment took a dramatic nosedive.

"Morning," Adam mumbled, pulling me to him.

I snuggled into him, wanting to enjoy the moment a little longer before the stress of the day fully took over. I smiled when he nuzzled my neck, and tried to ignore the thoughts that flew around my head.

"What's wrong?" Adam asked, propping himself on an elbow to look down at me.

"Nothing," I told him, running a finger along his shoulder. He looked at me intensely and I cracked. "Could you do something for me?" I asked, panic starting to take over. "Can you come on the show tonight?"

I felt him tense, and I could tell from the look on his face that he wouldn't do it.

"Don't ask me that," he sighed, lying back down to stare at the ceiling.

"I'd just feel better if you were with me."

He didn't say anything. I should probably have given up then and told him I was sorry for asking, but instead I went down the begging route. "Please?"

"You'll be fine," he told me, sitting up and swinging his legs off the bed, then reaching for his clothes. "You'll have the others around you."

"I want *you* there," I told him, while screaming at myself to shut up and stop being pathetic. I think part of me just wanted to test him – and it seemed that he was going to fail.

"I've already told them I'm not doing it," he told me, pulling his T-shirt over his head. He picked up his phone and wallet from the bedside table when he stood, shoving them into his pockets.

"Okay," I said, sitting up and pulling the duvet around me as I admitted defeat. "You don't want to do the show. You don't have to run away, though."

"I'm not." He smiled as he sat beside me. "I have to go into work to sign the contract. Sorry. What's everyone doing after the show? Shall I meet you at Dylan's or something?"

"I'm not sure," I told him.

"Okay, just let me know where you are and I'll come and find you." He leaned in to kiss me and then left me contemplating why I was so angry with him. I was so furious that I couldn't confine my anger to Adam; men in general and the universe at large were also in my bad books. Everything seemed to be going wrong, and I had a feeling my day would only get worse.

I felt better seeing the look on Chrissie's face when I calmly told her about Adam's refusal to come on the live show, and his abrupt exit from my bed. She'd skipped work and arrived at my door so we could be united in our panic about the upcoming TV appearance.

"What an idiot," she snapped, banging her coffee cup down on the table in the living room.

"I can sort of understand …" I immediately wanted to defend him, although I knew he didn't deserve it.

"Yeah, I know, we like Adam!" She grinned at me. "He's a nice guy. But he's abandoning you for a job in Spain, and now he can't even offer you some support with the TV show. I might call him and tell him what I think of him."

"No, you won't." I shot her a warning glance. "He's right; it wasn't really fair of me to ask him."

"But surely he can see how stressed you are about it? He shouldn't need to be asked. It's not really that big a deal for him, is it? One little TV interview. If it was the other way around and he asked you …"

I bit my lip. "If I didn't *have* to do the show?"

"You wouldn't do it, would you?" She erupted with laughter.

"Is that really the point?" I laughed with her, feeling better.

"No, it's not the point at all, but maybe we should keep that to ourselves all the same!"

Hannah Ellis

Chapter 43

"No!" I stared at the wardrobe lady, who was holding up a pair of black stilettos. "It's not possible for me to walk in those, so no! Take them away."

"That's all we've got in your size." She gave me a look that told me she was impervious to me and my demands. As though wanting shoes that I could walk in was some unreasonable diva-like request.

"I'll just wear my trainers then," I told her. She raised her eyebrows at me as I stood in front of the mirror and checked out my little black dress. "Fine." I took them from her. "Thank you!"

"You'll be okay," Kelly told me while she had her make-up done.

"I don't want to do this," I complained. Then my phone rang.

"Is that Adam?" Chrissie asked. "Answer it. You'll feel better if you speak to him."

"I'll either shout at him or get upset, and I'm struggling to keep it together as it is." I'd become increasingly annoyed with him as the day wore on, and this wasn't the first call of his I'd ignored. I reached for the phone and sent him a quick message saying I'd call him after the show – although I was so mad at him, I wasn't sure I would. He sent me a message back wishing me luck. I felt like throwing the phone across the room.

I'd seen Jessica when we arrived at the TV studios and managed to vent some of my anger on her. She'd been in the reception area, talking to an important-looking man in a suit, and she broke away, walking over to Chrissie and me when she saw us.

"All ready for the big show?" she'd asked, without preamble.

"No, not really," I said, my voice loud and angry. "I can't believe what you did. Do you have any idea what I've been through because of you?"

The smile remained on her face but she glanced around, looking awkward.

"You could at least apologise," I shot at her.

"Oh come on," she said impatiently. "It's not so bad. We told the truth; the public saw what actually happened. This could be life-changing; you were part of something cutting-edge. You should be thanking me!"

I looked at her to see if she was joking, but she wasn't. She genuinely believed she'd done me a favour. "Why don't you take a seat for a minute? Someone will come and show you around? You'll be well looked after today." She turned to leave but I called after her.

"Why me?" I asked, suddenly needing an explanation. She turned and looked at me questioningly. "Why did you make me look so bad? Why not the others?"

She motioned to the couches nearby and we took a seat.

"Honestly?" she began, her face softening slightly. "Just because it was easy."

"What's that supposed to mean?" Chrissie asked.

She drummed her nails on the couch. "You have to understand: we had a limited time to edit the show. We had no idea who we would end up with, and how things would work out. We did whatever was easiest. It wasn't difficult to portray Kelly as a dumb blonde, and it was straightforward enough to make Margaret into a Crocodile Dundee type. Dylan made a good brooding musician," she said with a shrug. "We took what was there and went with it. We made Ryan into a player and we played up the romance with Chrissie and Matt."

"But how could you have known something would happen with Matt and me from the very first day?" Chrissie jumped in.

Jessica raised her eyebrows. "Is that a serious question?"

"So you're saying that I looked crazy?" I asked incredulously.

"No," she said, looking at me intensely. "You caused us problems. You didn't fit easily into a mould. You were flirting with the cameraman and making friends with Matt and Chrissie. That's what you gave us to work with."

"So you mixed it together to create a monster?"

"We'd only intended to tweak things a bit, just to show how we could. But when it aired, there was such an intense reaction to you that we ran with it."

I sighed and leaned back against the couch, unsatisfied with her explanation. So there was no good reason why they'd picked on me? They just had.

Confronting Jessica hadn't made me feel any better, and I was still annoyed with the production team while I waited for the live show to start. I wanted to be anywhere but there.

"All ready?" A chirpy young girl with a headset appeared at the dressing room door.

"Not really, no," I told her. "I've still got to learn how to walk in stilettos."

"You'll be fine." She smiled kindly.

"Where are the boys?" Chrissie asked.

"They're waiting for you," headset girl told us. "Follow me!"

I shoved my feet into the ridiculously high shoes and caught Kelly's arm to steady myself. "I guess it doesn't really matter if I fall on my face. At least I might get a cheer then."

"It'll be fine," she told me.

"Could everyone please stop saying that?" I snapped and took a deep breath. All eyes shot to me. "Sorry. Okay, I'm ready. Let's get it over and done with."

We met the boys in the corridor and walked together to the studio, waiting backstage until the appropriate moment. "I feel ill," I told Dylan, slipping my hand into his when I heard the audience clapping. All I wanted to do was turn and run. I heard Chelsea's voice, and then Carl's. I couldn't hear what they were saying, just the hum of conversation punctuated by laughter from the audience. After five long minutes we were moving. Matt went first, drawing a cheer from the audience, then Chrissie, Kelly and Margaret followed. The applause grew louder when Ryan walked on stage – then I felt a hand on my arm when I set out to follow him.

"You go last," the smiley headset lady told me.

"No." I grabbed Dylan's hand again. "I don't want to go last!"

"It's okay," he reassured me. "Just follow me."

I'd wanted to slip in with everyone else, thinking I could keep my head down and go unnoticed.

"Now?" I asked her when I watched Dylan join the others on the crescent couch.

"Wait," she whispered, keeping her hand on my arm. "Now! Go." She gave me a nudge. I fixed my eyes on Dylan and my legs went into autopilot. My heart was pounding so hard that I barely heard anything at first, then everything started to come into focus. I plucked up the courage to look at the audience. Although the lights were low, I could see the first couple of rows, and people seemed to be smiling and cheering while they called my name. I'd wake up any second, I was sure of it.

I was in a state of shock by the time I made it to the couch and settled myself next to Dylan. Not only had I walked all the way across the room without falling in my ridiculously high heels, but I also seemed to be getting the most applause. I waved at the audience: a little gesture that would have made the queen proud. They calmed down then, so that Chelsea could speak.

"That was quite a welcome you got there." She smiled at me from her chair opposite us, seeming suddenly professional. I wondered whether her ditsy act while we were in Spain was just that: an act, put on to make the show seem less credible and further fool us into thinking it would never be aired. "How does it feel to be suddenly popular?"

There was a warmth to her voice which I'd not heard before.

341

"A bit weird, I guess." I glanced around, catching sight of the huge cameras in the studio. They were imposing and intimidating, making me look back at Chelsea and slip my hand discreetly into Dylan's.

"I think your story is the one that's really captured our viewers' interest, and we're dying to hear from you, but first, let's take a look at some of the highlights of the week." She turned to the screen behind her and I craned my neck to see. It made me smile watching us have so much fun, and my nerves settled slightly. Dylan gave my hand a squeeze.

When the clip came to an end, Chelsea began firing questions at us about our week in Majorca. It was fun watching Matt attempt to maintain his cool demeanour when he was quizzed about his feelings for Chrissie. He was obviously uncomfortable answering in front of a studio audience, never mind all the people at home. When it became clear he wasn't going to get away with sarcastic comments and avoidance tactics, he finally turned serious.

"I think I got very lucky meeting Chrissie," he said to Chelsea. "And you stopping me in the street might end up being the best thing that ever happened to me." Every woman in the room gave a sigh, and Chrissie reached up to kiss him on the cheek. "But that's enough about me!" Matt rubbed his hands together. "I bet people are dying to hear about Ryan's romantic escapades in the house." He grinned and the attention shifted from him to a surprisingly cool-looking Ryan.

I was amazed when Ryan confidently answered questions, coolly complimenting Margaret when the subject came up, praising vegetarians when asked about Matilda, and then expertly moving the conversation over to Kelly. Ryan was so polished I could've sworn he'd done some sort of media interview training. I wish I'd thought of that too.

It went on that way, with questions and conversation, interspersed with short clips on the screen. I think we all grew more relaxed as the hour rolled on. The boys got so carried away with their banter that Chelsea had to rein them in. Carl jumped in occasionally, his dry humour keeping the audience laughing.

Kelly brought a tear to my eye when she talked about how close we had become, and how she felt she had six new family members.

Margaret got choked up when she talked about leaving to go home to Australia. I had forgotten that this was just a very weird holiday for her, and she'd return to her own reality soon.

I wasn't sure when I'd relaxed enough to let go of Dylan's hand, but I reached for it again when Chelsea gave me a pointed look. So far I'd got away with making just a few vague comments, but I knew she'd get back to me eventually.

"First of all," she looked suddenly solemn, "I think we should talk about the way you were depicted in the first airing of the show. How did you feel when you realised you'd been portrayed so badly?"

"Angry," I told her thoughtfully. There was absolute silence in the room. "It was a shock – even to me – that I agreed to do the show. It was so out of character for me. My plan was to hide in the background and enjoy a free holiday, but then I relaxed when I met everyone, and had an amazing time. When I got back and found it had been aired while we were away and the public hated me ..." I stopped, a lump forming in my throat. "I was really angry. It felt as though my memories had been altered. I was on such a high, and then I watched myself on TV and felt sick."

"What kind of effect did that have on your life?"

"People were mean to me," I replied. "In shops, on the street, people shouted at me and told me what they thought of me. I just hid from everyone at first."

"That must have been a really hard time for you ..."

"Yes." I wavered. "And no ..." I thought back to the time since we'd returned from Spain and, actually, it wasn't the negative things that came to mind. "There were a few bad days, but then I met up with my friends, which helped. The people around me have been such an amazing support. These guys, and my family, made it all bearable. And Adam," I added without meaning to.

"I want to ask you about Adam in a moment," Chelsea told me. "But first, let's have a look at your time in Spain ..." She whipped around to the giant screen again and I watched my montage, tears filling my eyes while it played out.

"That was quite a transformation we saw you go through," Chelsea told me when it had ended. "You were so unsure of yourself when we met you, and by the end of the week you were dragging cameramen into cupboards!"

I wiped tears from my cheeks as I laughed.

"What was your favourite part of the week in Spain?"

"I don't think I could pick one thing," I told her. "I had such a great time. I made amazing friends, and I think that was the best part of it for me. I wasn't expecting that at all."

"Obviously, everyone is dying to hear about Adam." Chelsea smiled at me. "Unfortunately he couldn't be here today, but have you been in touch since arriving home?"

"Yes." I clammed up, remembering that I was mad at him. I wanted to correct her when she said he *couldn't* be here. He *could*, but he had chosen not to come.

"And how are things between you?" she asked.

"I don't really want to talk about Adam," I asserted. She shifted uncomfortably in her seat.

"I think everyone would love to know if you see a future with Adam."

"I don't know," I told her honestly, prompted by murmurs from the audience. "He's going back to Spain to do more filming, so I guess we'll just see what happens. We've not known each other very long, so it's difficult to say how a long-distance relationship will work."

"Well, I think it's safe to say everyone is behind you," Chelsea told me, her fake smile annoying me.

"I don't think everyone *is* behind us, actually," I told her, my anger bubbling to the surface. "You and your team at RDT have messed around with our lives. None of you are interested in us. You only care about ratings and money. We've not even had an apology!"

"The team at RDT are extremely grateful for the part you've all played in creating an extremely successful TV show," Chelsea told us. "And I can tell you that, to show our appreciation, you will each receive ten thousand pounds!" Her voice rose and she started clapping at the mention of money.

"I wasn't asking for thanks," I said, my voice getting lost in the applause that rippled around the studio. "I wanted an apology." I looked at the rest of my gang, who were clearly excited by the money. I guess it was as close I was going to get to an apology, and I wasn't about to look a gift horse in the mouth, especially since I was currently unemployed.

When the audience settled down again, Chelsea looked at Dylan and opened her mouth before stopping suddenly, touching her earpiece as though someone had shouted in her ear. She smiled blankly while we waited for her to go on.

"Sorry, but could we just go back to Lucy for a second? According to our producers, they met Adam this morning and he declined the offer of the job in Spain ..." She trailed off and stared at me.

"I don't know anything about that," I told her awkwardly. "And I'm not sure I trust your producers," I said, a vision of Jessica springing to mind.

"I can understand that," she said. "But if Adam wasn't going to Spain, would that change how you saw your future with him?" She looked slightly smug and I really didn't want to talk to her. I wanted to talk to Adam and find out if what she had said was true – and, if so, why he'd turned the job down.

"I really don't know," I snapped in response. "I've not got anything else to say. Talk to someone else." She looked slightly taken aback, but moved on to talk to Dylan. "Sorry," I said suddenly, getting to my feet and wobbling as I remembered I was wearing shoes I couldn't walk in. "I need to go."

Chelsea glared at me. "You can't just leave."

"I need to go and find Adam," I confessed. A murmur of approval washed around the room.

"You have to be here for the show," Chelsea told me firmly. I should never have signed that stupid contract, I thought in frustration.

"The show's nearly over. Who really cares?" I asked. The audience cheered their support.

Chelsea had her finger on her earpiece again. She clearly had no clue what to do, and was losing control of the show.

"If you get me a portable camera, I'll go with her," Carl offered.

"That would be acceptable." Chelsea nodded.

"You're kidding!" I said, looking from Chelsea to Carl. "Oh, whatever. Come on, Carl." I tottered across the studio floor and headed backstage. "I don't know what I'm doing," I confided to Carl once we were off stage. The adrenalin would probably wear off any minute and I'd realise that I was about to make a fool of myself.

I waited while people ran around giving Carl various pieces of equipment before we dashed through the building and out of a back door.

"Oh no!" Carl sighed dramatically when we reached the car park. I realised I didn't have my phone with me, and I had no idea where Adam was or how I would find him.

"What?" Carl pulled his earpiece out and moved the camera away from his face, tapping it gently.

"I don't think this thing's working properly." He shrugged. "I need to go and get a different one. Don't go anywhere without me, will you?" He winked and turned to go back inside.

"Carl," I called to him. "Where will he be?"

"I'm sure you'll find him if you look hard enough!" His grin lit up his face and I squinted at him in confusion. He gave me a quick wave and disappeared the way we'd come.

My feet were killing me so I slipped off my shoes. I was just wondering what my next move should be when a wolf-whistle drew my attention. I followed it to the figure leaning casually on a car bonnet at the far side of the car park.

"Nice sunglasses," I commented when I reached him.

"I'm incognito," he explained. "Due to the 'where's Adam?' campaign that's going around the internet."

"Would I get a reward for handing you in?"

"Probably," he said coyly. There was silence. "So my dad just called to tell me I'm an idiot …"

"A geek *and* an idiot? He must be very proud."

He looked sheepish. "He asked me why you were on TV holding hands with Dylan and I was nowhere in sight."

I felt anger rising up in me again. "I don't think you're in any position to say anything about me holding hands with Dylan!"

"I realise that," he said flatly, pulling off his sunglasses and taking a step towards me. I drew away from him.

"I wouldn't have had to hold Dylan's hand if you'd been there," I shot at him, tears springing to my eyes.

"I think that was my dad's point too."

"Just stop!" I shouted at him, holding up a hand. I knew that if he touched me my anger would fade to something else entirely – and I needed him to listen to me.

"Okay." He raised his hands and stayed put.

"You should've been there for me," I told him.

"I know," he replied, taking another step towards me and then stopping when I glared at him. "I'm an idiot."

"Yes! You are. Are you going to Spain?"

"Yes. But I—"

I cut him off. "Okay. Well, that's fine." My tone completely contradicted my words.

"Not for the job," he said, stepping forward and putting a hand to my face when I couldn't hold back the tears any longer.

"What do you mean?"

"I'm just going for a holiday," he said with a smile. "Just for a few days. I need a break. I turned down the job, though."

"Good." I sniffed, my voice filled with relief. "I didn't want you to move to Spain."

"You could have told me that before! I wasn't going to accept it at all until you started saying what a great opportunity it was and practically packed my bags for me."

"I didn't want you to turn it down because of me," I told him.

"I don't want to be away from you." He leaned back so he could look me in the eye. "But that's not the only reason I turned it down. I like the freedom of working freelance, and if I take the permanent contract I'll feel like they own me. I wouldn't have time to do any of my photography."

I felt a smile spread over my face. "I'm so glad you're not moving to Spain," I said, moving my face to his and kissing him deeply. "When are you going on holiday? How long for?"

"Tomorrow," he said, a look on his face that I couldn't read. "Just for four days."

"Okay," I said with a smile. "I think I can cope without you for four days."

He enveloped me in a huge hug before suggesting we move before someone came to find us.

"What's this?" I squinted at some tickets that lay on the passenger seat.

"Tickets for my holiday," he told me.

"But this one's got my name on it."

"I thought you might like to come with me, but since you said you'd be fine without me I can just get a refund." He reached out to take the ticket from me. I grinned as I whipped it away from him. "*Will* you come with me?" he asked, his face filled with uncertainty.

"Yes."

"Really?" he said. "I didn't know if it was too soon…"

"It's not as though it'll be the first time I've been on holiday with you!"

Epilogue

"Did you talk to Matt?" I asked Chrissie. She was washing her hands in the airport toilets, and I leaned against the sink next to her.

"Yeah. I told him I want to wait."

He'd asked her to move in with him, and Chrissie had been unsure.

"It's really soon, and I don't want to rush into it. It's a big step. I think it's better to wait."

"You're probably right. How did he take it?"

"Okay." She shrugged. "He'll get over it. I can't believe Margaret is leaving." Chrissie slipped her arm through mine while we walked back into the terminal.

"I know. This might be the last time all seven of us are together."

"Don't say that!" she snapped. "She'll be back."

"I hate goodbyes!" Margaret said when we walked up to her. "Quick hugs, and then I'm off to see what it's like in the first-class lounge! It's going to be weird to be back home and not be recognised wherever I go. You'll all come and visit, won't you?" She gave Ryan a quick hug, then moved on to Dylan.

"I'll be on my way as soon as the media attention dies down," Kelly promised her. "I just need to ride out this celebrity wave and then I'll be over to surf the waves down under!"

I smiled, not really able to imagine Kelly on a surfboard.

"Don't forget us," I told Margaret, feeling emotional when I hugged her.

"I couldn't if I tried!" she said. "It's been unbelievable. I'm going to miss you all." She got choked up embracing Chrissie and then laughed when Matt picked her up and swung her around. We moved in for a group hug as she clung to Matt. I felt sad for her. I wasn't sure how I would cope if I had to say goodbye to everyone. My life had changed so much in the past two months, and these people were the best friends I'd ever known.

"Right, I'm going!" She extracted herself from us and hurried away, her backpack over one shoulder. She turned on the escalator to wave at us, and we saw tears streaming down her face. We stood shoulder to shoulder, waving back at her until she was out of sight.

"And then there were six," Matt commented when we headed for the exit. "Please don't!" he shouted suddenly at a middle-aged man nearby. "We're having a moment; can't we get five minutes' peace? No photos! Just put the camera away and leave us alone!"

I giggled and Chrissie elbowed Matt in the ribs. This was his latest joke; whenever he saw *anyone* with a camera, he'd either strike a pose or raise a hand to his face and tell them not to take photos.

"You're quite embarrassing to be out in public with," I told him.

"Don't talk to me, Lucy. You're in my bad books. I'm not even sure I can look at you! I don't know how it's going to be at work. Just pretend you don't know me in the staff room, okay?" I was volunteering as a classroom assistant at Matt's school three days a week. I'd decided that, with the money from the TV show as a cushion, I could work part-time for a while and get some experience in a school to see if teaching was something I wanted to pursue. I wasn't sure what it would be like to spend so much time with Matt, but at least I wasn't in his classroom. I'd found a job in a café two days a week too: a family-owned place with a nice homely atmosphere.

"What have I done now?" I asked Matt.

"My girlfriend chose you over me," he told me. "Seems she'd rather cuddle up to you every night than me!"

"What are you talking about?" I looked at him and Chrissie, bemused.

"Do you want to move in with me?" Chrissie asked quietly.

"Are you serious?" I stopped in my tracks, tears filling my eyes.

"It's just an idea," Chrissie told me. "If you were thinking of moving in with Adam or something, just say so."

"I want to live with you," I told her, and I pulled her in for a hug. I'd already discussed our living arrangements with Adam, after deciding I couldn't cope with Melissa anymore, and we'd decided it was too soon for us to move in together. We'd rather carry on enjoying things the way they were.

"This is amazing!" Kelly screeched. "I'll come over all the time for girlie nights! We can give each other manicures and pedicures and facials—"

"And have pillow fights," Ryan suggested. "In your underwear." He stopped talking as we all glared at him. "What? That's what women do, isn't it?"

"Somebody hit him," I said with a sigh. Ryan took off through the airport, Matt and Dylan chasing him.

"It might be fun, though," Kelly mused.

"Pillow fights?" Chrissie asked.

"Yeah." She watched our reactions, and then cackled with laughter.

"Who's coming to Dylan's?" Matt asked when we caught up with them outside the terminal building.

"Well, I don't really drink," I told them seriously, before breaking into a grin.

"Next you'll be telling us you don't wear heels!" Chrissie said, looking down at my new cowboy boots, which had a low heel.

"Go on then – just one drink."

Then I caught sight of Adam walking towards us.

"Did I miss Margaret?" he asked.

"Yep," I told him. "She's gone."

"I got stuck at work."

"We're all going to Dylan's," I told him as we walked towards the car park.

"There's a surprise!"

"See you there," Matt called when we split up.

"I missed you." Adam turned to me when we reached his car.

"I only saw you yesterday." I grinned at him.

"I know." In the car, he kissed me, then reached behind my seat. "I've got a present for you."

I grinned, taking the flat package from him and pulling at the brown paper that covered it. "One of your photos?"

"What do you think?"

I opened it, uncovering a photo of a huge oak tree, halfway up a lush green field, a stream running in the foreground and the sky a beautiful bright blue above. A bench with a figure sitting on it was just visible in the background. I gasped. "It's amazing. Is this where we were the day you did the photo shoot for Angela?"

He nodded. "I'm calling it 'Lucy through the lens'."

"Oh!" I looked more closely at the figure sitting on the bench in the distance. "That's me! I love it. Thank you." I kissed him and looked again at the photo as Adam started the engine. "But I had all those bags at my feet … Where have they gone?"

He managed to keep a straight face while he reversed out of the parking space. "Do you really need me to explain the concept of editing?"

I smiled. "Actually, I think I know a bit about that already."

THE END

Made in the USA
Coppell, TX
22 November 2020

41892090R00208